BETRAYED

Sheppard & Sons Investigations, Book 4

Eveline Rose

Dedication

This book is dedicated to all the women who are stronger than they think are, and the men who love them.

Also by

WebPage

Eveline Rose About 84,000 words

evelinerose.author@gmail.com

BETRAYED
Sheppard & Sons Investigations Book 4
by Eveline Rose

Chapter 1

Blake

The hair on the back of my neck stood up as I entered the campus coffee shop. It wasn't the first time I'd had a feeling I was being watched. I paused and looked around, expecting to see some creeper watching me, but everyone looked normal. No one fit the movie-inspired image of a scary stalker I'd built up in my head.

Glancing over my shoulder as the door closed behind me, I noticed a guy staring. His attention made my skin crawl, but I forced myself to dismiss the feeling. *He's not looking at me.* It was the week before mid-terms and stress levels were high. *I'm imagining it.*

"Blake, over here!" Paige, my best friend and roommate, yelled, drawing my attention to the table she shared with Danny.

I waved and got in line to order a skinny latte with an extra shot.

"Can you believe how much reading we have to do this weekend?" Paige asked as soon as I sat down.

"It's not so bad," I replied. I liked reading case studies and looked forward to graduating in May. I couldn't wait to join a not-for-profit organization and help make the world a better place.

"That's because you love reading," Danny said, his voice thick with sarcasm.

"I wouldn't go that far," I replied.

"You like it a lot more than I do," he said.

"I love learning."

"Blake!" The barista called my name.

When I got up to grab my coffee, I looked for the staring guy. He wasn't there anymore, so I pushed it out of my mind and rejoined my friends. Our weekly Friday meetups helped me unwind before I headed home for the weekend. Unlike my friends, I only lived on campus during the week, my father insisting I go home on the weekends. Not that I minded. I loved my father, and weekends were the only time I got to see him.

"Are you coming to the party tonight?" Danny asked.

"No, my parents are hosting a dinner party and I promised my dad I'd go."

"Bummer, I'll have a shot or two for you." Paige laughed, knowing I wasn't a big party goer.

"She'll be sipping her fancy drink, the BriarRose, while we chug from a keg," he said, then turned to me. "Need a date?"

I wouldn't mind having a friend there, but I'd never ask Danny. It hadn't gone well last time, besides, it was too late.

My step-mother would have a fit if she had to re-arrange the seating chart.

"Thanks, but you know how Cilla is." Cilla was the nickname I gave Priscilla shortly after she married my dad, when her sweet demeanor turned rude and selfish. She'd married him for his money and status, and didn't give two shits about me.

"Yeah, the Wicked Witch of Texas," Paige said, rolling her eyes.

We all laughed. They'd met her, they knew. She was closer to my age than my father's and saw me as competition for his affection. I didn't expect Priscilla to poison my food or hire someone to kill me, but she wasn't interested in being my friend, either.

I clasped the gaudy diamond necklace around my neck. It wasn't my style, but Cilla wanted to show off the family's wealth. My mom had never forced me to wear anything I didn't like, but Priscilla would be unbearable if I didn't wear it. Besides, it was a simple thing to do to make her happy, and that made Daddy happy.

God, I miss my mom. She'd made this house a home; now it felt like a stranger's.

"It looks like a tiara on my neck." I shook my head, using the mirror to verify the pink streak in my shoulder-length blond hair was hidden. I refused to give Priscilla a reason to gripe at me.

I might not be a fan of frat parties, but I was sure Paige and Danny would have more fun than me tonight. *Unless there's a nice, smart guy my age I can talk to.*

A knock on my door interrupted my thoughts.

"Are you decent?" My dad's voice came through the door.

"Come in, Daddy." I turned to greet him, holding my arms out so he could see the new gown he'd insisted I needed despite the closet full of fancy, once-worn dresses.

He took my wrist in his hand, towering over me at only five-foot-ten, and spun me around. "You're a vision, Princess."

"You look handsome yourself." I pulled my hand away to adjust his tie. "Is this new?"

"Priscilla picked it out. It's flashier than I usually wear." He sounded unsure about the choice.

"It looks great, Daddy. You should wear ties like this more often." I wasn't exaggerating. Dad liked unicolor power ties, so wearing a brightly colored one with bold geometric patterns was out of his comfort zone. "Priscilla has good taste."

"Thanks." His smile made his brown eyes sparkle. "Are you ready?"

"I am." I put on my best smile; the one reserved for meeting my father's influential guests. It didn't matter if they were clients, the Dallas elite, or fellow politicians—they all got the same toothy smile. No one ever seemed to care if it was fake.

Priscilla gave me a once over when we reached the bottom of the curving grand staircase that brought us to the middle of the foyer, where we'd receive guests. Her disappointed look only lasted a second before she turned to greet my father with a smile, but I saw it. I didn't care. I was here for my father, not her.

I shook hands and accepted kisses on my cheeks, like a good daughter as my father introduced me to his guests. Before long, my cheeks hurt from holding the smile. *I can't wait until we're done and I can grab a BriarRose in the sitting room.* My father had a bartender create the cocktail for my twenty-first birthday, and served it at any dinner party I attended. I loved the hint of vanilla and rose, the pink color, and how the sparkling rosé topper tickled my nose.

It was fun having my own cocktail, and the guests got a kick out ordering it.

"Steven!" A male voice interrupted my thoughts. "This must be that daughter you're always bragging about."

"It is." Dad said with pride. "Blake, this is Jeffrey, a business associate."

"It's a pleasure to meet you, Blake." He held out his hand while his eyes roamed down my body. I fought back a disgusted shiver. *Why do men think it was okay to leer at women?* For a split second, I thought about asking him, but didn't want to upset my father, so I bit my tongue and smiled.

"Nice to meet you." I lied as I shook his hand. He grasped it in both of his before I could pull it away.

"You're even more beautiful than your father said."

Gross. "Thank you." I pulled my hand out of his. *His smile reminds me of a snake.* "It was nice meeting you."

He was the last guest to arrive, so Dad led him to the sitting room where they'd rub elbows and make deals before dinner.

Dad always said social engagements were an important part of business, especially for politicians. Attending events like this was one thing I wasn't looking forward to when I worked for a non-profit, but it was part of the job.

Wanting to create space between me and the creepy Jeffrey, I held back. *I wish Paige was here.*

During dinner, Priscilla sat on my father's left side instead of the other end of the table, while I sat in the middle. She couldn't stand my father paying attention to me, so she always made sure I was as far as she could reasonably put me. *At least I'm not sitting next to Jeffrey.*

I was between a guy named Carl, an intern at the Senator's office, and the young wife of a high-powered Dallas defense attorney. Carl was full of himself, but at least we were close in age and he could carry on an intelligent conversation. The woman on my other side was too busy gushing over her sugar daddy to talk to me.

Seriously, women like her made the rest of us look bad. We didn't all want to marry money and be mindless arm-candy. Some of us wanted careers and to make a real difference in the world. *Doesn't she have any dignity or pride?*

I counted down the minutes as I ate the last dish of the five course meal, knowing my obligation to my father ended when everyone moved back to the sitting room. I couldn't wait to change into leggings and a t-shirt and relax in front of the TV.

Chapter 2

AJ

After the officers released me, I drove to work. *Great, now I'm fucking late.* Resisting the urge to speed, I drove exactly five over the speed limit. I'd never been late before and hated that the first time was because of something out of my control. I typed the code to the security gate too fast and missed a digit. Swearing, I punched in the code slower, but with more force. If anyone was looking at the video feed, I'd never hear the end of it.

I grabbed my bag and forced myself to walk calmly to the door. *No point in running now.*

I didn't make it three steps into the lobby before I got called out.

"You're late, Janerek." John's voice boomed across the lobby. John Sheppard, the patriarch portion of Sheppard & Sons Investigations, was my boss. He started the company five years ago with two of his sons, Jamie and Jack.

Technically, they were all my bosses; but only John intimidated me.

"Sorry, sir," I said as I worked up the nerve to tell him why. Should I tell him everything? *Maybe he won't ask.*

"Care to tell me why?" he asked, his tone not changing, his face an emotionless mask.

Of course, he asked. I relaxed against the wall, swallowed my pride and said, "It's kind of a funny story. I'd just pulled out of the convenience store when I noticed Weatherford's finest, lights flashing, pulling up behind me. As soon as I stopped, another squad pulled in front of me." By now, Jamie, Jack, and Doug had come into the lobby to listen. Might as well make it worth their time. Hamming it up, I drawled, "Now, I'm no idiot-"

"Who told you that?" Jaden, the youngest Sheppard and newest addition to SSI, asked as he joined us.

I squinted at him and continued, "So, I pulled over, got out, and put my hands on my head." I wouldn't usually do that, but they gave the command over the squad PA.

"Why were your hands on your head?" Maxwell, our only female PI, asked as she joined the group.

Ignoring her question, I continued.

Meg, Jack's wife and SSI receptionist, bent over with one hand covering her mouth. *At least someone thinks I'm funny.*

"Luckily, one of the officers recognized me." I pretended I didn't hear the choked laughter in the room. "Apparently, some college chick called the cops and reported a scary guy with a gun, and gave them my plate number. Who does that?" I raised my hands in disbelief.

Seriously, this is fucking Texas. Who freaks out when they see a holstered gun?

"Oh my God." Jack said as he bent over, holding his gut. Jaden, who everyone called Jay, was openly cackling while he pointed at me. Jamie and Doug were more reserved, but no less entertained. Maxwell shook her head and rolled her eyes, her laugh more a huff.

The left side of John's lip lifted as his amber eyes sparkled. *He knew.* What the fuck! If he knew, why the show?

He punked me? Never in a million years would I have expected that. He said, "I got a call from Officer Sanders, he wanted me to know one of my guys was terrorizing tourists."

Terrorizing? "What the fuck?" I half laughed, half barked. It wasn't bad enough it had happened, but Weatherford PD called John? The price I paid for moving to a small town where everyone knows everyone. Hell, John and Jamie had both been local cops before starting SSI.

"That explains why she called the cops. No Texan would have," Jamie said.

"Dude, what'd you do to scare her?" Jay asked.

I bought some fucking batteries. I didn't have time to answer before Meg piped up, her attempt to hold in her laughter a complete failure, "It's okay AJ, it could've happened to anyone."

"It's never happened to me, and I lived in Chicago." Doug said, making everyone bust out laughing again. Except Maxwell, she just shook her head in disbelief. She was still getting used to the vibe here after working at the FBI for the last three years—we weren't half as stiff or formal as her former co-workers.

"Not helpful, Sharpe." I glared at him. *I'll never hear the end of this.*

"Alright, that's enough terrorizing AJ for the day," John said, earning more laughs by emphasizing the word terrorizing. "Let's get back to work."

When did John get a sense of humor? That wasn't accurate; I'd seen him tease Jamie, Jack, and Meg, but that made sense—they were family.

I poured a cup of coffee before following Jack to his office. He didn't bother waiting until I sat to give me shit.

"Leave it to you to scare a tourist," he said as he opened his laptop.

"Shit way to start the day." I admitted.

"At least it's Friday and you have the weekend off."

"Amen to that, Brother." I lifted my coffee mug. Weekends off were a luxury in our line of work. As private investigators who also provided personal protection details, we worked more weekends than not. I was single and loved my job, so I didn't mind.

"Any fun plans?" Jack asked.

"I might see if Ashley's free."

Jack laughed. "She's not," he looked up from his screen, "she'll be with Meg and Emily." Emily was Jamie's fiancé. She and Ashley had been friends since grade school, and had welcomed Meg into their inner circle with open arms.

If Ashley and I were dating, I'd be worried about the potential for disaster given her relationship with Emily and

Meg. But we weren't. We hooked up once in a while; neither of us wanted anything more.

"Good to know. You busy?" I asked.

"I told Meg I'd paint the spare room this weekend. Want to help?"

"Sure. I'll expect my usual fee."

"Beer and pizza?"

"Beer and pizza."

"You're still a cheap date, Janerek."

"Maybe, but I won't put out for anything less than lobster and champagne."

"Get back to work," he ordered with a laugh.

"Yes, sir." I saluted him as I walked out. You'd think it'd be weird working for my best friend, but thankfully, it wasn't an issue.

Chapter 3

Blake

I came downstairs late Sunday morning knowing I'd missed breakfast but dying for a coffee. Listening to Priscilla recap the party and brag about how successful it was, knowing she hadn't done any of the work didn't sound like fun, so I decided to go to my favorite coffee shop and do some homework.

As I reached for the door handle, I noticed a small white envelope on the floor. I covered a yawn as I bent over to pick it up.

That's weird.

No name. I turned it over. Unsealed. When I lifted the flap, I could see thick card stock inside.

Maybe someone dropped it last night. *I'll just see who it's for.* I slipped the letter out and unfolded it. Scanning the first few words, I looked for a name. I didn't intend to read the whole thing—until I saw my name.

> Davenport, Your daughter Blake is captivating. It'd be a shame if something happened to her before she graduates. Honor your word and nothing will.

I gasped as I backed away from the door.

It's a joke. A sick one, but still a joke. It had to be.

Only, it wasn't funny and I wasn't laughing.

"Dad!" I yelled as I ran to his office. Expecting someone to jump out at me, I looked around every corner. My heart racing with every step.

I almost crashed into him when I rounded the corner.

"Why are you yelling?" Priscilla demanded from behind him.

Dad put his hands on my shoulders and stepped back so he could see me. I must have looked terrified because he asked, "What's wrong? Are you hurt?"

I shook my head. "No, but," I looked down at the card clutched in my hand. "I found this." I held it out for him.

"Seriously? All that for a card?" Priscilla dismissed me and went back to playing on her phone while my father took the now wrinkled paper.

He turned towards his desk as he pulled the paper flat. His abrupt stop told me he'd read it. His sharp intake of breath told me he didn't think it was a joke.

Someone was threatening me. *Us.* But why?

Priscilla, engrossed in her phone, hadn't noticed his reaction, but looked up when she heard the fear in his voice.

"Blake, I don't want you leaving the house today."

Any hope I had of dismissing the threat disappeared with his order.

"Yes, Daddy." I couldn't hide the worry in my voice. I wanted to ask if he knew who sent it, or what it was about, but Priscilla beat me to it.

"What's going on, Steve?" Priscilla asked, a hint of concern in her voice.

"I'm sure it's nothing. Just a prank," he said as he waved the letter around. "I'll call Dallas PD and report it. Just in case."

Priscilla relaxed, but his tone did nothing to put me at ease. It was easy for her to dismiss; she didn't know what it said.

I'm the one being threatened.

I went back to my room and tried to focus on my case studies, but it was useless. I couldn't stop thinking about the letter. The threat.

"I'm sure it's just a prank, like Daddy said." I muttered as I closed the file. My father was a District Attorney, so there were criminals out there who blamed him for being in jail. But why would someone threaten me? And what did they mean by "honor your word"?

Probably just some stupid joke one of his buddies thought would be funny.

By the time my phone buzzed with a text from Danny asking if I wanted to meet for lunch, I'd convinced myself it was a joke and was more pissed than scared.

He was teasing, but his words were irritatingly accurate. It sucked being stuck at home because someone was playing a prank on my dad.

Knowing he'd pester me with questions I couldn't answer, I decided not to tell Danny what happened.

I have to study.

How about dinner tonight?

Sorry, I'm having dinner with my parents.

You'd rather have dinner with them than me? You don't even like Cilla.

Danny was my friend, but his whining could be annoying.

We'll have lunch tomorrow.

Okay, but it's on you for blowing me off tonight. {wink emoji}

Okay.

We hadn't made plans, so I wasn't actually blowing him off, but I could afford to treat him to lunch. And it was easier than arguing with him.

My father refused to let me leave again on Sunday, saying he'd feel better if I stayed home. I hated being trapped inside all day, but at least I had plenty of time to read and start studying for my mid-terms.

During Sunday dinner, Dad announced we had an appointment with a personal protection company first thing in the morning.

"What does that mean?" I asked, more from shock than ignorance.

"I'm hiring an executive protection detail for you."

My fork clattered on my plate. "What? I thought you said it's probably a prank," I said.

"Be careful," Priscilla warned me. I doubted the three-inch drop caused any damage to her precious china.

"It may be, but I'd rather be safe than sorry," Dad answered. "I'm not willing to risk anything happening to you."

Despite the anxiety in his eyes, I refused to entertain the possibility of the threat being real. Not after spending the last two days convincing myself it wasn't.

"I don't want a bodyguard," I argued. I didn't want some big, dumb guy following me around. What would my friends think? Would my professors have an issue with someone tagging along in the classroom?

"I know, Princess, but it's only for a few days while we sort this out."

"Do you know who sent the card?" I asked, letting my irritation seep into my voice. It was easier than feeling afraid.

He shook his head back and forth as he lifted his wineglass. "Not yet."

"What about my morning class?" I asked, hoping he'd let me skip the meeting. "You know I can't afford to miss a class this close to mid-terms."

"I asked him to meet us early; with any luck you'll still make your class."

With any luck? That did nothing to improve my mood.

Neither did seeing the look of jealousy and irritation on Priscilla's face.

Chapter 4

AJ

"Morning, Mary. Morning, Beth." I called as I walked into Grannie's Coffee Bar bright and early Monday morning.

"Morning AJ. What brings you in this morning?" Mary asked.

"Treating the office to the best coffee in town." It never hurt to kiss up to the boss's wife.

Mary Sheppard was an amazing woman in her own right. She and John had been married, well I didn't know for sure, but, over thirty years, given Jamie's age. She was a strong, loving mother; the kind I wished I'd had growing up. Mary inherited Grannie's from her grandmother, and treated everyone who worked for her like family. She was the Mama Bear at the coffee shop and at SSI. Those of us not related by blood or marriage weren't exempt from her tough love if she thought we needed it. *She and John have that in common.*

"This have anything to do with scaring a tourist on Friday?" Beth asked.

Fucking Doug. He and Beth had been dating about six months. Technically, they were pre-engaged, after an accidental proposal, but he hadn't officially proposed yet. *I should have known he'd tell her.* I'd put money on Mary knowing, too.

"It does. I figure it can't hurt to suck up a little." I wasn't really worried about my reputation, but knew they'd appreciate my effort.

"John knows it'll never happen again," Mary said before asking, "How many do you need?"

"Eight." I'd get murdered if I didn't get coffee for everyone. "And a mocha for Meg."

I arrived at the SSI office, holding nine large cups of coffee, twenty minutes earlier than requested. John had called yesterday afternoon, asking everyone to come in early at the request of a big client.

My goal was to arrive first, and I did. Barely. John arrived a few seconds after me. Just in time to unlock the back door and hold it open for me.

"Good morning, sir." I said, handing him a coffee with one hand while carefully balancing the trays holding the remaining eight on the other. It didn't lighten my load much, but it took the precariously balanced cup off the top.

"Morning." His grin, so like Jack's, told me he was expecting my coffee suck-up. Once again, reminding me how impossible it was to keep a secret around here. Though,

I hadn't actually told Mary it was a secret when I admitted I was sucking up to her husband.

"Thanks," he said as he looked me over. I was wearing a plain black polo and khaki slacks. It was my typical work wear, unless I was protecting a rich or high-profile client. Then I'd be in a suit and tie. "You have a clean SSI polo here?"

"Yeah, should I change?" It was a stupid question. He wouldn't have said anything otherwise.

"Yes. We're meeting with Steven Davenport, District Attorney out of Dallas." We treated all our clients with the same courtesy and respect, but some commanded more professional attire than others.

"Yes, sir." I set the trays on Meg's desk, placing her mocha in front of her monitor before grabbing my coffee and heading to the office I shared with Doug. We all kept clean clothes in the office, never knowing when we'd need to change. We also kept bags with our tactical gear in our cars, so we'd be ready faster when shit hit the fan.

Which happened more often as our client base increased and we took on more dangerous jobs.

By the time I came out of my office, the rest of the guys were in and holding their coffees. We looked sharp in our matching navy polos, the SSI logo embroidered on the upper left chest.

"Thanks for the mocha," Meg said as she lifted her cup in my direction before setting it down without taking a drink.

"You're welcome." I lifted my cup back at her.

"Thanks, man. You should be late more often," Jay said. He only thought so because, as the new guy, it was his job to get

Grannie's coffee for the office. Before him, it was Maxwell's job.

She'd bitched about it, thinking it was a pick-on-the-new-girl thing, emphasis on girl, but Doug and I quickly corrected her. It was a pick-on-the-new-person thing, emphasis on new. She was skeptical, but as soon as Jay started, the task fell to him and she shut up about it.

Given her resume, I'd expected Max to be serious, but not quite so uptight. If she didn't remove the stick up her ass and relax once in a while, she'd be miserable working with us at SSI.

We took our job seriously but let loose when it was just us, sharing the typical dark humor found in the military and law enforcement. Jamie was the only full-time person on the team who hadn't served in the military, but he had SWAT training, which was close. That shared experience was how the hazing ritual started.

As far as hazing went, it was enjoyable. The new guy, or girl, had to pick up coffee for the office. And while more expensive than when I started—it was just John, Jamie, and Jack back then—it still wasn't hard on anyone's wallet because Mary gave us the employee discount.

Plus, Meg had started a coffee fund shortly after she started working here. Not because she didn't want to pay when it was her turn; *it was never her turn*, but because she recognized the growing expense as the team expanded. Probably a good thing; SSI had doubled in size since I signed my contract. Tripled if you included the part-time help.

"So, who's the client we're meeting?" Doug asked.

"District Attorney Steven Davenport. He received a note threatening his daughter and wants us to provide twenty-four-seven protection for her while investigating who sent the note," John answered as he looked at his watch.

Great, a politician's bratty daughter.

John, Jack and Jamie would handle the investigation, Doug and Maxwell had previous assignments, and Jay was still too green. Which meant I'd get the lion's share of protection duty.

Spoiled rich kids are the worst.

"Is it a credible threat, sir?" Maxwell asked. She commanded respect in her smart suit and military tight bun.

"I don't know yet. Davenport hinted it might be a prank, but doesn't want to take any chances." He filled a carafe with the coffee and handed it to Jack. "I'll meet you in the conference room. Review the files I left on the table."

We filed up the stairs. In the conference room, we each grabbed a folder before taking our seats. According to the file, DA Davenport had family money and high political aspirations. I flipped to the next page and forgot how to breathe as I stared into the most gorgeous cobalt blue eyes I'd ever seen.

They belonged to Davenport's college-aged daughter, Blake.

The room disappeared as I forced air into my lungs. It wasn't her beauty that held me captive; it was what I saw in the depth of her eyes. The windows to her soul displayed love, compassion, and intelligence; a person could drown in those beautiful blue eyes.

I hadn't met her yet, but Blake Davenport held the power to level me.

"AJ!" Jack's voice ripped me back to the room.

I tore my gaze away from the page. "What?" I said, miffed he'd forced me to look away.

"What the fuck, dude?" Jack's expression asked more than his words did.

No way in hell was I telling him I'd fallen into Blake's eyes and gotten lost. What the fuck was right. *It's just a picture.*

He glanced at the file I hadn't finished reading. Shit. *How long was I staring at her pictures?*

"Dad's on his way up." His look told me he'd be interrogating me later. "You should probably finish reading that," he said, nodding at the file.

"Yes, sir." I said with an exaggerated salute before licking my finger and turning the page. "Right away, sir." Sarcasm was my default setting when I felt uncomfortable.

The next page had a photo of the note. My blood boiled as everything in front of me turned a frightening shade of red.

Taking a deep breath, I reminded myself that this was just another job. I wasn't the fall in love at first sight kind of guy. *Besides, I'm sure her spoiled rich kid attitude will kill any potential feelings.*

Chapter 5

Blake

At breakfast, I tried arguing again. I didn't want or need a bodyguard. Once again, I lost. When I tried to get out of going to the meeting, using my morning class as an excuse, dad put his foot down, saying, "Blake, you're going, it's not up for debate."

Dad's harsh tone put an end to my argument.

"Yes, Daddy." I told myself he wasn't mad at me. *He's just worried.*

I texted Paige, asking her to take notes for me. Not wanting to explain why, I gave the 'something came up' excuse when she asked. I assured her I was okay when she said she was worried; I never missed class. A few minutes later, while I was packing my backpack, I got a text from Danny asking if I was still meeting him for lunch.

I hope so. I accepted that I'd most likely miss my first class, but didn't want to miss anything else because of this stupid meeting.

I used the long drive to study. It was a better use of my time than worrying if the threat was a joke, or listening to my step-mother prattle on about whatever stupid celebrity she was talking about.

Ninety minutes later, I read the sign out loud as our driver parked. "Sheppard & Sons Investigations. Why did we come all the way to Weatherford when there are a ton of security companies in Dallas?" It made no sense. What could a small-town company offer that a big city one couldn't?

"They have a good reputation. And I'd rather not use someone in Dallas, since I don't know who's behind the threat."

"Why does that matter?" I asked. My dad's anxiety putting me on edge. Why'd we have to come so far away? Was he actually worried a local PI could be bribed by whoever sent the note? And why aren't we going to the police?

None of this makes any sense!

Priscilla tapped her fingers on her Prada purse while she waited for Dad to open her door. I rolled my eyes as I opened my door, once again thankful my mom raised me to be an independent woman. I wasn't completely anti-chivalry, I'd let a date open the door if I was wearing a fancy dress, but I didn't expect any man to open my door.

A man greeted us as soon as we walked in, introducing himself as John Sheppard. Given he looked older than my dad, I guessed he wasn't one of the sons. He had short wavy brown hair peppered with silver, and friendly amber eyes.

Paige would call him a silver fox. I held back my smile at the thought.

John was the same height as my dad, but he had a lot more muscle. It was obvious he didn't sit at a desk all day. The corners of John's kind eyes crinkled as he shook my hand.

"You must be Blake. It's nice to meet you."

"Nice to meet you too, Mr. Sheppard."

"Feel free to call me John," he said with a friendly smile.

I nodded. When I looked down, I noticed his gun. Surely, he didn't need to be wearing a gun in the office. What did he think we were going to do, attack him?

A part of my brain recognized this was an investigation and security company, which meant they were probably all armed all the time, but it still made me nervous. I looked at clouds through the vaulted ceiling skylight to distract myself.

"The team is waiting upstairs in the conference room." John indicated the stairs to the right of the spacious, comfortably furnished lobby. "This way, please."

"It's not what I expected," Priscilla said. "It's nothing like the PI offices in movies."

I had to agree; the plants were a nice touch.

John chuckled. "We have my wife and daughter-in-law to thank for that." He looked around, pausing at one of the large trees near the stairs. "Our old office was pretty bare bones."

I glanced at the receptionist, who looked about my age, and returned her smile when we made eye contact. It was impossible not to notice her striking emerald green eyes and friendly smile.

My father ushered Priscilla ahead of us, then put his arm around my shoulder and led me to the stairs. "It'll be okay, Princess. You'll see."

John led us to a large, crowded conference room. The glass walls lining the hall allowed me to see inside.

"Why are there so many people?" I whispered to my dad.

"I'm sure it's normal," he answered.

I was sure it wasn't, not to investigate a prank. I was still telling myself this whole thing was a stupid joke made in poor taste. *People don't go around leaving threatening notes in real life.*

John held the door and pointed to seats at the head of the table. My father was the perfect gentleman and pulled out Priscilla's chair for her before turning to help me. I smiled and thanked him. From my seat.

Six people sat around the table, with John taking the chair next to me. They all had laptops and files in front of them. The only woman, with her red hair pulled back in a severe bun and wearing a tailored black suit, sat at the other end. She looked out of place in a room full of men wearing matching polos. They were all big guys who towered above me, even sitting, and looked like they spent more time in the gym than was necessary.

At least there's one woman. I bet she'll be the one protecting me. With all this toxic masculinity, I'd expected the receptionist to be the only female, so it was refreshing seeing a woman in the room. I tried to make eye contact with her, but she was staring at her screen.

"This is DA Davenport, his wife, Priscilla, and his daughter, Blake." John introduced us to everyone in the room, then introduced his team. The woman's name was Catelyn, but he said she went by Max, and most of the guys had names that started with J.

How am I supposed to remember them all?

Dad explained what had happened, then held out the note and envelope for John, who put on gloves before taking it and placing it in a plastic bag.

He's preserving evidence, treating this like a crime. My heart sped up as fear surged.

I convinced myself it meant nothing; he was just doing his job.

"Has anyone else touched the note?" John asked.

"Just Blake and me," Dad answered.

"Good, we'll get it to a lab to look for fingerprints and anything else they might find."

I stared at my hands. *It's just a prank. He's just being thorough.* I kept trying to convince myself, but it felt less and less likely with each passing minute. I chewed on my thumbnail, not caring that Priscilla would give me shit on the ride home if she saw me.

This can't be happening. My nerves got the best of me and I blurted out, "I'm sure it's just a prank."

"Perhaps, but we'll treat it as a threat until we know otherwise," John said.

"I'm sure you're right, but like I said, better to be safe than sorry," my dad said as he patted my hand.

"I'm with your father on this. It never hurts to be cautious."

Easy for him to say; he wants to get paid. He wouldn't have some big oaf following him around all day interfering with his life. How was I supposed to focus on mid-terms with someone hovering over me?

"Mr. Davenport, you mentioned wanting twenty-four-seven full coverage for Blake. Will you also need coverage for yourself or Mrs. Davenport?" John asked.

"No, just Blake. I'm either at my office in the Dallas Court Building, or at home with the security system armed."

"What about me?" Priscilla asked in her high-pitched, whiny voice. *She wasn't worried before, but now she wants security?* No doubt it was a ploy for attention from a new audience.

"Darling, the threat was directed at Blake. You aren't in any danger," Dad reasoned with her.

His condescending tone didn't seem to bother her, but it bothered me. I loved my dad, but hated how he talked down to her. It didn't matter that I didn't like her, it still grated on my nerves.

"I don't need someone following me around campus, Dad." Maybe I could convince him to hire someone to drive me and wait in the car. When I suggested as much, I was shut down, not just by my dad but by John as well.

"Blake, I understand you don't want a protection detail, but college campuses are dynamic and chaotic. It'd be easy for someone to carry out the threat and disappear," a guy at the other end of the table said. Jimmy? Jake? I couldn't remember.

"Jamie's right. The best way to protect you is for someone to be with you at all times. We'll make sure the person assigned to you is discreet. You have my word," John promised.

"I stay in the dorms Monday through Friday." I said, thinking I'd be able to ditch them at least part of the time, since we couldn't have overnight guests in our rooms.

"I want you coming home every night right after class," my father said.

"But Daddy." I sounded far whinier than I'd wanted to.

"No. I won't risk your safety." His tone was harsher than he usually used. It had been last night too, and I didn't like it. "This will all be over soon. I promise."

I glared at the note. I should have thrown the damn thing away.

My life was being turned upside down because some asshole thought a threat was a funny prank.

"Are you my bodyguard?" I asked, looking down the table at Max.

"No, I'll be in court all week," she answered flatly.

Then why are you even here?

Knowing I couldn't talk my father out of hiring a bodyguard, I gave up arguing. I'd be the good little girl he expected me to be so we could get this stupid meeting over with, and I could get to class.

Chapter 6

AJ

Blake was even more captivating in person, despite her bratty attitude and the scowl on her face. I forced myself to look away whenever I caught myself staring. Which was a lot.

When she turned her head, her shoulder-length blond hair moved just enough to reveal a pink stripe. Rebellion? Lost a bet? School spirit? All the cool kids were doing it? I couldn't help but wonder why a rich politician's daughter would dye her hair with a bright pink stripe.

My eyes drifted to Blake repeatedly, as if they had a mind of their own. I watched as she struggled to hide her fear and annoyance. I wasn't a profiler like Maxwell, or an experienced detective like John, but my gut said this wasn't a prank. She could insist it was a prank until the cows came home, but I wasn't buying it.

Her father played with his class ring, a sign he believed the threat was real, even if Blake didn't. Something about his behavior felt off. *What isn't he telling us?*

His young wife, the epitome of a trophy wife, with her perfectly styled hair, excessive bling, and manicured nails, looked irritated.

At the situation? At Blake?

To limit how much time I spent staring at Blake, I noted my observations, forcing myself to be more detailed than necessary. My behavior was borderline creepy. Not that she'd noticed; Blake avoided making eye contact with everyone except John and Max.

It made sense she'd expect to find a kindred spirit in Max, but the joke was on her—Maxwell was one of the toughest people I knew. She wasn't a *let's do our nails and talk about our feelings* kind of girl. She held her own any time she faced one of us on the mat, her gender and size irrelevant when facing us in unarmed combat. *Well, some of us.* She had yet to beat me or Doug. And she was a badass on the range, too.

"I'll have Meg draw up the contract for twenty-four-seven coverage for Ms. Davenport, including a car and driver," John said. "We'll order forensics on the note and investigate to determine who sent the threat."

Blake had given up arguing, but I saw her roll her eyes when John said driver. Her picture might have captured my heart, but her attitude was a turnoff. She needed to stop acting like a spoiled teenager and accept reality.

If this was a prank, someone would have come forward by now. No one would let something like this go on long enough to scare the prankee.

"Given the personal detail in the note, it may be from someone who attended your dinner party on Friday. If you could email a list of the attendees, we'll start there."

Blake's head shot up. The look of fear in her eyes as she looked at John felt like a shot to my gut.

Protect her! The desire to eliminate any and every threat so she'd never feel fear again flooded my system. It didn't make sense, but I couldn't deny the strongest desire to protect anyone I'd ever felt in my life.

Fuck. Was this what the guys felt when they fell in love? Love?

Double fuck. They'd never let me hear the end of it if they could read my mind.

"I'll email the list later today," Mr. Davenport said.

"Thank you," John said before addressing Blake. "Ms. Davenport, I understand this is disruptive and I assure you, we'll do everything in our power to sort this out as quickly as we can," John said.

"Thank you." She said the words, but they lacked sentiment.

The meeting was almost over when Blake finally looked up and made eye contact. Anger flashed across her features before she looked away.

What the hell did I do to piss her off?

"Can I go now?" Blake asked.

John made eye contact, a silent question in his expression. I nodded. I only needed a few minutes to gear up and grab the keys to one of the SSI bulletproof sedans.

I stood as John re-introduced me, "This is AJ Janerek. He'll be with you for the next two days. Jaden Sheppard will be outside the house in the evenings." Jaden stood and nodded towards Blake.

Blake glared at me. *Damn!* So much attitude in one look. How was I so drawn to her when she couldn't even look at me without a scowl on her beautiful face? I broke eye contact and closed my laptop.

"I'll escort you downstairs. AJ will be right behind us. He'll be ready to leave in ten minutes."

My boss was one hell of a leader; who else could give an order without actually issuing an order? There was no doubt I'd be ready to go in eight, because after what happened last week there was no way in hell I'd be late.

After they left, Jamie asked, "What are your thoughts, Max?"

"I'd get more from the note if it was hand-written, but given the word choice and details, I'd say it's real. Davenport's scared, despite his attempts to hide it." She tapped her pen on the table. Something else was bothering her.

"I got the same impression," Jack added. "Blake doesn't want to believe it's real, but she's scared, too."

I'll kill anyone who tries to hurt her.

"Feel free to email me if anything comes up. I'll do what I can around my trial schedule."

I didn't envy her the next few days; she'd be stuck sitting in a courtroom waiting to be called to testify for a case she'd helped solve as an FBI profiler. We were lucky Maxwell could attend the early meeting to get a read on the Davenports and analyze the note before heading to Dallas. She might not be buddy-buddy with the rest of us, but she was a team player and dedicated to her work and we knew she'd make herself available in the evenings if we needed her.

"Did anyone else notice the looks Priscilla was giving Blake?" I asked.

"Yeah, she almost looked jealous, which is insane," Max agreed. I was glad I wasn't the only one who'd noticed. "It's worth looking into."

"Agreed. Women who marry for money and status often go to extreme lengths to get, and keep, what they want," Jack said.

I looked at my watch and was about to leave when Jamie said, "AJ, it goes without saying, but I'll say it anyway. College campuses are a hive of activity, so keep your eyes up and your head on a swivel. And wear your vest."

"Yes, sir." He was right—it didn't need to be said. "Text me with updates. I'm going back to college." I chuckled. Having earned my degree online, I'd never attended a class on a college campus.

Though I've spent the night in a dorm room or two.

Jack stopped me just outside the conference room door. "You okay?"

"Yeah, why?"

"You don't seem like yourself, and you were staring at Blake like a man possessed," Jack said.

"Just looking for clues, honing my PI skills." I laughed it off. "I gotta run. Can't be late twice in… well, ever."

Jack clapped me on the shoulder with a laugh. "Be careful."

"Always." I said as I headed for the stairs, taking them two at a time as I rushed to my office. I grabbed my rifle, just in case, and soft vest from the gear locker in my office. Knowing my fitted SSI polo wouldn't hide it, I changed into a looser t-shirt, then tossed on a flannel. I didn't know how college kids dressed, but this would have to do for today.

When I walked into the lobby with a minute to spare, Blake greeted me with an impatiently tapping foot and a look that could freeze a flame.

"Ms. Davenport, I'm AJ." I stuck out my hand to offer a formal introduction. It wasn't necessary, but I hoped to lessen her animosity towards me.

She craned her head back so her heart-crushing blue eyes could look up at me. I'd noticed she was short when she walked into the conference room, but didn't realize just how short until I was standing next to her. Towering over her. *She can't be more than five-foot-four.* I amended my guess when I saw her heels; five-foot-two.

Blake huffed as she reluctantly shook my hand. "Can we go now?"

Ignoring the zing dancing up my arm, I answered, "Yes, ma'am. The car's in the back." We had a fenced-in lot in the back for company and personal vehicles. It wouldn't stop determined thieves, but the cameras, motion sensor lights, and alarms would keep most out.

She didn't like being called ma'am, according to her flared nostrils and squinted eyes. *Damn, she's sexy when she's mad.*

Nope. I couldn't think about that. Football stats, they were safe.

"Bye, Daddy," Blake said as she hugged him. She didn't bother saying bye to her step-mother.

Blake didn't want me here. She'd made that perfectly clear on the drive over, but I had a job to do.

I had a feeling she wouldn't make it easy for me. When I suggested she switch things up, like where she sits in class, she refused. When I told her I'd be within arm's reach at all times, she'd told me to keep my distance.

I was ready to lay my life down to protect her, but she couldn't be bothered to sit in a different seat or take a different route to class. *Definitely a spoiled rich kid.* My opinion felt at odds with the jolt of emotion her picture had inspired.

Sitting behind her in class, I spent ninety minutes observing the two entry doors; one behind the professor, the other behind the students. Nothing stood out, and no one acted suspiciously.

I also kept a watchful eye on Blake, which was, by far, the easiest part of the job. My hands itched to massage the stress and fear from her tense shoulders.

She'd probably threaten to break my hand if she knew I wanted to touch her.

After class, she hung out with her roommate in the quad. I was standing a few feet away, watching the crowd, when I noticed a big guy sneaking up behind her, a determined look on his face as he closed the distance.

Hell no. No one touches Blake.

In a flash, I stepped behind Blake, intercepting him. Reaching out and grabbing one wrist, I twisted it as I forced him to his knees.

Blake turned around when she heard the commotion, just as her roommate screamed.

Blake yelled, "What the fuck are you doing? Let him go."

The guy pleaded his innocence while I held him on his knees. "He was coming at you." Heads turned towards us as a crowd formed. I released his fat wrist, glad my hand was large enough to hold it.

"I was sneaking up to give you a hug," the guy said to Blake, sounding like a wounded animal. His tone turned angry when faced me. "What the fuck is wrong with you, man? Back off!"

He acted tough now that I wasn't holding him down. It might have been more convincing had he been standing.

Her other friend glared at me from behind Blake's back. *Damn, who needs enemies with friends like that?* What kind of friend sneaks up on someone with a protection detail, or glares at the guy protecting her friend?

Unless... She didn't tell them. *Shit.* I gave the guy some space but didn't offer to help him stand.

Blake hugged him after helping him up, her arms barely reaching around his waist, then pulled back and asked, "Are you okay?" Her eyes roamed over him, looking for injuries.

Fuckface said, "No, I'm not. This asshole tackled me for no reason."

I didn't tackle him. "I had a reason, I was-"

Blake put her hands on her hips, cutting me off. "No, you didn't. You had no right to tackle him. You totally over-reacted you big dumb ogre."

I'd been called a lot of things in my life, many of them unsavory, but never an ogre. *Jack will laugh his ass off when I tell him.*

I scanned the crowd, glad they were dispersing now that the action had ended.

My nostrils flared as I watched him hug her again, his hands on her back, his body rubbing against hers.

That I had zero right to be jealous didn't matter one bit. Watching him touch her pissed me right the fuck off.

Mine! Except she wasn't mine. Hell, she couldn't stand me. It didn't matter; I couldn't shake the feeling that Blake was mine to protect. And protect her, I would.

Whether she likes it or not.

"Blake, can I talk to you?" I asked, indicating we needed privacy.

"You don't need to listen to him," Fuckface said.

"Blake?" I asked again, this time with some urgency in my voice.

Her other friend stood behind them, glaring at me. She rubbed Blake's back and said, "We should call 9-1-1."

"Blake." I channeled John, making it clear I was no longer asking.

Blake turned to her friend. "It's okay. I'll be right back."

Her friends continued to glare as Blake turned and stepped up to me. "Fine," she spat out. "But make it fast."

Refusing to let my anger take over, I forced my body to relax as I prepared to follow her a few steps away from her friends.

As she brushed past me, her crossed arms resting on her ample chest, the scent of vanilla and wildflowers filled my nose. *Holy hell, she smells fucking amazing.*

Chapter 7

Blake

I thought about refusing, because the stupid asshole had just hurt my friend, but I didn't want him causing a bigger scene. Better to get it over with. Plus, I didn't want my friends listening.

I probably should have warned them I have a bodyguard.

As soon as we were out of earshot, I said, "What the fuck was that? You're supposed to protect me, not hurt my friends."

"I didn't know he was your friend." He scanned the crowd over my head as he answered. "I did my job."

"Well, you shouldn't have." I crossed my arms over my chest.

"That's where you're wrong, Princess. I absolutely should have," he said. "And just so we're on the same page, I'll do it again if I have to."

Who the fuck does he think he is, calling me Princess?

"Don't call me Princess, asshole."

The asshole grinned. "You need to tell your friends that you have a protection detail. Anyone assigned to you would've done the same."

I didn't think Maxwell would've tackled Danny. *I hope she's assigned to me sooner rather than later.*

"Maxwell wouldn't have." I sneered at him.

The asshole ogre had the balls to laugh. "Trust me, she would have. Don't assume because she's a woman she's not willing or capable of taking down assholes who look like they're about to attack you."

I rolled my eyes and said, "He wasn't trying to attack me. How many times do I have to tell you that?"

"How many times do I have to tell you it doesn't matter what he was trying to do? What matters is what it looked like he was trying to do. He looked like he was going to attack you, and that's all I had to go on."

There was a part of me that knew he was right; AJ was doing the job my father paid him to do. So why was I so pissed off? Because I didn't want him here. I didn't ask for protection detail, and I sure as hell didn't ask to be humiliated in the quad.

I pointed at his chest. "Wait until I tell my father about this. He'll make sure you get fired." I sounded like a petulant child, not a woman in her last year of law school.

"Do your best, Princess."

He sounded so smug, and his big stupid grin made me want to punch his dumb face. But I didn't believe in violence.

"Ugh!!" Clenching my fists, I screamed through gritted teeth before turning on my heels and marching away from him. When I rejoined my friends, I told them I was going home for the day. All because I didn't want to risk my big, dumb bodyguard tackling anyone else. It didn't matter he hadn't actually tackled Danny. I wouldn't risk anymore embarrassing situations. *And I want to tell my dad what he did.*

Danny whined about me bailing on lunch again, so I told him I'd make it up to him. When Paige asked if I wanted to order takeout later for dinner, I admitted I wouldn't be staying on campus for a while.

"What? Why?" Paige asked, her voice thick with disappointment.

"Does this have something to do with the Sasquatch who tackled me?"

It did, but I didn't want to talk about it anymore.

"I'll fill you guys in later. Right now, I just want to go home."

At least there I wouldn't have to deal with AJ.

Chapter 8

AJ

Blake fumed the entire drive back to her dad's house. I didn't have to look to know she was glaring at me from the back seat—I could feel it.

Had I over-reacted and handled her friend too violently? I kept telling myself no, but somewhere deep inside, doubt started brewing. Had my anger caused me to act like a jealous asshole instead of a trained professional?

No. I was in control the entire time, and it wasn't my fault he was a whiny little bitch. It wasn't like I broke his wrist or anything. If questioned, I could justify my actions.

Was that what my father did? I felt sick to my stomach as I turned onto the street that would take me to the Davenport estate.

I punched in the gate code and waited for the large wrought-iron gate to roll to the side. The long driveway ending in a circle with a large sculpted Pegasus fountain in the center. Water rolled over the spread wings and fell in sheets back into the pool below the horse's hooves.

Damn! I'd seen pictures of the house, but still wasn't prepared for the enormity of it. The house, *mansion*, had columns supporting the roof of the wrap-around porch. It was pristine white with pine green shutters framing the second-story windows, and the professionally landscaped flower beds erupted in a rainbow of spring blooms.

Blake reached for the door as soon as I pulled up to the steps leading to the front door.

"At least let me put the car in park before you try to jump out."

"Whatever," she hissed at me, but let go of the door handle.

"Wait here," I ordered as I got out and scanned for threats while I walked around the front of the car. The coast was clear, so I opened Blake's door.

"I can open my own door. I don't need some stupid man doing it for me," Blake huffed.

She'd said the same thing earlier when I insisted on opening her door on campus. "I'm not doing it to be chivalrous," I couldn't help the grin forming in response to her stubbornness. "Like I said before, the car is bulletproof. Me opening your door is the sign that the coast is clear and it's safe for you to get out." I over-explained just to get a rise out of her.

"Whatever, mansplainer." She slung her backpack over one shoulder and stomped up the steps. At the top, she stopped suddenly and spun around, crashing into me because I was only a half step behind her. She yelped and stepped back, knocking herself off balance.

Without thinking, I reached out, grabbing her full waist to steady her. "Are you okay?"

"I'm fine. Why are you so close?"

So much attitude in such a short body.

"I wasn't until you stopped," I said. My body reacting to her closeness, despite my irritation. When she blushed; her cheeks turned a shade darker than the pink stripe in her hair.

She looked like she might apologize, but she huffed instead. "I suppose you need to open this door, too."

"I'd be happy to open the door for you." I held out my hand for the key.

She looked at my hand and huffed again.

Blake pulled her keys out of her bag, shot me a look meant to freeze my blood, turned and shoved the key in the lock. I watched as she cranked the key and shoved the door open.

After stepping inside, she turned and made eye contact before slamming the door in my face.

I laughed as I walked back to the car. *She's going to be a handful.*

Chapter 9

Blake

Who did he think he was treating me like a damsel in distress? I wasn't some princess who needed a dashing hero to come save her. *He probably thinks he's God's gift to women.* Well, he wasn't.

I wasn't attracted to guys like AJ. Tall, muscular guys with penetrating dark brown eyes and dimples that split his cheeks when he grinned. I was a modern, independent woman, and I didn't need big stupid men doing things for me. And I sure as hell didn't need him intimidating my friends.

I yanked my laptop and books out of my backpack and tossed them on the couch.

Before starting my school work, I pulled out my phone to text an apology to Paige and Danny for what happened earlier. Not that it was my fault, but I had to admit, Danny wouldn't have tried sneaking up on me if he'd known I had a bodyguard.

Hey guys, sorry about earlier. I should have told you, I have a bodyguard for a few days.

Danny, I hope you're okay.

Paige: Why do you need a bodyguard?

Danny: Can't you find someone less violent?

It shouldn't surprise me that Danny thought of himself first. He was my friend, but he could be selfish.

Someone sent a threatening note to my dad, until they figure out who and why I have protection.

Paige: Is that why you can't stay on campus?

Yeah, until it's settled I have to come home at night.

Danny: That sucks. I hope they find him soon so you can get rid of that asshole.

Paige: Danny, he thought you were going to hurt Blake.

Thank you Paige. I didn't have the energy to deal with Danny's attitude.

Danny: He didn't need to be so violent.

Paige: He was excessively violent.

Danny: You should demand someone else.

I wish I could, but I can't.

Danny: Does he have to go with you everywhere? I'm sure you're safe at school.

Paige: I doubt anyone would try anything here. Too many witnesses.

After her initial show of concern, I couldn't help but notice how Paige parroted everything Danny said. It was happening more and more, and I didn't understand it. *Maybe it's because he's mean to people who disagree with him.* God knew I'd agreed with him to avoid a fight on more than one occasion.

He'll be with me for a few days {eye roll emoji}

Danny: Can you ditch him for lunch tomorrow?

I can't. But I won't let him sit with us.

We made plans to meet at our favorite off campus bar for lunch. I figured the least I could do was buy Danny a beer or two after what happened.

"Hey Princess, how was your day?" my dad asked as I sat down for dinner. Funny how being called Princess only pissed me off when AJ said it.

"It sucked having AJ hovering over me all day. I came home early, so I didn't have to deal with him."

Priscilla rolled her eyes, mumbling how I shouldn't complain because at least I could leave the house without worrying I'd be attacked. I ignored her. Dad patted her hand and consoled her by promising to take her on a vacation when this was all over.

I decided not to share the real reason I came home early. Not because I thought AJ was right or because I didn't want him to get in trouble; he most definitely deserved to after what he pulled. But because Dad had huge, dark bags under his eyes. He looked exhausted and sad. He'd clearly had a bad day at work and Priscilla wasn't helping. I didn't want to add to his stress.

Did they figure out who sent the note? It'd only been one day, not even a full twenty-four hours, so I doubted they had any answers, but that didn't stop me from asking.

"Not yet. I'm sure it'll all be over soon." Dad kept glancing at his phone. Another sign of his stress—he rarely brought his phone to the dinner table.

"I hope so." I didn't think I could handle having AJ around for more than a couple of days.

Chapter 10

AJ

When Jay relieved me at five, I pulled out of the parking spot where I had a view of the front door and driveway so he could park. He rolled down his window as I walked over. "It's been quiet, but that doesn't mean you can let your guard down."

"I know how to do my job," he responded. Jaden Sheppard was nothing like his two older brothers. I'd expected him to be easygoing and maybe a bit of a wild child, given all the stories I'd heard. But he had a boulder-sized chip on his shoulder. Three weeks in and he was already earning a 'doesn't play well with others' reputation around the office.

"Right. Anyway, call if anything comes up." I trusted him to do his job. He was a former Marine Raider, and from what I heard, a damn good one, but I didn't feel comfortable with Blake's safety in anyone's hands but my own.

And doesn't that realization just fucking suck? It did, because I wasn't a warm and fuzzy, relationship-having kind of guy.

"Thanks." Sarcasm, thick as molasses, coated his reply.

"Good night."

"Night." He saluted with his shiny new SSI travel mug.

I walked away wondering what had happened to turn a special operations team guy into a lone wolf.

Those of us who were available met at the office gym for our monthly team workout and sparring session. I was the reigning champ, but didn't think I'd hold the title for long.

"I've got a twenty on you taking Doug down tonight," Jack said as we walked to the gym.

"Who bet on Doug?"

"Meg and Jamie." He laughed and clapped me on the back. "Don't let me down."

"I'll do my best." I never gave anything less in the ring.

I opened the door and held it for him. "Who will you pick when I go against Jay?" I was a Brazilian Ju Jitsu black belt, but so was Jay. A fight between us would be an epic battle.

"Jay. He's younger and fresh off the battlefield," Jack said. "Sorry, Bro."

I laughed. He was right. Plus, he was full of anger and constantly itching for a fight. *And he's watching over Blake. How will he react if she wants to go out? Will he remain professional or take the bait when she stirs the pot?*

I fought the urge to call, focusing on the training ahead instead of checking on him.

We started with a thirty-minute workout. Jamie and Jack hit the free weights, spotting for each other. They weren't worried about winning on the mat. They could hold their own in any street fight, and always gave it their all in the ring, but neither was a match for Doug or me.

Doug hopped on the treadmill next to me and smiled. He had the same idea I did—reserving his strength for the fight.

John pulled a name from a hat, Doug. No one challenged him, so John picked again: Jamie.

Doug won. When Jack looked at me; I lifted an eyebrow and grinned. This was his chance to choose his opponent. Sensing my pent up frustration, Jack challenged Doug.

Smart move. He lasted longer than Jamie, but in the end, he tapped out.

My turn. I stretched my neck and cracked my knuckles before putting on my padded gear. The mat was the perfect place to release my energy. And remove the image of Blake and her sexy anger flushed cheeks from my mind.

Doug and I faced off. He was three inches taller and just as solid. We were evenly matched despite different disciplines, and I always enjoyed sparring with him.

I started out fine, but when I took Doug to a knee; the image of doing the same earlier to protect Blake flashed through my mind. The two second distraction was all Doug needed. I barely had time to snap back to the present before I was flat on my back with a grinning red head straddling me, pinning my arms.

I'm so fucked.

In the locker room, Jack asked me what happened.

"I lost. It's not the first time."

"No, but it's the first time you've had a weird grin on your face half a second before getting your ass kicked."

Fucking Jack. He was too observant for his own good.

"What are you talking about?"

"You saw it, right Jamie?" Jack asked.

"What, the weird look on AJ's face right before Doug kicked his ass? Nah, I missed it." He raised his eyebrows like Groucho Marx and laughed.

Fucking Jamie.

"If it makes you feel any better, I didn't see it," Doug said as he walked up behind me. He turned towards Jack and asked, "Think the cameras captured it?"

He moved out of the way just in time to avoid my elbow hitting his ribs. "You're getting slow, Janerek," he said, laughing.

Fucking Sharpe.

"I need a beer. Anyone interested?" They weren't. They all had women waiting for them at home.

Sometimes, I envied them.

I'd sworn myself to a life of bachelorhood, knowing I couldn't, wouldn't, risk getting married. I was just like my father, who'd ruled his house with anger and violence. Just like his father before him. They'd destroyed the lives of the people they claimed to love and I'd rather be alone than end up like them.

Chapter 11

Blake

Immediately after dinner, my dad locked himself away in his office. Which wasn't like him. I grabbed a sweater and went out back to take a walk.

Fresh air and exercise will help me work off my anxiety. I walked along the side garden path to the front of the house. The burst of color and floral scents of the spring blooms always soothed my nerves. I was finally feeling better when I stepped around the corner and spotted the dark sedan parked near the circular driveway.

My heart beat a little faster as I approached. Not because I wanted to see AJ, but because it reminded me I, we, needed protection. I told myself I wasn't disappointed when the man who got out of the car and turned towards me had longer, lighter colored, wavy hair.

It shouldn't have surprised me; John said someone else would be here at night. The guy introduced himself as Jaden and asked if everything was okay.

"Just taking a walk," I answered.

"Okay, let me know if you want to leave. Or if you want company, I'd be happy to walk with you."

He'd be happy, my ass. His job was to make sure I didn't leave the house unattended.

"Thanks, but I think I'll go back inside." Seeing him negated the calming effect of the garden. *Maybe I'll take a long hot bubble bath and have a glass of wine.*

Half a bottle later, I stepped out of the now bubble-less, tepid water and dried off. *Much better.* I corked the wine and blew out the lavender vanilla candle. After putting the leftover wine in my mini fridge, I grabbed my text book and got under my down comforter.

I must have fallen asleep because my book fell to the floor when I sat up in a panic a few hours later.

It was a dream. The faceless man wasn't real. *I'm okay.*

I padded down the stairs and peeked out a front window. Jaden leaned on the hood of his car, stretching his arms over his head. Unlike earlier, his presence was comforting.

Everything's okay. It was just a dream. *No one is trying to kill you.*

I told myself the whole thing was just a stupid prank. *Tomorrow, one of Dad's friends will own up to it and we'll have a good laugh.*

I'd have to force mine, because I didn't think this was funny. Not one bit.

Chapter 12

Blake

Much to my disappointment, AJ waiting for me when I walked out the door Tuesday morning. He looked relaxed, leaning against the side of the car, but his eyes never stopped moving.

Until he heard the door slam.

Then his intense dark eyes focused on me as he closed the distance to the bottom of the porch steps so he could escort me to the car. *Like I need help walking a few lousy feet.*

He opened the rear passenger door before I reached it.

"I'm not helpless, you know. I can open my own doors." It was bitchy, and not who I believed myself to be, but I hated when men treated women like they were helpless.

"Just doing my job, Ms. Davenport." He grinned, pissing me off even more.

"Whatever." I got in the car and tried to slam the door, but he held it until I gave up. He made a production out of closing it softly.

Big, stupid jerk with his big muscles trying to intimidate me.

I glared as he walked around the front of the car, willing him to notice me, but he was looking left and right. When he finally got in and glanced at me in the review mirror, I scowled.

He fucking smiled, causing his dimples to crease like crescent moons in his cheeks.

"Which lot do we need to park in today?" he asked calmly.

"The same one as yesterday." I barked at him, then looked away from his stupid face. It was like he was trying to piss me off by being polite. *Who fucking does that?*

"Buckle up." After a short pause, he added, "Please."

I buckled up. Not because he wanted me to, but because it was the law.

"I'm meeting some friends for lunch today. Can you try not to attack them for no reason?" I didn't think of myself as a rude person, but AJ incited my snarky side.

"Sure, just make sure they know not to sneak up on you." At least he was looking ahead now, so he couldn't see me roll my eyes. *Is twenty-four too old to roll your eyes?* I didn't care.

"They know. And no hovering over me. I need my space," I huffed at him.

Logically, I understood he was just doing his job, but it didn't matter. I gave him attitude anyway. His smugness irritated me, and I hated needing a bodyguard.

"I'll stay as close as necessary to do my job." He made eye contact in the mirror. "I'll give you privacy, but not at the risk of your safety."

How the fuck am I supposed to argue with that?

I couldn't, so I mumbled, "Fine. Whatever." Acting more like a bratty pre-teen than a woman who was about to graduate from law school.

Crossing my arms over my chest, I said, "I'm sure you can protect me from a distance."

"Not if I have to take a bullet for you."

I jerked my head up. Seeing the commitment in his dark, piercing eyes crushed the fight out of me.

But it's not real. It couldn't be. *It's just a prank.* If I repeated it enough, I'd believe it again. I had to. Because things like this didn't happen in real life, at least not to me.

"Wait for me to open the door, please," AJ said as he parked and cut the engine.

I waited, but ignored his proffered hand. My nerves were on edge as I looked around, expecting someone to charge at me from every direction.

"No one will hurt you, Blake. I promise."

I don't know if it was because he used my name for the first time, or the conviction behind his promise, but it short-circuited my brain. I tried to find a smartass response, but failed.

Not wanting to look weak or scared, I squared my shoulders and held my head high before nodding and walking away.

Knowing AJ stayed a few steps behind me should have been a comfort, but it wasn't. His presence forced me to accept the reality I'd been doing my damnedest to ignore.

My life is in danger.

I tried to blame my rudeness on my exhaustion, but knew deep down it was because I no longer believed the note was a prank. And it scared me. Surely, the person who left it would have said something by now. *Plus, my father's acting weird.* Not to mention the constant reminder in the form of a tall, hulking bodyguard hovering all day.

The nightmare keeping me up all night was just the icing on the cake.

Unable to concentrate during class, I looked around. I kept expecting someone to jump out at me at any second. About thirty minutes into the lecture, I felt a tap on my shoulder.

Concern written all over his face, AJ leaned in—close enough for me to feel his warm breath on my neck—and whispered, "Are you okay?"

You're not supposed to be nice! "I'm fine," I huffed as much as I could while whispering.

He nodded as he leaned back. I faced forward and forced myself to focus on the lecture. *Fuck my life.*

When class was over, I stayed in my seat until most of the students had cleared out. It wasn't because I was nervous, I just didn't feel like getting jostled in the rush.

I'm not even good at lying to myself anymore.

My favorite pub, where I was meeting Paige and Danny, was only a few blocks away from campus, so I usually walked. But AJ insisted on driving, for my safety. Too tired to argue, I gave him the silent treatment instead.

I need a drink. Thankfully, I was done with my only class for the day, and was thinking I'd have more than one. *Why shouldn't I? It's not like I'm driving.*

Normally, I loved having lunch with Danny and Paige. Today, I dreaded seeing them, knowing they'd be upset I couldn't ditch AJ.

Part of me wanted to avoid them. *That's not who I am.* I could do this. I could put on a smile and get through the rest of the day. Who knows, maybe they wouldn't say anything, and I'd enjoy having a beer with my friends. Something I desperately needed.

Paige and Danny waited for me at a high top. Danny leaned back and dropped his arms to his sides, staring at AJ as we approached. I checked to see if AJ was offended, half hoping he would be. Nope, he was shaking his head back and forth, looking amused, as he read Danny's t-shirt: Violence is never the answer.

Paige's rainbow hoodie, with the words Make Love not War, painted across the front, was more subtle.

"I'll be right over there." AJ said, pointing at the bar.

"Okay." Then, because I didn't want to appear rude in public, I added, "Thanks."

"Why are you being nice to him?" Danny whined.

"I wasn't being nice." I just wasn't being rude.

"Are you getting your usual?" Paige asked, quickly changing the subject.

"I think I'll try something different today."

We ordered a round of beers to start, then looked at the menu. "Anyone want to share some nachos?" I asked.

"Only if we get them without meat," Danny replied.

Ugh. I wanted meat on mine. "Paige?"

She looked torn. Unlike Danny, she ate meat, but she didn't want to upset him. Neither of us usually opposed Danny when he was in a mood, often choosing vegetarian options when he was with us. "I'm fine with nachos without meat," she said while playing with a napkin.

"Fine," When I ordered, I asked the server to put the meat on the side. Then I ordered a burger with bacon and fries, instead of my usual Greek salad, reveling in the look of disgust on Danny's face. Apparently, I had the maturity of a nine-year-old today.

"What's gotten into you?" Danny huffed after chugging a third of his beer. The table wobbling as he set the pint glass down with a thud. Danny was a big boy, and often used more force than was necessary to do things. He wasn't muscular or strong, he just wanted everyone to think he was tough.

I looked over towards the bar in time to see AJ push up his sleeves. His forearms weren't fat. *I bet he doesn't have an ounce of fat on him.* Not that I cared. I wasn't attracted to guys just because they were tall, dark, and gorgeous. Or because they had sexy, muscular forearms. Being smart, caring, and kind were way more important than being tall, sexy, and covered in muscles.

"Sorry, I'm just tired. I had a really bad nightmare last night."

Paige said sorry, but I barely heard it over Danny saying, "Well, you're awake now. I bet you'll forget all about it after a beer or two."

Maybe he was right, and all I needed to shake off the lingering fear was an afternoon with friends, food, and a few beers.

I raised my glass and took a generous swig of the cool amber liquid; the bubbles tickled my nose and making me laugh. *Yeah, this is exactly what I need.* I glanced over at AJ, who was looking around the room.

I was adjusting to his presence, though I wished he'd leave his gun in the car. I asked him to do so, but got a hard no in reply. He claimed it was necessary to do his job, but that didn't mean I had to like it.

God, I miss my mom. She'd know how to help me deal with all of this. I missed her every day, but on hard days like this, her loss hit me harder.

Our server interrupted my pity party when she delivered our nachos and my side of seasoned ground beef. We kept the conversation light, talking about classes and our upcoming midterms, while we ate. I prided myself on working hard and earning good grades, and was worried all this stress and disruption would interfere with my studying time.

What if I fail?

I didn't have time to freak out because Stan Lancaster the Fourth walked over. We weren't friends, but we had acquaintances in common. He was a snob and his ego rubbed me the wrong way. He'd asked me out a few times, but I'd always said no.

Every so often, he'd try again. I thought it was because he wasn't used to hearing no. Paige thought it was because he was interested in my father's political connections.

He wouldn't be the first.

"Hi Blake," Stan greeted me, but no one else. *Rude.* I glanced up and saw AJ's back stiffen. "Mind if I join you?" Stan asked as he pulled out the fourth chair. He hadn't bothered to look, and the sudden movement caused Danny's bag to fall off.

"Dude, be careful," Danny yelled, before picking up his bag.

AJ stood up, facing us.

Stan didn't bother looking at Danny as he said sorry, his tone confirming my suspicion he wasn't.

God, he can be an obnoxious ass. Refusing to create a scene that would get AJ's attention, I plastered a fake smile on my face.

Chapter 13

AJ

From my spot at the bar, I could see Blake and the rest of the dining room. I ordered a coke with a lime wedge making it look like a mixed drink.

Blake didn't look like she was having a good time, but that was none of my business. I chuckled as I caught sight of Fuckface's t-shirt again. He tried to get a rise out of me by proudly displaying the words, "Violence is never the answer," stretched over his thick midsection. *Did he really think I'd react to a t-shirt?*

I understood him being upset about getting dropped to his knees, but I wasn't the enemy. You'd think he'd let it go after learning Blake had a bodyguard. But no, he needed to make it about him.

I laughed. If he wanted to pretend he was a victim and tell everyone who'd listen I'd committed some violent crime against him, he could. But what I'd done to protect Blake wasn't violence.

He has no idea what real violence is.

I did. I'd experienced it firsthand. The senseless violence, committed under the umbrella of war, leaving innocent bodies dead in the streets, and the necessary violence of my job, which left human traffickers and abusive exes dead on the floor.

Like the trafficker who'd taken Meg to exact his revenge, and the drunken ex who beat Emily and her parents while holding them at gun point.

"Violence is never the answer," I whispered to my drink.

Sometimes, violence is the only answer.

At least Paige's shirt was subtler, and she didn't look pissed off to see me.

I was sitting close enough to hear snippets of their conversation during lulls in the room volume, but mostly, I relied on reading Blake's facial expressions and body language.

I could see the tension in her shoulders under the cream-colored snug sweater she wore. It wasn't low-cut, but it emphasized her ample breasts none-the-less. It hung low, drawing my eyes to her ass, framed in shiny black leggings. She had curves in all the right places. I had to force myself to look away as I'd walked behind her.

Nope. I adjusted myself on the stool and scanned the room. *Get your head in the game.*

Blake tensed when a pretentious-looking guy approached the table. I stood, ready to pounce, no longer hiding the fact I was watching them.

He created a ruckus when he pulled the chair out too quickly and a bag fell off. *If he damaged Blake's laptop…*

Fuckface complained about his bag, but I didn't care about his shit.

The guy was singularly focused on Blake as he prattled on, either oblivious to or ignoring the fact she didn't want him there. I didn't have a reason to act, yet, so I watched and waited.

Blake's strained smile was like a bat signal. I stood poised, ready to strike the instant she gave the word, because she clearly didn't want to talk to this idiot.

Get a clue, dumbass. I worked my way towards the table, appearing calm and controlled. Two words in complete opposition to how I felt.

Things would go much better if he'd leave without me having to step in.

Then he put his hand on Blake's shoulder.

Seeing her flinch, I decided I didn't need words. *No one touches her.*

I closed the remaining distance at lightning speed, grabbed the guy by the wrist, twisting it as I pulled him away from her.

He cried out as I released him with a push.

"Blake, are you okay?" I turned just enough so I could see them both, my body positioned between them.

"I'm fine," she answered, irritation and gratitude sharing space in her expression.

"Who the fuck are you?" the guy asked with as much bravado as he could muster while looking up at me.

We both knew he wouldn't challenge me.

"Her bodyguard." Fuckface's voice dripped with disdain. *I should learn his name.* Nah, Fuckface suited him.

"Sorry, Stan," Blake apologized, though she shouldn't have. He was the one who should be apologizing. I considered forcing the issue, but it wasn't my place, so I let it go.

"No worries." Stan, not that I gave two fucks about knowing his name, leaned on the back of the chair and asked her out. Like I wasn't still standing there.

Discomfort radiated off her. How fucking self-absorbed was this guy that he didn't notice? And why weren't her friends stepping in to help her?

"I, um, don't think that's a good idea right now." She glanced at me.

"Him?" he asked, ignoring my death stare and looming presence. "Ditch him," Stan said with a smile so slimy it'd make a used car salesman look honest.

"I can't," Blake answered without looking at him.

"Time for you to go, Stan." I shifted, so I was between them again.

Stan tried to step around me. "Blake?"

Dude wasn't used to hearing the word no. I shifted, blocking his access. He didn't deserve to be in her presence, let alone look at her.

"You should go," she whispered from behind me.

He looked at me before saying, "Fine. Whatever." Blake's shoulders relaxed as he stormed off.

Ignoring the looks and comments from her friends, I asked Blake, "Are you ready to go?"

"But we haven't finished lunch yet," Paige said, sounding nervous.

"I'm not hungry anymore," Blake answered.

"But you said you'd buy us lunch," Fuckface whined.

I really don't like this guy. My gut told me he was using her, and I didn't understand what Blake saw in him. As far as I could tell, he was an awful friend and a leech. *I wonder if he's ever asked her out.*

"Right, sorry, Danny."

Knowing his name wouldn't stop me from calling him Fuckface.

She reached into her purse, pulled out her wallet, and put some cash on the table. At a quick glance, it looked like enough to cover all three lunches and another round of drinks.

"It's raining. Can we get a ride back with you?" Fuckface asked.

Blake's eyes flicked in my direction; her silent plea for help loud and clear.

"I'm sorry." I had to stop myself from calling him Fuckface. "That's not allowed." I was happy to take the blame, so she didn't have to.

"We'll go out when this is all over. Okay?" Blake asked. I hated how sad and small she sounded. *Fucking assholes.*

"Okay," Paige said. She wasn't nearly as bad as Fuckface. I had a feeling he intimidated her, because she'd looked apologetic a few times, but her expression always changed after looking at him.

Fuckface fit him perfectly.

"Fine. As long as he doesn't come." He straightened out his shirt, so I'd be sure to see it.

Ignoring the movement, Blake said, "Bye guys, I'll call later."

"Bye," they said together.

I took Blake's backpack and shouldered it, grateful she didn't argue.

I opened the door for her and instinctively put my hand on her lower back. It was a move we used with clients to control their movements. But that wasn't the only reason I did it—I wanted to stake my claim for everyone to see.

She didn't pull away, her warmth bleeding through the sweater to my hand.

I am right and truly fucked.

I had to find a way to get her out of my head because she'd never go for a guy like me. We were complete opposites; Blake Davenport hated everything I stood for, everything I was. And she had every reason to be afraid of me.

Chapter 14

Blake

I wanted to be pissed off at AJ for stepping in and chasing Stan away. After all, I was a modern, independent woman and didn't need some man coming to my rescue. But the only emotion I could find was gratitude. Stan had been getting progressively more insistent, and more handsy, each time he asked me out, refusing to accept I wasn't interested.

His ego was bigger than AJ's biceps.

Which were huge and bulging against his sleeves.

I let him open the bar door for me and looked at the ground as I walked by, hating how far I had to tilt my head back if I wanted to look him in the eyes.

I rarely cared about my height, or having plenty of padding. But AJ's physique made me acutely aware of my short and curvy body.

Most days, I didn't care about not being skinny and felt comfortable in my skin, but anytime I was near AJ, I felt like a fat little shrub standing next to a giant redwood. Priscilla's voice rang out in my head. "You're too young to let yourself go. You should cut back on your carbs."

Bitch. I was a smart, kind, and confident woman. I didn't-

The gentle pressure of AJ's hand on my lower back sent an electric shock up my spine, short-circuiting my brain.

I should've called him out for touching me, but I couldn't find the words. And if I was being completely honest with myself, I kind of liked the comfort of his touch.

Not because I liked AJ, I didn't.

A few steps past the door, AJ asked, "Where to?"

I shrugged, missing the warmth when he lowered his hand.

I turned my head and got an eyeful of solid chest muscles. *How often does he work out?* I glanced down at his abs. Of course, his stomach was flat. I bet he had a six-pack under his shirt. *Is a twelve-pack a thing for abs?* If it was, he probably had one.

When I finally lifted my eyes to his face, he grinned. *Great.* He noticed me staring. He was just arrogant enough to assume it meant I was into him. Which I wasn't.

"Want to get out here, away from all this," he swept his hand out, "for a few hours?"

Before I could stop myself, I said, "Yeah, that actually sounds good."

AJ suggested going to Weatherford. "There's a great local coffee shop, Grannie's, where you can relax and get some homework done."

Wow, that was remarkably nice of him. Maybe there was more to AJ than just muscles. I had to admit, he'd done his best to give me space at lunch, until Stan acted up. Now he was offering to drive me ninety minutes away so I could have some peace and quiet to do my homework. *And he didn't do anything too violent to Stan.* Even though he could have taken him down as easily as he had Danny. I forced myself not to laugh.

I wasn't the type of person who laughed at other people's pain.

Once we were in the car, I contemplated asking him to take me home, but decided I really wanted to get away.

"Can you let your dad know you'll be out for the afternoon so he doesn't worry?"

I hadn't even thought about telling my dad. I guess it makes sense he would, since my dad was paying him. "When will I be back?" I asked.

"I'll bring you back whenever you want. Just say the word."

I texted my dad to let him know I was going to a coffee shop to do my homework, adding I was with AJ so he wouldn't worry.

"Sent."

"Thank you," AJ said with a smile.

I couldn't help but notice the cute little pockets just above the line of his neatly trimmed beard. I'd always thought dimples on a guy were cute; but something about AJ's were sexy. I felt the heat rush to my cheeks and hoped he didn't notice.

I texted Paige and Danny, apologizing for leaving early and suggesting going out for dinner later in the week, away from campus. Paige accepted my apology and said she had plans Friday but could go on Saturday. Danny said he only go if I left the "big dumb bully" at home, claiming he couldn't have fun when he was worried about getting beat up or watching someone else get beat up.

After typing and erasing my response three times, I gave up. I didn't have the energy to argue with him. Besides, I might not need a bodyguard by the weekend, and if I did, it might be someone else.

I finally replied and suggested we plan for Saturday.

Maybe I'll be lucky and this will all be over by then.

Paige: I hope so, I want my roomie back {smiley face}

Needing a break from Danny, I put my phone down before he replied.

I don't know how long I stared out the window before AJ's deep voice brought my attention back to the car.

"I'm sorry. What was that?" I asked, turning my attention to him.

"What kind of law do you study?"

"Business." I had an internship lined up after graduation with a not-for-profit in Ft. Worth, but I didn't think he'd care. "You know you don't have to make small talk. I know it's not in the job description."

He didn't deserve my attitude, but I was still upset after the conversation with Danny and venting my frustrations.

"True, but it's better to talk than sit and stew." His smile was softer this time. *Is he trying to help me feel better?* I hadn't expected that from him. But he was right—talking was better than stewing.

"Sorry, that was rude." I might be upset with Danny and freaked out by my circumstances, but that didn't give me the right to be rude. That wasn't who I wanted to be. Besides, my mother taught me better than that.

"It's okay, you've had a rough few days."

Understanding and compassionate. I yawned and thought about asking him to stop at a coffee shop when I remembered he was taking me to one in Weatherford.

"I can't wait to get a big ass cup of coffee," I said to lighten the tension in the car.

"You're in for a treat. Grannie's has the best coffee around, and the shop has a fun, old style saloon feel to it."

"That's weird." I was trying to imagine the coffee shop, but all I could picture was old saloons from black and white movies.

"The building was a saloon before Mary's grandmother turned it into a coffee shop. She liked the idea of keeping the saloon decor. You wouldn't think so, but it works," he said. There was a hint of pride in his voice.

"Now I'm curious to see it." Much to my surprise, I was looking forward to my field trip with AJ.

I covered another yawn with my hand.

"Late night studying?"

Before I could stop myself, I admitted, "I had nightmares all night."

"I'm sorry. Want to tell me about it?"

What? I figured he's blow me off like my friends, but he sounded genuinely interested. I was still thinking about whether to share when he said, "Sometimes it lessens the impact if you give voice to it."

I didn't know if he was right, but I wanted to talk to someone about it.

"I was being chased, but I couldn't see his face. No matter how fast I ran, I couldn't get away."

AJ was right; it felt less scary when I summed it up. I wouldn't admit it to AJ, but it felt good telling someone about it. My dad would've listened, but he had enough on his plate and I didn't want to add more.

I expected AJ to make fun of me or downplay it.

"I'm not surprised, given the circumstances." His voice had an unexpected note of empathy.

Was this an act, or was I wrong about AJ being a big, dumb ogre?

Chapter 15

AJ

Blake needed to make a pit stop, so I stopped at a travel center. I expected her to argue when I followed her into the store and stood outside the restroom, but she didn't. While grateful she wasn't arguing, I missed her fiery side.

While I waited, I called Meg, explaining the situation and asking if she could meet us at Grannie's. I figured Blake could use a break and some supportive company. Blake could always decline the offer if she didn't want company.

Meg suggested bringing Emily and said, "We'll help Blake feel right at home."

Of course they would.

"Thanks, Meg." I could hear someone talking to her in the background.

"Hang on, Jack wants to talk to you."

A few seconds later, Jack asked, "Everything okay?"

"Yeah, Blake wanted to get away from campus, so I suggested Grannie's."

"I'm sure Mom will be thrilled, but why'd you suggested a coffee shop ninety minutes away?"

Good question.

Because I wanted to get to know her during the drive.

Because I wanted to be her knight in shining armor.

Because I wanted her to meet the people in my life.

"I thought it'd help Blake relax if she was out of her normal environment." *And her friends are shit.*

"Okay." I knew that tone—he didn't believe me. "I found some inconsistencies in our research. I'll stop by Grannie's and fill you in."

"I'll let you know when I'm close." The restroom door opened. "Gotta run." I disconnected the call without waiting for a response.

"Need a water or snack for the road?" I asked.

"I'm good. Thanks."

When we got back to the car, I reached to open the back door, but Blake stopped me.

"Would it, um, be okay if I sat in the front?" she asked, looking at her boots. "I don't like feeling like I'm being chauffeured around." My dad had a driver, but I usually preferred to drive myself.

Hell yeah, it's okay.

"Of course." I opened the passenger door.

"Thank you."

I closed the door and jogged to the driver's side. Before opening my door, I wiped the goofy grin off my face.

We'd only been on the road for a few minutes when Blake broke the silence. "What does AJ stand for?"

"Andrew Janerek." No one had called me by my first name, the one I shared with my father, since the day he left and I swore to never use it again. "But no one calls me Andrew."

Ever.

"What's your middle name?"

"I don't have one. My mother and father couldn't agree, so they didn't give me one." Later in life, I heard my father was so pissed off at my mom for daring to argue about my middle name that he smacked her around as soon as they got home from the hospital.

Unfortunately, I inherited his temper.

"What about you? Do you have a middle name?"

"Promise you won't laugh?"

"No." I smiled. If she was asking, then I probably would. "Come on, out with it." I prodded.

"Edith." she said, her eyes daring me to laugh. "It was my grandmother's name."

I didn't think her middle name was laughable.

Blake Edith Davenport.

"Your initials spell bed." *Don't go there.*

"They do." She tried to be serious, but the smile on her face gave away her amusement.

We settled into comfortable conversation for the rest of the drive.

When we got to Grannie's, Jack was waiting by the door. I dropped Blake off, leaving her in his care while I parked.

By the time the bells above the door chimed my entrance, Jack had introduced Blake to Meg, Emily, Beth, and Mary. Surrounded by the outgoing, friendly women, Blake looked like a deer in the headlights. Their efforts to make her feel welcome having the opposite effect.

I stepped up behind Blake, offering my silent comfort. My right hand wanted to reach out and touch her, but I knew that'd be a problem. Not only would it piss off Blake, but the gesture wouldn't go unnoticed.

Jack wasn't the only one in the room with eagle-eyed observation skills.

Mary looked at me over Blake's head. "I hear my coffee is worth driving ninety minutes to try," she said with a laugh.

"Without a doubt." I smiled.

"Blake, would you like to sit with us and relax for a bit, or do you need to study?" Meg asked.

Blake looked at me, several emotions crossing her face.

"They'll understand if you can't," I whispered.

Tension drained from her body as she smiled. "I can sit for a few minutes. Thank you."

"What would you like to drink?" Beth asked.

"A skinny latte, please." She reached into her bag and pulled out her wallet.

"First one's on the house," Mary said as she and Beth headed to the counter to make our drinks. "AJ, the usual?"

"Yes, ma'am."

"You mispronounced Mary again," she called out with a chuckle. She was always reminding me to call her Mary, but it never felt right.

Blake's laugh reduced me to mush.

I stared. Openly fucking stared as she walked away with Meg and Emily.

The hair on the back of my neck stood up as Jack's voice broke my trance. "Come on, Janerek."

Hopefully, no one else noticed me staring.

We sat at a high top in the middle of the dining room. From our position, we could see out the windows lining the front of the café. We were in the perfect position to intercept if anyone came in and tried anything. Not just for Blake, but for the other women, too.

"Wanna tell me what that was all about?" he asked.

"Nothing." Something.

"Right, that didn't look-"

"What'd you find out?" I cut him off. I couldn't act on my attraction to Blake, so there was no point talking about it. The very thought of losing my temper and hurting her scared the shit out of me. I couldn't, wouldn't, risk it. She deserved so much better.

Jack paused before shaking his head and shifting gears. "Doug and I have been looking into Davenport's case history to see if anything or anyone stands out."

"And?"

"And things aren't adding up. He has a track record of cases getting dismissed for petty reasons. We compared it to other DAs in the area, and his percentage is well above average. Doug dug deep and connected a few of the cases, but it wasn't easy."

"You think he's dirty?" I looked at Blake; it'd kill her to learn her father was crooked.

"Too early to say," he glanced at Blake, "but there are a few red flags. We've got a list of people to interview."

"Could the threat be because he didn't take a bribe?" I wanted him to be innocent, for Blake's sake.

"It could be, but we're not making any assumptions."

I nodded, knowing I could hope and wish all I wanted, but it wouldn't change the outcome.

Laughter floated over to us from the booth where our girls were sitting. The sound made my chest constrict. I glanced over; Blake was relaxed and enjoying herself.

My heart leaped in my chest when Blake turned and smiled at me. *She's beautiful, classy, intelligent, and so far out of my league we might as well be on different planets.*

"Jamie's free tomorrow if you want a break," Jack's smug tone interrupted my train of thought.

"No."

Damn it. I took the bait.

He grinned. "Yeah, I figured as much."

"What's that supposed to mean?" I knew exactly what he meant. It'd be a cold day in hell before I let anyone take over the day shift.

Instead of answering, Jack exaggerated his movements to look at his watch. "By the time you leave, it'll be Jay's shift." He picked up his phone. "Want me to ask him to start early and drive Blake back?"

My best friend is an asshole. Glancing at Blake, I grumbled, "That won't be necessary."

Chapter 16

Blake

AJ was right. The coffee shop had the typical barista counter, but the decor belonged in an old-fashioned saloon. The high top tables in the center looked like they belonged in a bar, not a coffee shop. Old photos, and new ones in black and white, decorated the walls along with shelves filled with old colorful bottles and cowboy hats.

Somehow, it worked, providing a comfortable, relaxing atmosphere.

"You remember Meg?" Jack asked.

"Hi. It's nice to meet you, again," I shook her offered hand.

"It's nice to see you," she said. "This is Emily, Jamie's fiancé."

By the time AJ came in, Jack had also introduced me to Mary, John's wife, Jack's mother, and owner of Grannie's, and Beth, Doug's fiancé, Mary's best friend, and café manager.

Talk about a small town. It seemed like everyone was related to, or married to, someone from Sheppard and Sons.

Within seconds I could tell these women were close. So, not only did I feel like an outsider intruding, but it reminded me of what I didn't have—women in my life who loved or supported me the way these women did for each other.

My mom had, but I'd lost her after graduating from high school. And Paige used to, but lately she hadn't been there for me.

I missed them both.

I plastered on a smile. Faking comfort in group settings was nothing new to me. If I could do it for an entire evening at one of Daddy's parties, I could do it here for a few minutes. Then I could go hide in a corner and study.

When I sensed AJ standing near me, my shoulders relaxed, and it took less effort to smile. *What's that about?* I told myself it was because he was my bodyguard and his presence meant safety. As much as I hated to admit it, I was getting used to him being around.

More than that, his presence comforted me. *I'm more afraid than I care to admit.*

When Meg invited me to sit with them, I sensed an energy shift. Had AJ asked them to come here? Was I some kind of charity chase? Was her invitation to make AJ happy?

Part of me wanted to decline the invitation, storm off and wallow in my anger at AJ for setting this up.

But I didn't. Even if he set it up, they didn't deserve my wrath. As far as I could tell, their invitation seemed genuine.

The other part appreciated the distraction, and if I was being completely honest with myself, it was thoughtful of AJ to think of it.

God only knows why AJ's reassurance had made the decision easier, but it did.

I accepted the invitation. I could always say I had to study and escape if I was uncomfortable.

Except I wasn't, and an hour flew by in the blink of an eye as I learned more about each of them. I loved how they all had their own careers, even if it surprised me. I assumed all alpha men were toxic and wanted their wives to stay home. The words 'barefoot and pregnant' crossed my mind. But I was clearly wrong. *At least for this group.*

When asked, I confessed I wasn't seeing anyone. I didn't miss Meg glancing at Jack and AJ with a devilish grin on her face. *Must be an inside joke with Jack.*

Mary excused herself to cover the counter during the shift change and came back with a plate of pastries a few minutes later. I loved baked treats but rarely ordered them, knowing they'd go straight to my hips and ass. Neither needed any more padding.

I compared my short, full figure with each of them. I shouldn't have, but I did. Emily and Meg were both thin and fit. Mary and Beth weren't as thin, but that made sense, they were older and had kids. My only excuse was bad genes and a carb craving. Priscilla, the queen of starving herself and Zumba, was always telling me I needed to eat less and work out more.

"What about us?" Jack asked as he approached our corner booth.

Mary raised an eyebrow.

"Right. I'll just slink back to my table with my tail between my legs." His words in complete opposition to the playful expression on his face.

"Nina, would you please be so kind as to give Jack and AJ a couple of cookies before they waste away to nothing?" Mary called over to the counter.

"Of course," Nina said before asking. "What kind do you want?"

"I still can't believe you poached Chase's favorite babysitter," Beth said with a grin.

"Hey!" Meg pretended offense.

"You're his favorite aunt." Beth soothed her.

"What did you expect after giving her a glowing recommendation and insisting I hire her?" Mary defended herself.

"Right, I did that, didn't I?" Beth admitted. She turned to me and explained, "She's paying her way through college and needed a job. Her old boss was a bit handsy." She wiggled her hands. "And we needed a new barista."

"Hiring her was a no-brainer," Mary added. "And Chase still has my girls to watch him when Nina's not available." She beamed at Meg and Emily.

"I'm just happy I've graduated from Ms. Emily to Auntie Emily," Emily added.

"Hopefully you two will claim the title mom soon, and give me some grandbabies," Mary said as she pointed between Meg and Emily.

Meg and Emily looked at each other, shrugged, and said, "Someday."

Beth and Mary got up occasionally to help in the café, but otherwise the conversation flowed without interruption. I opened up a little and told them about my mom.

I inherited my height and blue eyes from her, and she was the one who'd taught me to respect everyone and to work for what I wanted in life. She was the reason I'd worked so hard to earn scholarships, despite knowing my parents could afford my college tuition.

I'd loved her, and she'd loved me. The complete opposite of my relationship with Priscilla.

"Well, not the complete opposite. We don't hate each other," I corrected myself. "We tend to avoid each other as much as possible; me ignoring her constant criticism and her ignoring my constant snark." I didn't tell them I frequently compared her to evil stepmom characters.

We kept talking, and before long, over two hours had passed.

Knowing my dad expected me home for dinner, and needing to do some homework before then, I reluctantly stood up and excused myself.

After a round of friendly goodbyes, AJ left to get the car. While Jack waited with me; Meg and Mary invited me to visit them any time I wanted.

I had a feeling I'd want to. Despite the early awkwardness, I now felt relaxed and rejuvenated. Time away from Dallas was exactly what I'd needed.

AJ must have told Jack I wanted to sit up front because he opened the passenger door. Then he put my backpack, the one he insisted on carrying for me, in the back seat. When I tried to argue, Meg told me not to bother, adding, "The guys all have old school gentlemanly manners."

To which Mary said, glowing with pride, "Damn straight."

Their behavior made sense now; she'd raised her sons to be old-fashioned gentlemen. I remembered John giving off southern gentleman vibes, too. It'd make sense for him to demand that behavior from his sons and employees.

Mary didn't strike me as someone who'd encourage her sons to believe women were weak. *I bet no one thinks she's weak.*

Grief washed over me. *I miss my mom so much.* I bet she and Mary would've liked each other.

Her loss had hit me hard. When she died, I was so lost in my grief I almost quit college before my first semester started. But my dad reminded me she wouldn't want me to give up. He'd told me, "She wanted you to get your degree and do good in the world. You can honor her memory by going to school and making her proud."

That was exactly what I did. I went to school, worked my ass off to get mostly A's, and would graduate law school with honors in May.

"Did you have a good time?" AJ's question brought me back to the present.

"I did."

"Sorry I surprised you. I was afraid you'd ask me to bring you home if you knew."

I probably would have. *Probably?* I one-hundred percent would have. "I was mad at first, but turns out, it was exactly what I needed." After a pause, I turned towards him. "Thank you."

"I'm glad." AJ's soft smile did weird things to my insides.

I squashed them. He wasn't my type. Sure he was surprisingly sensitive and considerate. *Don't forget easy on the eyes.* Like I could forget that tidbit of information with him sitting a few feet away. *He smells good too.* But he was rough around the edges, and nothing like the men I usually dated.

I felt heat flood my cheeks as I looked away.

"Is today the last day you're stuck with me?" Somewhere in my mind I remembered John saying AJ would be with me for the first part of the week and then someone else would take over.

"I'm not stuck with you," he answered. Something about the way he said it made me blush again. "But you're stuck with me all week."

The corner of his mouth lifted in a smile, softening his normally gruff features. *He looks friendlier when he smiles.*

Oh my God. *How dare I think that?* How many times had I been told I'd look prettier if I smiled? How many times had I wanted to punch someone for saying it? I'd never hit someone, but that didn't mean I hadn't thought about it.

I wasn't as extreme as Danny, but I didn't like violence and believed communication could resolve most issues.

We talked about random things for the rest of the drive. It was after five by the time AJ parked in the driveway.

"Jaden will relieve me at six," AJ informed me as he walked me to the door.

"Okay." I didn't really care who'd be here since I wouldn't be leaving the house again until tomorrow, when AJ picked me up for class. Wait, why didn't he have Jaden drive me home?

My head snapped up when I heard AJ's voice. "Have a good night." He handed me a business card. "My cell is on there. Call me if you need anything or if just want to talk."

I didn't think I would, but I took the card anyway. It was probably a good idea for me to have his phone number. *Does he have mine?* Would he call me if I volunteered to give it to him? It didn't matter; it wasn't like I wanted us to be friends.

But he should have my number, just in case.

"Thanks. Should I give you mine?"

"I have it, and your father's." He grinned, showing off his dimples.

"Right, of course. Good night, AJ."

"Good night, Blake." I didn't mind that he'd stopped calling me Ms. Davenport. Not one bit.

Chapter 17

AJ

Dreams of Blake kept me up most of the night, so after taking a shower, cold enough to make a polar bear happy, I stopped by Grannie's for a large coffee before driving to Dallas.

I texted Jay when I was twenty minutes out so he'd know to expect me early.

Blake occupied my thoughts far more than I cared to admit. More than I wanted. Seeing her relaxed and laughing had done funny things to my heart.

Getting to know her better on the ride home had put her front and center in my mind, and fantasies, all night. I'd need a coffee IV to get through the day.

And the will of a saint.

"Thanks, man," Jay said when I handed him the coffee I'd grabbed in town. We stood beside his car, enjoying the early morning sun as we talked. The forecast called for perfect spring weather, with sunny skies and warm temperatures.

"Anytime. All good here?"

"Quiet night." He sipped his coffee. "I'll be glad when I get to see some real action."

My anger flared, because in this instance action meant a threat to Blake, but I choked it down and reminded myself he didn't mean it that way. He was young, and used to the action that came with being in the Special Forces. Overnight security duties would seem boring in comparison.

"Give it time, we all started out doing the boring jobs," I said. "And remember, in our line of work, boring is good."

"That's what everyone keeps telling me," he said. "If you're good, I'll take off."

"Yeah, I'm good." I clapped him on the back and said, "Go get some rest."

Thankfully, Jay didn't ask me why I was early. He didn't need to know it was getting harder to leave Blake's safety in anyone else's hands, no matter how much I trusted them.

An hour later, my phone buzzed.

"Janerek," I answered.

"Jay says you relieved him early?" I could hear the laughter in Jack's voice.

I should've known he'd mention it.

"Is that a problem?" I asked.

"No. Not as long as we're providing the coverage we promised."

I grunted and scanned the area to remind myself I was there to do a job, not to see Blake.

"You got it bad, dude." Jack didn't bother to hide his laughter. "I've never seen you look at or react to anyone the way you do to Blake."

"Fuck you, Sheppard." *Great come back, idiot.* I had a better chance of being crowned Miss America than I did of convincing Jack I wasn't falling for Blake.

"That's what I thought." He paused. "Listen, I'm the last person to tell you not to get involved, but you have a job to do. Don't let your emotions be a distraction."

"Yes, sir." I was being an ass to my best friend. "Sorry, man, I don't know what's gotten into me."

"I do, you're in love."

Fuck.

"Hell no." That couldn't happen. Not only would she never feel the same way about me, but I'd vowed to never get married or have kids. I couldn't turn into an abusive husband or father if I didn't have a wife or kids.

Of course, Jack didn't know that. He only knew the lame excuse I'd given; there were too many beautiful women in the world to settle down.

He laughed again. "Let me know if you need anything."

"Will do." I disconnected the call before he could say anything else.

Not wanting to be alone with my thoughts, I stared at the front door, willing Blake to come out early. When that didn't work, I walked the driveway, making sure I never lost sight of the door.

After what felt like a million years, the door opened. I started to move before seeing Blake, eating up the distance to the steps in a few long strides.

"Good morning," I said as I waited for her at the bottom.

"Morning." Her sad smile made me want to swoop in and destroy whoever or whatever had caused it.

I stepped in behind her and escorted her to the sedan. "Front or back today?" *Please say the front.*

"Front, if that's okay."

It was more than okay.

"Of course." I tried to sound neutral as I opened her door.

I wanted to ask her if she'd had more nightmares, but knew from experience it was never a good idea to ask a woman anything she might interpret to mean she didn't look good.

Blake was quiet, staring out the window most of the ride. I wanted to offer her comfort, an ear to bend or a shoulder to cry on, but it wasn't my place to pry. No matter how badly I wanted to.

I'll have to settle for being the strong, silent type, and hope she reaches out.

She didn't.

Not long after getting to campus, I figured out one reason she was upset. Her friends, though I was loath to call them that, were ignoring her. Fuckface shot daggers at me as we approached. Before Blake could say hi; he walked away, dragging Paige with him. Paige shot Blake an apologetic look over her shoulder.

Who needs enemies with friends like that?

Blake sat in the back of the class, packing up and leaving before the professor finished the lecture.

"Can we go off campus for lunch?" she asked.

"Of course. Do you have somewhere in mind?"

She did. When we got to the restaurant, she asked me if I wanted to sit with her.

Hell yeah. This wasn't a date, but that didn't mean I couldn't keep her company, and maybe get to know her better.

"Unless it's against the rules." She sounded sad and defeated.

I missed her feisty side. Hell, I'd let her call me an ogre a thousand times if it'd bring back the spark in her eyes.

"It's not." When the hostess seated us, Blake claimed the chair facing the door before she realized I'd pulled out the other one for her. I fully expected to get an earful for being chivalrous, even if it wasn't the main reason.

"Can you sit here, please?" I asked.

"Sure, but why?"

Hearing her agree, without so much as a hint of irritation, made me want to show Fuckface what it really felt like to be tackled. He deserved it for making her feel like shit. Blake had no control over the circumstances making me necessary.

"So I can see the door." I said as I pointed. As much a reminder to myself as to explain to Blake, because my thoughts were dangerously close to overprotective boyfriend territory.

After the server took our orders, Blake asked me if I ate alone often when I was working.

"Depends on the job, but I suppose I eat alone more often than most people." Eating alone, or in the car, was a normal part of the job.

"I hate eating alone."

Which explained why she asked me to sit with her. Not because she wanted me here, but because she didn't want to eat alone.

At least she thinks eating with me is better than eating alone.

It wasn't much, but it was an improvement over how she felt two days ago.

Chapter 18

Blake

How lame was I that I had to ask AJ to sit with me so I wouldn't look pathetic, or feel so lonely, after my friends deserted me. Danny had texted me last night, saying he spoke for himself and Paige when he gave me an ultimatum—them or AJ.

It didn't matter that it wasn't my choice to have a bodyguard or that my life was in danger. Danny complained about the stress being around AJ caused him and said he wouldn't subject himself to that kind of trauma. He was being over-dramatic, even for him, and it hurt.

It wasn't bad enough he felt the need to abandon me, but he included Paige. When had she let him start speaking for her? How had I never noticed how selfish he was?

Maybe it's time to reevaluate my friendships.

Oddly enough, AJ was being nicer to me than my so-called friends. He'd shown a level of compassion and 'friendliness' that I knew wasn't part of the job. I'd known plenty of people with personal security, and I didn't think any of them had ever been brought to their bodyguard's hometown because they'd had a bad day.

AJ did that for me. Not only did he bring me to Weatherford, he set up a meet and greet with his friends to help me relax. And now he's having lunch with me. Not that I'd call him a friend, but he was being nice, even though he didn't have to be.

Our conversation flowed. To my surprise, he didn't ask about my friends or pry for information about the note and who might have sent it.

"Did you always know you wanted to be a lawyer?"

"No, I wanted to be a few different things when I was a kid." Mostly I wanted to be a ballerina, but the generic answer felt safer.

"Like what?" he asked before dipping a fry in ketchup and popping it into his mouth.

"When I was a little girl, I wanted to be a ballerina." *Why did I tell him?* I expected him to make fun of me like most people usually did.

"What made you change your mind?"

I'm too short and too round to be a dancer.

"I sucked." I chuckled. "My parents spent a fortune on private lessons hoping I'd get better, but my pudgy body and two left feet refused to improve." It crushed twelve-year-old Blake to give up her dream.

I'd never told anyone before. *So why did I tell AJ?*

Maybe it was because he gave me his full attention, except for the occasional glance around the room. Maybe it was because I never felt like he judged me.

Having that much focused attention was flattering and unnerving. People were rarely as interested in what I had to say as AJ was. None of my boyfriends had ever paid such close attention.

What would it be like to have AJ as a boyfriend? Would he be generous and kind, or demanding and selfish? Was he the type of guy who gave multiple orgasms, like the ones I read about in rom-coms?

I bet he is. I watched the muscles in his neck work as he scanned the room again. *Who has muscles in their neck?* Heat crept up my neck and across my cheeks.

"Blake, are you okay?"

Shit.

As I slowly lifted my eyes to make eye contact, I noticed his full lips. I couldn't help staring at his dimples as he grinned.

More heat flooded my face.

If my face gets any hotter, I'll spontaneously combust. I suddenly felt like one of those southern belles who needed to fan her face to keep from fainting, only it was March and I wasn't wearing a corset.

"Blake?"

"I'm okay," I answered. The humor in his voice hinted he hadn't missed my reaction.

Kill me now.

I spent the rest of lunch staring at my plate. When the check came, I tried to pick it up, but AJ beat me to it.

That was new, too. My friends rarely paid for their own lunches, and never insisted on paying for mine. Not that they couldn't afford it, they just never offered.

I need new friends. Friends who acted more like AJ than Danny. Paige fell somewhere in the middle, but was too easily influenced by Danny. She wasn't always like that, but over time, she'd given up being herself when he was around.

Someone like AJ, but not him. AJ and I couldn't date. Maybe if things were different, but we lived in two very different worlds. And he was too macho-man for my tastes. Too controlling. Too alpha male.

I wanted a calm, polite, professional man. Someone like Daddy. He had a great job, served his community, was polite and kind to everyone. He even hosted dinner parties for friends and colleagues.

I don't think he's ever raised a fist to anyone.

AJ was the complete opposite of what I wanted. So why couldn't I stop thinking about him? *Why do I blush every time I see his dimples pop when he grins?*

And why was I thinking of him in terms of dating rather than friendship?

Concentrating during my second class of the day was nearly impossible. It was bad enough someone had threatened me and disrupted my life, but did they had to do it a week before mid-terms?

I prided myself on being a good student and the idea of my GPA suffering because of some asshole pissed me off.

After class, I told AJ I wanted to go to the library. Hopefully, the normalcy would help me relax so I could study. I expected an argument, but all he said was, "Lead the way."

I could feel his powerful presence just behind me, off to the right. When we changed directions after crossing the quad, his shadow engulfed me.

As we approached the library, a guy came up and asked me to sign his petition.

Before I could ask what it was for, AJ waved him off. Undeterred, the guy asked again, shoving the clipboard at my chest.

I instinctively reached for it, but AJ slapped it back as he stepped between us.

Damn it! I didn't need AJ causing another scene.

AJ squared his shoulders as he stood at his full height and told the guy to back off.

The poor guy looked like he wanted to piss his pants as he slinked away.

I yanked on AJ's arm to turn him around.

"That was not necessary," I said, exasperated by his need to use violence when a polite word would do.

"What wasn't necessary?" He scanned the crowd over my head.

I fought back the urge to scream. "Using violence and scaring him," I answered as evenly as I could.

"How was that violent? I never touched the guy." He kept his voice low as he argued.

Technically, that was true, but he had physically intimidated the poor guy.

Deciding it wasn't worth arguing over, I rolled my eyes before turning and walking away. I didn't like this AJ; he was a brute. The AJ I had lunch with was a lot nicer.

"I've changed my mind. I want to go home." I wouldn't be able to concentrate if I had to worry about him scaring anyone who talked to me.

Chapter 19

AJ

Blake didn't get it, and it pissed me off. Her life was in danger, and she refused to accept it was my job to keep threats at a safe distance. She didn't have to like it, but she had to accept it. And things would go a hell of a lot smoother if she stopped arguing about it.

Was I more assertive than necessary when I stopped that kid?

No. Well, maybe.

Okay, yes. But Blake was mine to protect and I wouldn't let anyone get close enough to hurt or intimidate her. And while she may not remember flinching when that guy got too close; I couldn't forget it. Hell, she probably didn't even realize she had. That asshole made my woman flinch.

Unacceptable.

When did I start referring to her as mine? I need to cut that shit out and focus.

When she walked to the rear door of the car and threw it open, I knew it'd be a long, silent drive back to her father's house. And I was right; her frosty silence was deafening.

She didn't wait for me after I parked. Instead, shoving the door open, getting pissed when it bounced back at her, and pushing it open again. When she finally got out, she practically ran to the door.

It would have been comical if I wasn't the reason she was angry.

I made sure she got in safely before parking and waiting impatiently for Eric to relieve me for the night.

Why didn't she understand I was there to protect her? And while she didn't think it was true, everyone else on the team would react the same way. Almost. To do our job, we had to assume anyone acting aggressively—no matter who—was a threat until proven otherwise.

For all I knew, that kid had a knife or a needle so letting him get close enough to make contact was out of the question.

The drive back to Weatherford did nothing to improve my mood. I was stupid for letting her get to me. It wasn't like I was her boyfriend, or even her friend. I was her bodyguard. *A bodyguard she doesn't want, let alone like.* Nothing more.

Part of me couldn't wait until Maxwell took over the day shift, so I could be free of her attitude.

Part of me wanted to be on duty twenty-four-seven.

Part of me wanted to forget I'd ever laid eyes on Blake Edith Davenport.

All of me wanted to shove my hands into her sassy pink-striped, blond hair, pull her head back until she had no choice but to look at me, and kiss her until the annoyingly sexy, irritating, sassy attitude drained right the fuck out of her.

I slammed my hands on the steering wheel.

I am so fucking fucked. Blake was under my skin, living rent free in my head, and turning my world inside out.

And I wasn't happy about it. I didn't want to fall in love. *I can't.* What if I turned out like my father?

I slammed my hands on the steering wheel again.

A call interrupted the radio and my spiraling thoughts.

"Janerek," I barked after hitting accept.

"Dude, who pissed you off?" Jack's question echoed in the car.

"Nothing," I forced myself to calm down.

"Whatever, dude. Can you meet me for dinner? I want to update you on the Davenport investigation."

The hair on the back of my neck stood up.

"What'd you find?" I had a feeling I wouldn't like what I heard.

"Not over the phone."

I definitely won't like what I hear. My knuckles turned white as I gripped the steering wheel and applied more pressure to the gas pedal.

"Where are we meeting?"

Dreading what Jack had to say only added to my foul mood. I walked into the bar and scanned; Jack and Meg were in a corner booth.

"Thank God you're here. I'm starving," Meg said when I sat down.

"You didn't have to wait for me," I said, knowing it wouldn't make a difference. Meg was too polite not to wait.

"We only half waited. The appetizers should be out soon," she admitted. I'd only known Jack for about ten years, but I was confident Meg was the best thing that had ever happened to him. And I knew beyond the shadow of a doubt he was the best thing to happen to her.

"Thanks."

Jack waited until the server took our orders before starting. "You won't like this," he said.

"Just tell me." I hadn't told a single soul about my attraction to Blake, but Jack knew. Sometimes his observational skills made it seem like he had a sixth sense.

Turns out, Jack and Doug ran into a lot of resistance when they started questioning people about DA Steven Davenport. He'd dismissed a lot of charges against associates of known crime bosses under questionable circumstances.

"We got a lot of doors slammed in our faces, figuratively and literally," Jack said.

"You think he's dirty?" I asked.

Jack's hesitation was answer enough. "I think he pissed someone off enough for them to use Aurora to get to him," Jack finally answered.

We used Blake's call sign and talked in hushed tones despite the noise in the bar being loud enough to keep most people from hearing us. *One can never be too careful.*

Giving our female clients Disney princess call signs was Meg's idea back when she first started at SSI, after John poached her from Mary. Hers was Cinderella when we saved her from Sullivan's revenge. Meg believed every girl dreamed of being a princess, even if they wouldn't admit it.

I didn't think it was true, but the system worked for us.

We'd called Emily Snow White when she was a client. When her best friend, Ashley, asked for one, I'd suggested one of the seven dwarves, but she didn't think the names fit. I couldn't remember who suggested creating an eighth dwarf, Flirty, but it fit her to a tee. And Ashley had loved it.

Damn. I hadn't thought about Ashley since I started this detail. We hooked up regularly, and I usually thought about her every couple of days. Especially if I had a bad day and wanted a couple of beers. *Or some physical stress relief.* She was the perfect friend-with-benefits. Neither of us wanted a commitment, we had a lot of fun together, and by being each other's dates for Sheppard events, we kept everyone off our backs.

"Has Blake said anything?" Jack asked.

What the fuck kind of question is that?

"You mean has she made some grand confession of her father's guilt that I swept under the rug? No, she hasn't." How dare he imply Blake might have knowledge of, or be involved in, her father's alleged illegal activity? Or that I wouldn't tell him the instant I heard it.

Jack held his hands up in surrender. "Sorry, man, I didn't mean it like that, but I had to ask."

"No. You didn't." I leaned back and crossed my arms, daring him to say something else.

He nodded, but kept his mouth shut. *Smart man.*

"Should we have two people at the house?" I asked, suddenly worried one wasn't enough.

"Eric knows to be on high alert, and Dean is on standby in the area."

I nodded. Worried the person who sent the note would act sooner rather than later, I debated packing a suitcase and heading to Dallas for the foreseeable future.

"We're increasing her coverage during the day; I'll be your backup on campus tomorrow. Jamie, Dad, and Doug will keep pulling threads. Maxwell agreed to reach out to the FBI and see what they know."

When I didn't answer, Jack asked, "We good?"

"Yeah." I nodded and leaned forward. "Thanks." Jack questioning Blake's character might have pissed me off, but it was temporary. He was doing his job, which sometimes meant asking stupid questions.

Knowing Jack would have my back the next day made me feel better. We'd faced hell together in the Middle East, and I trusted him with my life.

I trust him with Blake's life.

Which meant so much more.

Chapter 20

Blake

Fuck AJ and fuck SSI. I can't believe AJ almost attacked that poor guy just because he asked for a signature on his petition. *Seriously, who does that?*

I tossed my bag on the floor and stormed down the hall to my father's office.

Why is his fucking door closed? He never closed it when he worked from home. At least I'd never seen him do it.

I tried the handle. Locked. Pissed off at AJ but blaming my mood on my father's locked door, I pounded my fist on the hard wood.

"Priscilla, I told you I'm busy!" The door muffled his yell.

It wasn't like him to snap at her. I wonder what did she did.

"It's me, Daddy."

"Just a second, Princess," his voice softened as he called through the door.

I tapped my foot as I waited for him to let me in, trying to imagine what was taking so long. After what felt like forever, he opened the door.

"Sorry, I was on an important call." He gave me a hug. "Now, what's got you so upset you tried to bust down my door?"

"I don't want a bodyguard anymore. AJ almost attacked a guy because he got too close." I paced around his office. "All he wanted was a signature on his petition."

"Blake, honey, I'm paying SSI to make sure no one gets close enough to hurt you. He was just doing his job."

I didn't appreciate his condescending tone.

"But Daddy, he's ruining my life," I pouted and crossed my arms across my chest.

"You're so dramatic," Priscilla said as she walked in and plopped into one of the oversized leather chairs in front of Daddy's desk.

I ignored her. My father greeted her.

He looks so tired. "Are you feeling okay?" He had dark bags under his bloodshot eyes and I'd swear he had more gray in his hair. "Maybe you should go away for a relaxing weekend."

"We can't go away because we're paying for your stupid bodyguard," Priscilla whined. The look she gave me reminded me just how young she was.

"Priscilla, that's enough," he chided her.

When had they ever been worried about money?

"This wouldn't be a problem if your father hadn't left everything to *her* in a trust fund," she snapped at him in her high-pitched voice.

Is that what this was about? *She's pissed about my inheritance.* Priscilla married my father, expecting him to inherit my grandfather's millions. It wasn't my fault they didn't find out grandpa left most of his fortune to me, in a trust fund, until after they were married. It'd been a shock when we found out at the reading of the will. And boy was Priscilla angry. When I asked, Dad said he didn't know why Grandpa had changed his will.

Unless Grandpa included a letter explaining it, for me to open on my birthday, I'd never know why.

In two weeks, when I turn twenty-five, I'll be a millionaire. It felt surreal.

"That's enough," Daddy barked.

Something was definitely wrong; he never barked at either of us.

"Blake, I'm fine. Just worried about you, that's all."

He avoided making eye contact, which was a huge red flag. There had to be something he wasn't telling me. Was he really having money problems, or was Cilla being a bitch? Was he worried I'd judge him if he had money problems?

"You don't need to worry about me. I'm fine."

"Well, I'm not fine. And I don't think Blake needs protection anymore. It's been days and nothing has happened." Priscilla glared at me like all this was my fault. "It's not enough we're paying for her college tuition, but we have to fork over thousands for her to have a bodyguard, too."

I'd had enough of her constantly complaining about me and snapped. "The scholarships I earned covered more than half my college expenses," I argued back. "It's not like you had to give up your weekly waxes or mani/pedis." Priscilla lived the life of a spoiled politician's wife.

Sometimes I wondered why my dad married her. *He can't possibly love her.* Not like he loved my mom. Priscilla was a spoiled, self-centered gold digger who was way too young for him. The complete opposite of my mom.

Priscilla was wrong about my college expenses being a financial burden, but she was right about the bodyguard thing. *I can't believe I'm agreeing with her.* I turned back to my dad.

"But she's right about SSI. I'm sure whoever left the note meant it as a joke and is afraid to say anything because you hired security." It was the only thing that made sense. No one had so much as given me a dirty look. Well, no strangers at least.

"Priscilla, will you give us the room?"

"Fine." She huffed as she stomped her fuzzy slipper clad feet out of the room.

My father followed behind her and shut the door.

"I know this is disruptive, but, um, I think, SSI thinks the threat is real and I, we, have to defer to their expertise."

He still wasn't making eye contact. *And why is he stuttering?* My father was a brilliant prosecutor and an elegant speaker. He didn't stutter, stammer, or get tongue tied. *He's beyond stressed, and I'm making it worse.*

"I'm sorry. I'll stop complaining." It was the least I could do to help him.

"Thank you. And you know none of this is your fault, right?"

I did. "Are we really having money issues?" I asked, half expecting him to laugh it off.

When he looked at me, the fear in his eyes was more than I could bear. I rushed over to him.

"Priscilla is exaggerating. I asked her not to go shopping for a while, thinking it'd be safer for her to stay home, and she assumed it's because we have money issues."

That didn't ring true; she shopped a lot on line.

"Are you sure? I'd be happy to help when I get my inheritance."

"No, no, that's not necessary." He dismissed my offer. "There's nothing to worry about." He rubbed my back to comfort me like he did when I was a kid.

I wasn't convinced, but there wasn't much I could do if he wouldn't talk to me. "Okay, Daddy." I pulled back and kissed him on the cheek. "I'll let you get back to work."

"I'll see you at dinner," he said as he sat back down and focused on his monitor.

I had a feeling he wasn't being honest about their money problems. If it was a safety issue, Priscilla could shop online. Did he owe someone money? Was that why they threatened him, me? I'd be happy to give them what they wanted if it meant things could go back to normal.

I needed to study but couldn't concentrate. After an hour of reading the same sentence over and over, I gave up and closed my laptop. Hoping it'd help me relax, I drank half a bottle of wine while taking a long, hot bubble bath.

Sadly, it wasn't enough to prevent the nightmares from ruining my sleep.

I hugged my pillow as snapshots from the dream filled my mind. A large tattooed hand reaching for me. A bone-chilling laugh from a faceless man. A long, bright white hall with only one exit. The walls stretching with every step I took—making escape impossible.

Chapter 21

AJ

Too worked up to sit behind the wheel, I leaned against the hood of the car after relieving Eric. Jack kept me company via the ear-piece as he drove directly to campus. He had Blake's schedule, and I'd marked a map with her normal routes; the plan was for him to watch over us from a distance. We'd marked alternate routes; with any luck, Blake would be open to using them.

I hated needing extra coverage, but was grateful for the second set of eyes.

We considered not telling Blake, but Meg had argued, "It might scare her to know what was going on, but at least she'll be prepared." She was right. Knowing would most likely cause Blake to feel more nervous, but at least she'd know what was going on.

Unfortunately for me, it was my job to update her during the ride to campus. *This would be so much easier if she wasn't pissed at me.*

Much to my relief, we agreed not to tell her about her father's questionable practices. There wasn't enough evidence to justify upsetting her. And selfishly, I didn't want to give her a reason to be even more angry with me.

"Aurora is leaving the castle," I whispered into the comms as Blake opened the door.

"Copy that," Jack's voice was in one ear while I tuned the other one to listen to Blake's loving goodbye to her father.

I nodded to Mr. Davenport as I met Blake at the bottom of the steps. She opened her mouth to argue when I opened the front passenger door.

I cut her off, asking, "Please?"

She sighed and rolled her eyes, but got in.

No time like the present. I took a deep, calming breath and ripped off the Band-Aid. "We have to talk," I said once we were on the road.

I could go the rest of my life without ever again seeing the I'm-so-done-with-you look she sent my way. Her disgust and irritation hung thick between us.

"Jack is going to be shadowing us toda–"

"What? Why?"

"Keep it simple," Jack said in my ear.

"Right," I whispered before taking a deep breath.

"Right what?" Confusion mixed with her frustration.

"Sorry, I was talking to Jack." To help Blake feel more comfortable, I wouldn't use our call signs unless there was an immediate threat.

Her glare bore a hole in the side of my head, but she didn't speak, so I continued, "I know this isn't what you want." She huffed and crossed her arms. "But we're concerned our investigation may cause whoever sent the note to act sooner rather than later."

Not wanting to risk upsetting Blake more, I tapped my mic when I heard Jack say, "Well done."

Blake didn't talk to me the rest of the ride. Something about her body language hinted her silence was about something other than having an extra bodyguard.

Jack's update broke the silence; he had parked.

I expected Blake to bolt from the car as soon as I parked, but she stared out the windshield instead.

She jumped when I reached out and gently touched her shoulder. "Blake, are you okay?" It was a stupid question, but I didn't know what else to ask.

She turned her head, but not her eyes. When they finally caught up and met mine, I could see the depth of her fear. Hell, I could almost feel it.

"This is really real. Someone wants to hurt me."

She sounded small and defeated as she fought back her tears.

She's trying so hard to be strong.

I wanted nothing more than to pull her into my arms and hug her. I'd give anything to tell her this was all just a bad dream. But I couldn't.

"I'm sorry." I looked out the window and saw Jack making his way towards us. Not caring that he could hear me, I said, "I swear I won't let anyone hurt you."

I ignored Jack as I watched Blake blink back tears. She said thank you as she turned away. Her voice was almost drowned out by the click as she released her seat belt.

Before getting out, I reminded her to ignore Jack if she noticed him.

Blake sat in the back, in the seat closest to the aisle, during her first class. I had to scoot her over so I could sit between her and the door. Not that I minded standing for the ninety minutes, but it would have attracted unwanted attention.

Jack kept me entertained by making random comments as the professor droned on.

Blake was packed up and ready to go before the professor dismissed the class, so we left early. I let Jack know which exit we'd use, then steered her in that direction. She showed some of her earlier sass by rolling her eyes, but followed my lead without a word.

Blake tried to be strong, but fear had driven out most of her fight. I missed her yelling at me for opening her door.

We were crossing the quad when I heard Jack say, "You have a shadow."

"Copy that," I answered, stepping closer to Blake. Wanting to look casual, I put an arm around her shoulder and leaned in.

I smiled as I whispered in her ear. "Please don't pull away; someone is following us." I felt her stiffen, but to her credit, she didn't move away from me or freak out.

"Where?" she asked as she started to turn her head.

"Don't look," I said, grabbing her chin and forcing her to look up at me. "Jack's watching him and relaying info. You're safe."

"He's at your five and picking up speed." Jack's voice interrupted me. "I'm closing in."

"Blake, don't panic, but I need you to do exactly what I say when I say it. Please."

Fear radiated off her as she nodded. Having memorized the buildings around the quad, I knew there was a bookstore and café up ahead and to the left. If I could get her inside, out of his line of sight, we could disappear without causing a scene. *I only need a few seconds.* Not wanting to give away our destination, in case he was close enough to hear me, I told Jack my plan in code.

My heart raced, and my breathing sped up. *I can't let anything happen to her.* Refusing to let my nerves get the best of me, I ignored my reflexive need to look behind me and focused on my breathing as I led Blake towards the building housing the campus bookstore.

"He's fifteen yards out and picking up speed. Moving to intercept."

Jack would take care of the threat, but that didn't mean we could stop. Just because Jack had only identified one; didn't mean he was alone.

Shit. They may be leading us in to a trap.

I heard the commotion, in real time and over comms, before I heard Jack say, "Fuck!"

Fuck!

I didn't need to look to know whatever had happened accomplished two things; it created a scene, capturing everyone's attention, and left me without backup. *Shit.*

I heard Jack say, "get off me," as I urged Blake to walk faster.

"Just keep walking," I said to Blake with a quick glance behind us. I couldn't see the guy trailing us as everyone rushed to see what was happening by Jack.

"Shit, I lost my line of sight." I could hear the frustration in Jack's voice. I tuned out the sound of Jack untangling himself from the crowd and focused on getting Blake to safety.

I could hear Blake's heavy breathing as panic set in.

"It'll be okay, just keep moving and follow my directions." She nodded.

"Tango ten yards out," Jack said. "I'm on my way but won't make it in time to intercept."

We were on our own.

Ten yards. Thirty feet. That was all that stood between Blake and the threat. I kept leading Blake as Jack kept me updated, dropping the threat's distance every couple of words. He was moving fast, but not running.

When the guy was three yards out, Jack told me there was no one between him and me. Nine feet.

Given his height, he only had to take seven or eight steps.

I trusted my ability to handle the guy—as long as weapons weren't drawn. Because I was bound by the law, and my conscience, I wouldn't draw my gun and risk hurting innocent bystanders. I doubted the Tango cared about either.

"No matter what happens, stay behind me." I used my left arm to force her behind my back as I turned to face the threat. My right hand up and ready to intercept.

Shock registered on his face when I spun around. His quarter-second pause was all I needed.

A quick glance told me his hands were empty. *Thank God.* I exceeded at unarmed combat and wouldn't hesitate to demonstrate my skills on the fucker who was stupid enough to threaten my girl.

To gain the upper hand, I closed the distance, my right fist connecting with his face in a nose-breaking crunch. Unfazed by the pain or blood spattering across his lower face, he drew back to return the favor. I blocked it and trapped his arm, using it to pull him closer as I brought my knee up to his ribs. He tried to connect a punch with his free hand, but my next move twisted him into a choke hold.

I glanced over to make sure Blake was safe. Her expressive eyes were the size of saucers as she ignored the crowd forming around us.

Not wanting to see the disgust in her eyes, I avoided making eye contact as I tightened my arm around the guy's neck.

He clawed at me and tried stomping on my feet as he struggled.

He's lucky I'm choking him out and not snapping his neck.

I tightened the sleeper chokehold, forcing him to pass out sooner.

"Sierra Four! Let go!" Jack's voice cut through the red haze that had over-taken my mind. I relaxed my grip and set the guy on the ground, noticing the noise of the crowd around us for the first time. They were loud but giving us a wide berth.

"I've got him. See to Aurora." Jack was standing next to Blake, protecting her as he led her towards me. The shock and fear on her face was enough to snap me fully back to the present. I replaced Jack at Blake's side while he knelt over the limp body.

"I got this," Jack said, letting me know he didn't need my help zip-tying an unconscious man.

I gave Blake my full attention.

Her unblinking eyes stared at the guy on the ground.

"Are you okay?" I asked, stepping in front of her to block her view.

She didn't move. Didn't even blink.

The only thing I could think of was to physically pull her out of the trance. *It'll scare her.* Knowing it needed to be done didn't help me feel any better about it.

When I gently shook her shoulders, she yelped and jumped back.

The fear in her eyes was like a dagger through my heart.

Shutting down my emotions, I focused on my goal—get Blake to safety.

Just because we hadn't seen anyone else didn't mean the threat didn't have backup.

Jack relayed information as he searched the guy for weapons. So far, he'd found a gun and a full syringe.

Keeping my body between Blake and Jack, I glanced over my shoulder. "You good?" I whispered into my comms.

"Yeah, get her out of here. I'll deal with campus police."

No doubt they were already on their way and would want to take our statements, but they'd have to wait. Getting Blake to safety was more important. Luckily, John had told them Blake had an armed escort, so it wouldn't surprise them to see SSI on the scene.

"Are you hurt?" I asked as I tried to turn her away from the scene.

Blake refused to budge. "Is he dead?" she asked, her eyes once again glued to the guy lying at Jack's feet.

"No. Just unconscious."

The energy shifted as the crowd grew restless.

"Get her out of here," Jack ordered.

"Let's go," I said, sounding harsher than I'd intended.

She still didn't move. Her freeze response had kicked in, cementing her feet to the ground.

I don't have time for this. Knowing it'd look bad if I flung her over my shoulder, I scooped her up like a newlywed carrying his bride over the threshold.

The movement snapped her out of it and she whimpered, burying her face in my neck as her short arms clung to me for dear life.

"I got you. You're okay." I wasn't sure my words had registered until I felt her delayed nod. Blake's sheltered life had just been cracked open. Her innocence shattered.

I glanced behind me as I jogged to the car, relieved no one was following us.

Blake's death grip on my neck tightened when I tried to set her down so I could open her door.

"It's okay, I'm not going anywhere." I tried to set her down again, but she curled into me. I rubbed her back as I spoke in hushed tones, "Blake, Sweetheart, I have to put you down to open the door."

She nodded and slowly released her grip. Releasing her legs, it hit me—I didn't want to let go of her any more than she wanted me to. When her feet touched the ground, I wrapped my arms around her, stroking her back and holding her head to my chest as I swore I'd never let anyone hurt her.

I'll face the devil himself if I have to.

I helped her into the passenger seat, where I could keep an eye on her, and buckled her seatbelt. I clicked the door lock as I ran around the front to the driver's side, scanning as I went.

What a fucking day. And it wasn't even noon.

Chapter 22

Blake

This can't be real. He tried to kill me. And I just stood there like an idiot.

My stupid body had refused to move, even after Jack got there and tied the guy up.

And how humiliating was it that AJ had to carry me? He kept telling me I was safe, promising to protect me, as he carried me to the car. He was surprisingly gentle with me after almost killing a guy with his bare hands.

He could have killed him.

But he didn't.

He looked so angry.

He saved you.

I warred with myself.

AJ's ruthless violence shocked me, but I was grateful he'd stepped in and stopped the guy.

The situation confused me; I hated violence, but was grateful for AJ and his brute strength.

I'd be dead if it wasn't for him.

And I couldn't forget how gentle he was, how safe I felt, when he wrapped me in the protective cloak of his body.

AJ held the steering wheel in a vise grip as he drove us away from campus, rolling through most of the stop signs along the way.

The tense silence in the car wasn't helping me feel any better. Even when AJ said something, he wasn't talking to me. I listened, but he used code and clipped sentences so I was no better off than if I couldn't hear him at all.

"How are you holding up?" he asked, turning his head towards me.

"I, um, I guess I'm okay." I wasn't. How could I be? Someone tried to kill me. "What's going on?"

"I'm sorry, Blake. I know you're scared, but please don't shoot the messenger." He reached over and grabbed my hand. "But this could get worse before it gets better."

My breath caught in my throat. How could it get worse? "What do you mean?" My voice sounded small and weak.

"You're safe," he said. "But to keep you that way, I need you to turn off your phone."

"What? Why?" I hadn't turned off my phone since, well, ever.

"It's harder to track a phone if it's turned off," he explained.

Track my phone? Was that how they found me? "Okay." My fingers trembled as I reluctantly turned it off.

"Thank you. I wish I didn't have to, but I'm taking you to the SSI office. It's not safe to take you home."

My home isn't safe?

"Oaky." I hated how scared I sounded. "When will I be able to go home?"

AJ turned, empathy in his eyes. "I don't know. SSI is close to finding answers, but we can't give you a time frame."

"Can I at least pack a bag and see my dad?"

He shook his head back and forth. "I'm sorry, we can't risk it. We'll get you everything you need."

If it wasn't safe for me, was it safe for my father?

"John is calling him. We warned him in the beginning we might need to take you to a safe house, so he won't be surprised."

Why hadn't he warned me? I was going to a safe house, with nothing but my schoolbag and the clothes I was wearing. Clothes that now reeked from nervous sweat.

Why is this happening? Someone wanted to kill me, and now I had to hide away. *I'll probably miss midterms.* It'd be impossible to fix my grades, so I'd have to withdraw to save my GPA.

I won't graduate. *I'll lose my internship.* I was so freaked out I didn't realize I was hyperventilating until I felt AJ's hand gently squeezing my shoulder.

"Blake? Talk to me. Do I need to pull over?" AJ asked.

I put my hand over my heaving chest and leaned forward, trying to force air into my lungs.

Wanting to run away and be anywhere but here, I tried to get out as the car rolled to a stop. But I wasn't thinking clearly and opened the door before releasing my seatbelt. Before I could reach the release button, AJ shoved the car in park and grabbed my hand.

"Blake, you can't get out of the car," he said, turning towards me.

"I have to, I, I can't breathe," I huffed out as I gasped for air, the walls of the car closing in around me.

"Blake, can you close the door?"

Close the door? No, I need to get out. I pulled away and turned towards the door, but I wasn't fast enough. AJ grabbed my shoulder and pulled me back. I still had a death grip on the door, so it pulled closed when he pushed me back against the seat. My chest rising and falling in rapid bursts as I tried to suck air into my lungs.

"Look at me." He waited, but I couldn't move. "Blake, please, look at me." He reached over and gently turned my head.

When I finally made eye contact, the concern in his eyes nearly pushed me over the edge. AJ spoke softly as he gave me instructions. "Here's what we're going to do." He grabbed my hands and held them, rubbing the backs with his thumbs. "You're going to follow my lead while we do some breathing exercises, okay?"

It was too hard to talk while my lungs screamed for air, so I nodded.

"Breathe in nice and slow, like this." He counted to four as he inhaled. I only made it to two before I exhaled. "Good."

How was that good? I only made it halfway.

"Let's try again."

I don't know how long we sat there before I got my breathing and heartbeat under control, but it felt like forever.

"I'm okay now." *At least I think I am.*

"All good in the carriage. Aurora is Oscar Mike again."

I remembered them telling me they'd refer to me as Aurora if things went bad. Apparently, Meg had a thing for princesses. I didn't think much about it, other than being annoyed. I didn't care if it was ironic that I hated being called a princess when my father called me his princess.

That was different. He meant it as an honorific, the daughter of a king; SSI meant it as a damsel in distress. When I said I didn't want a code name; John said it was standard operating procedure.

I'd foolishly believed they wouldn't need to use it.

And who the fuck is Oscar?

"Who's Oscar Mike?"

"Sorry, military speak for on the move."

"Right. Will everything be in code now?" I couldn't keep the irritation out of my voice. I was smart enough to know I was acting out because of my fear, but couldn't stop myself from doing it.

"Some of it will. I know this is stressful and frustrating for you, but there's a reason for everything we do."

"Fine." I leaned back and rested my head against the headrest, praying my alarm clock would go off and end this nightmare.

But this wasn't a nightmare, and no amount of praying would change that. *Neither will acting like a bitch.* I needed to put on my big girl pants and deal with reality. And that started with apologizing.

"AJ?"

"Yeah."

"I'm sorry. You just saved my life and I'm being a bitch," my voice still shaky as I answered.

"It's okay. It's actually a normal reaction."

Who knew? Not that it made me feel any better. A few seconds later it occurred to me I hadn't thanked him.

"AJ?" I tried to sound friendly and calm.

"Yeah?" He turned to me with a soft smile.

"Thank you."

"You're welcome."

"Is Jack okay?"

"He is. He gave his statement to the campus PD, and is on his way back to the office. We'll give our statements via a video call later."

My statement wouldn't help much. I didn't see anything until AJ turned to stop the guy, and everything after that was a blur.

Oh my God. Did Jack hear me freak out?

"Did he hear me have my panic attack?" I didn't know why it mattered, but it did. I didn't want him thinking I was weak.

"No, I shut the mic off until it was over."

He did? Really? AJ continued to surprise me. Maybe he wasn't an ogre, like I'd originally thought. Even if he did choke that guy. Would he get in trouble for it?

My chest tightened as panic threatened to take over again. Remembering AJ's earlier breathing technique, I took a deep breath and released it slowly.

"Do you have a code name?" I asked, needing to occupy my mind, so I didn't panic again.

"I do. Sierra Four."

"What does it mean?"

"Sierra is the military phonetic for the letter S, and we each have a number. Sierra Three has been with us all day."

So Jack was Sierra Three.

"How'd you pick your numbers?"

"They're based on the order we signed our contracts. I was the fourth."

I asked AJ if he minded me asking questions. He said he didn't, so I kept asking. Talking helped keep me from freaking out.

We were about fifteen minutes from the office when AJ signaled he was listening to Jack.

"Copy that. See you in a few," he said, then turned to me. "Change of plans; we're not going to the office, we're going to Snow's Castle."

I laughed. Not a little feminine laugh, but a deranged cackle. What was it with these people and their princess references?

"Snow's Castle." I asked, "Seriously?" My voice thick with loathing.

"Yup," he answered. "What do you have against princesses?"

"Nothing, I just don't think it's something girls should aspire to. Why do we encourage young girls to think they need a man to save them?" I realized the irony of my statement as soon as it came out of my mouth.

AJ raised an eyebrow and grinned. I waited for him to call me out on my hypocrisy, but he didn't. He let his expression do the talking.

I'd just needed a man had to save me. *And keep me from having a panic attack.*

Defending my position, I said, "What happened today isn't normal. Most girls won't need a bodyguard at college. Or ever."

"If you say so." The humor in his voice annoyed me. I planned to tell him just that, but before I could come up with a clever comeback, he said, "Five minutes out."

"What?" I asked before realizing he must be talking to Jack.

Chapter 23

AJ

Blake stayed silent for the rest of the drive. Which was good, since I had to focus on not reacting to Jack's continuous stream of updates while watching Blake for signs of another panic attack.

I appreciated Jack updating me on the big picture stuff, but it was hard not letting my anger show.

SSI moved fast to get information on the attacker. He worked for one of the guys at the top of our suspect list. An untouchable, career criminal who everyone suspected had DA Davenport on his payroll. Davenport had a significantly higher than average history of not prosecuting several of the people on our list. Often citing lack of evidence, mishandled investigations, or some random undotted I or uncrossed T in the paperwork.

My orders were to keep Blake in the dark. I refused to believe she was involved in any way, but that didn't mean she was ignorant about her father's activity. Jack's voice sounded off in my head. "Don't let your feelings get in the way."

My feelings weren't the reason I believed Blake was innocent; her actions and reactions were. *You can't fake that kind of panic.*

When we got to Jamie's, he met us in the driveway. It was a risk having us meet here, but it was less obvious than the office.

Plus, Jay was staying with Jamie and Emily until he found a place of his own, and Jack would be there soon. Emily would be there to offer moral support, and Meg said she'd be there too. I didn't have the words to convey how much their support meant to me, knowing Blake would need their comfort.

I could tell by Jack's tone he wasn't happy his wife put herself in the line of fire, but Meg was a force to be reckoned with and wouldn't back down. Emily was a little less forceful, but she wouldn't back down either, and I was one hundred percent sure Jamie was freaking out about it.

Emily played hostess to Blake while Jamie and I locked everything down. He had a top of the line security system, including cameras covering every inch of the house's exterior. Jack did too. It went without saying that Doug had installed the same system in the house he now shared with Beth. Shockingly, John hadn't yet. But then, he was old school.

Just as we were finishing up, Jack and Meg arrived. Once Blake was settled at the table with Meg and Emily, the rest of us went to Jamie's office.

"You should sit," Jack said when I leaned against the wall.

"That bad?"

"Yes, and no." His answer wasn't helpful.

I sat. "What'd you find out?"

"The guy who attacked Blake works for Richard Roman. And while we don't have anything concrete, there's a mountain of circumstantial evidence linking Davenport and Roman," Jamie said.

"Why the threat?" That part still didn't make sense. If he was dirty, what caused them to threaten Blake?

Unless.

"Do you think he's trying to cut ties?" That would explain the wording on the note. They'd be pissed off if he decided to clean up his act.

"It's possible, but it's only speculation," Jamie answered. Jack nodded in agreement.

"You've spent the most time with her. Has she said anything that might help us?"

I counted to ten before unclenching my fists. Jack wasn't accusing her, and it was a logical question, but that didn't mean I didn't want to punch him for asking it.

That violent reflex is exactly why you can never be with Blake, my inner voice reminded me.

"No, she hasn't. She has an innocent's trust in her father." I thought back to the few conversations we'd had. "There's no way she knows anything. She's genuinely confused about the entire situation."

Jack and Jamie shared a look. That was never a good thing.

"Spill it."

"We think they're targeting Blake for her money," Jack said, not giving me much to go on.

"You mean hold her for ransom?" If her father was taking bribes, why would they hold his daughter for ransom? Did her father borrow money from the wrong guy? Did he take payment and not deliver as expected?

"No. Blake is due to inherit millions when she turns twenty-five," Jamie answered.

Millions? I felt like I did a good job of not letting my eyes pop out of my head, but it was hard to know for sure.

"Say that again."

"Blake's grandfather was a millionaire." Jack sounded exasperated.

I knew that.

"He left most of his wealth to Blake," Jamie said.

I didn't know that, but judging by Jamie's tone, I should have. It was probably in the part of the file I didn't read because Blake's picture had hypnotized me.

"That explains her friends." I used air quotes, which triggered Jack to ask, "What about them?"

I could practically hear the investigator wheels turning in his head. Could one of them be behind the threat? I doubted it. *But then again, you never know.*

"They all want something from her. Especially Danny. He's a whiney little bitch, and he's clearly using her." They nodded. My opinion of Danny wasn't a secret. "Let's just say Blake's too trusting, and people abuse it."

"That sucks," Jack said.

It did. I'd be her friend, a real one, if she'd let me. *Who am I kidding? I want to be a lot more than friends.*

I'd gotten glimpses of the real Blake, and I wanted more. She hid who she was because she hung around with people who didn't really care.

But I cared. I wanted to know everything about her. To show her what it felt like to be supported and loved for who she was, not what she stood to inherit.

"Is her father having money issues?"

"He is, but it's not public knowledge. His wife is still spending money like they have it to burn," Jamie said.

"Rumor has it Priscilla married Davenport, thinking he'd inherit the millions. She wasn't pleased to find out it was left to Blake."

"Is she a person of interest?"

"Not really. We can't find a shred of evidence against her," Jack answered.

Jamie added, "Though we haven't removed her from the list."

"We've secured a safe house. Jay is picking up supplies, groceries, and some clothes for Blake," Jamie said.

Jaden was picking out clothes? That sounded like a disaster waiting to happen.

Jack was quick to put my fears to rest. "Don't worry, Meg is helping him via text."

I sighed in relief. "That's good." Meg would do right by Blake.

I texted Meg with my best guess of Blake's size and what she liked to wear. Meg replied she'd have Jay pick up things in different sizes, just in case.

"He'll take her to the safe ho-"

I cut him off. "I'll take her."

Jack huffed out a laugh. "Told you," he said to Jamie.

"Fine, you'll take Blake to the safe house. We'll assign Jay to over-watch for the night. Dean can have the night off."

I nodded. "Has Davenport asked for security for himself?"

"No, we suggested it, but he refused. Said they have a state-of-the-art security system at home, and his office is a secure government building. Plus, his driver doubles as security." Jamie sounded as skeptical as I felt.

I scratched my chin. "Blake won't be happy about this," I said.

"Maybe not, but she seems to understand the threat is real now, so it shouldn't be too hard to convince her it's for her safety," Jack said. He'd overheard most of our conversation on the drive here.

"Maybe." I knew better. She was scared and transferring her fear to something she could control. For her, that meant freaking out about missing classes, and failing mid-terms—it was easier than focusing reality.

I have my work cut out for me.

Chapter 24

Blake

After confiscating my phone and laptop, then having the audacity to ask if I was okay, AJ disappeared to Jamie's office. He left me sitting at the table with Meg and Emily, two perfect hostesses, or in my case, babysitters.

It's not their fault, they're just doing what they were told to do.

I wasn't upset with them, but with the situation. Being kept in the dark upset me. Losing my autonomy upset me.

Not wanting to go down that path, I focused on the two women in front of me. I noticed how relaxed and easy their conversation flowed, and once again found myself wishing I had a friendship like theirs.

Jealousy joined fear and frustration as I talked to them, playing with the tea bag string hanging from my mug. I doubted any of my friends would have made me peppermint chamomile tea to help soothe my nerves after a horrible day.

They're probably only doing it because their husbands told them to be nice.

I chided myself for judging them unfairly. *That's not who I want to be.*

When Meg and Emily told me about the times they needed help from SSI, I assumed they did it to help me feel better, but it didn't work.

I never would have guessed they'd lived through such horrors. Meg was targeted by a trafficker, and Emily by her abusive ex. It seemed crazy to me they'd both hired SSI to protect them. *And they both fell in love with the guy who protected them.*

I couldn't imagine it happening to me. AJ was the only person protecting me. Well, the only one during the day, and he and I couldn't be more different if we tried. Meg and Emily may have found their happily ever after with men from SSI, but I wouldn't.

They shared more stories while we waited for the guys to decide my fate. The longer I waited, the more my anger built. Being left out of the decision pissed me off something fierce, though I tried not to take my anger out on Meg and Emily. They weren't the ones interfering with my life.

No, it was their egotistical, toxic, alpha male husbands who thought they had the right to take away my phone and laptop and tell me what to do.

I didn't care that Jamie and Emily weren't married yet.

In an effort to help me feel more comfortable having a call sign (they'd corrected me when I called it a code name, though it seemed like they were the same thing to me), Emily told me hers was Snow White, and Meg's was Cinderella.

It shocked me how two women who seemed so strong didn't mind being referred to as helpless princesses. Meg confessed to liking her call sign, and referring to their houses as 'castles' when they were used for work.

"And sometimes just for fun," Meg said.

While I understood the logic of not using real names or locations for safety, it still bothered me. Why couldn't we have warrior or Goddess names? I worked myself into a mood, not understanding how they could deal with overbearing, bossy husbands treating them like they were helpless.

"Doesn't it bother you?" I blurted out. "Them making decisions for you, telling you what to do, treating you like you're helpless?" I was about to apologize for being rude, but Meg laughed.

She literally laughed out loud. Emily chuckled and shook her head.

"They don't make decisions for us. In fact, they tried to send us to their mom's so we'd be out of harm's way." Meg rolled her eyes. "Like we'd ever leave you alone with them."

They refused to leave? So they could be here for me? God, I'm a bitch.

"Their hearts are in the right place when they get all over protective. Unfortunately, it interferes with their brains, so we have to set them straight," Emily added.

"We don't need them to do all the old school chivalric things, but we appreciate that they want to. For Jack and

I, it's a delicate balance that isn't always easy to achieve. He's an over-protective, southern gentleman, and I'm fiercely independent."

"I like that Jamie's old school. It's refreshing," Emily admitted.

As I learned a little more about them and their past traumas, I realized I'd misjudged them. And their men.

"Jack once told me, when I was arguing about his need to protect me, that he doesn't protect me because I'm weak, but because I'm important."

Emily added, "There was a point when I'd convinced myself Jamie thought I wasn't capable of taking care of myself. When I started a fight about it, he said he didn't do because he thought I couldn't, but because he loved me and wanted to treat me how I deserved to be treated."

Listening to them talk, I realized their husband's behavior didn't diminish their strength—it amplified it.

My shoulders sagged as my chin dropped to my chest. "I'm sorry, I shouldn't have assumed." My voice was barely above a whisper.

"It's okay." Emily said.

"You're under a lot of stress, and they're in a room making decisions for you, so it's understandable," Meg added.

"No, no way am I leaving my phone and laptop. I can't."

Jamie had just told me they'd secured a safe house, and I'd be going there in the morning. With AJ. He'd be with me twenty-four-seven. *Why does it have to be AJ? Why not someone else, someone who isn't confusing my emotions?*

Fear fueled my anger at having no say in the planning or control over my situation.

"They can be tracked, so you can't take them to the safe house," Jamie patiently explained. AJ had told me all that before, but surely I'd be safe at the safe house. It was in the fucking name. After fuming for a few seconds, I asked, "How am I supposed to attend classes or do my homework without my laptop or phone?" I'd come up with a plan to ask my professors to let me attend classes virtually. Hiding away shouldn't mean I had to fail the semester.

Their identical expressions made it clear I wouldn't like the answer.

"You don't. I'm sorry, but we can't risk it," Jack answered.

"You can message your professors before you leave here, and let them know what's happening," Jamie said.

"So I can have my phone back?"

Jamie answered, "No, you'll have to message them from one of SSI's secure servers and I'll need to read it before you send it."

He needs to read my email? I rolled my eyes and huffed in disbelief. What did they think I'd say?

"I know it seems like overkill, but your phone doesn't need to be on for long to be traced, and I won't risk anyone's safety." Jamie looked at Emily as he responded. Love, concern, and determination written all over his face.

AJ leaned against the counter as Jack and Jamie answered my questions and countered my arguments. *Why isn't he saying anything?* Maybe he had nothing to say. Maybe it was because Jack and Jamie were his bosses. I shook my head; it wasn't what mattered.

"How will I talk to my dad? My friends?" I asked. The idea of being alone with AJ, unable to contact anyone else, filled me with dread.

"We can relay messages to your father, but he's the only person you'll have outside contact with," Jack answered. "Blake, I know this is hard, but everything we're doing is for your safety. And while I can't promise you it'll be over soon, I can promise we're doing everything we can to bring this to an end as quickly as possible."

My eyes stung with unshed tears. *I can't believe this is happening.* By now, everyone on campus had probably heard about what happened. Paige and Danny must be worried out of their minds. *Well, Paige, at least.*

"Can I get a burner phone, like they always do on TV?" I asked, feeling smart for suggesting a solution to my problem they hadn't considered.

"Blake, that only works on TV. The minute you contact your father, the person looking for you will trace the call back. It's frightening how easy it is to track people these days." Jack's answer wiped away my smugness.

"But they can't track yours?"

"Yes, and no. We'll contact your father from the office. If they trace the call; it won't lead them to you," Jamie answered.

AJ still hadn't answered any of my questions, which bothered me for no other reason than he usually had something to say. And in a way, I missed it.

Before I had time to process that revelation, a new question occurred to me.

"Will AJ have his phone?" I asked, frustration lacing every word.

"No. He'll have a company burner phone to contact SSI," Jack answered.

"And Doug will monitor it, so we'll know if it's traced," Jamie added.

"Can't you do that for my dad's phone?" Desperation filled my voice.

Jamie and Jack shared a look, their hesitation obvious as tension filled the stretching silence. More and more, I sensed they were hiding things from me.

I had to assume they thought my father had done something illegal, provoking the threat against me.

But he wouldn't. My dad was a good guy. He upheld the law and put criminals in jail. He was a respected member of the community.

They only suspected him because they didn't know him like I did.

"We asked him if we could monitor his phone," Jamie finally said, compassion filled his voice. "But he declined."

He said it like it proved Daddy was a criminal, but he worked with a lot of high-powered clients and important political figures. I couldn't blame him for saying no. He had to protect his attorney-client privileges.

"Blake, I know this is hard, but the person looking for you isn't messing around. The guy they sent for you today had a syringe in his pocket, and I'd put money on the lab verifying it's a sedative," Jack said.

A sedative? My heart beat a little faster.

AJ uncrossed his arms, stepped away from the island, and walked towards me.

"In our experience, the first attempt is usually the weakest. Next time, they'll send more than one guy, and they'll be a lot more aggressive," Jamie added. "Right now, the best way to keep you safe is for you to be out of sight while we sort this out."

"We're doing everything we can to find out who's responsible and bring this to an end," Jack said.

AJ still hadn't said anything, but I could feel his presence behind me.

"Do you know anything yet?" I hadn't meant to sound snarky, but I was 'this close' to losing it. They didn't deserve my attitude, so I reframed the question, dialing it back as I asked again, "Who's so mad at my father that they want to hurt me?"

"We don't know, yet, but the evidence leads to a known criminal your father has," Jamie paused and looked over my shoulder at AJ, "dealt with in the past."

What was he going to say before he looked at AJ? What did he mean dealt with? *Is he accusing my father?*

"My father is not a criminal!" I yelled, emphasizing each word.

AJ stepped up beside me and placed a large, warm hand on the small of my back. "No one is saying he is. But someone he works with could be."

AJ's words sounded hollow, but his touch comforted me. It shouldn't have. I wished it didn't. I don't want to be comforted by a big, dumb ogre who works for a company that thinks my father might be a criminal or have ties to one or whatever it is they think.

"He'd never do anything to hurt me," I said as tears filled in my eyes. This time, I didn't bother holding them back.

"Of course not. He'd never intentionally do anything to hurt you," AJ said.

I was months away from earning my law degree, so I didn't miss his use of the word intentionally. *Words matter.* Despite what he'd said, he thinks my father is somehow involved.

Could this nightmare get any worse?

Chapter 25

AJ

Watching Blake react while Jack and Jamie explained the situation was killing me. There was nothing I wanted more than to hold her in my arms and comfort her, but I couldn't. It wasn't only because I had to keep it professional; she still hadn't recovered from the shock of the attack.

Hearing the fear in Blake's voice when she defended her father was more than I could handle. *I have to at least try to comfort her.* I moved to her side and put my hand on the small of her back. To my surprise, she didn't flinch or pull away.

When I spoke for the first time, I chose my words carefully. I wanted to put her fears at bay, but wouldn't lie. The more evidence we uncovered, the more it pointed to Davenport having ties to the person threatening Blake. Not that I believed he'd intentionally hurt her, but choosing to do business with people who targeted innocent victims meant he was at least partially responsible.

"Jay's here," Meg said. "We'll help him get stuff put away."

I walked Blake to the couch and sat down with her. She hugged her knees to her chest, rocking back and forth.

"Blake," I risked pulling her small trembling hands into mine, "this won't be for long. And I'll be with you every step of the way." I wasn't sure my promise would comfort her, but I offered it anyway.

Fear, confusion, and hope filled her eyes when they met mine.

"Why do you care so much?" she asked as the door opened, pulling her attention away from me.

Jay, Meg, and Emily came in carrying assorted bags of food, supplies, and clothes.

"I have everything we need to survive the next few days," Jay announced, without reading the room, as he walked in.

Blake's grip tightened as she stiffened beside me.

Apparently, no one had updated him, so he didn't know I'd be staying with Blake.

Jack answered, "Change of plans. You're on over watch, AJ will stay with Blake."

I tried not to let my hope soar when I felt Blake's hands relax. *Is it because she's relieved I'm staying with her?* I shook my head. No point in wondering why; the answer wouldn't change anything. She'd never feel the same way for me, nor should she. I wasn't a bad guy, but I was too violent for Blake Davenport.

"Over watch again? When are you guys going to trust me to do more than sit in a car and stare at houses?" Jay's irritation ruffled my feathers.

I growled. "This isn't-"

Jack put his hand on my shoulder as he cut me off. "Jay, over watch is an important job. One we've all done more often than not."

Jay looked at Jack, then at me. I saw the instant he registered my scowl and my hand holding Blake's. His amber eyes, so much like his father's and Jack's, opened wide for a split second before he grinned. "I get it."

I clenched my free hand to control the burning desire to wipe the smirk off his face.

He saw it and backed away. "Don't worry, Big Guy." His laugh was like a cheese grater on my nerves. He shifted his focus to Blake. "I got you some clothes. I hope they're okay," he said, placing the bags on the floor.

Blake finally spoke, asking, "You what?"

"Don't worry, I told him what to buy and made him send pictures so we could approve his choices," Meg quickly put Blake's mind at ease. "I couldn't go," she rolled her eyes at Jack, "but that doesn't mean I couldn't help."

"How'd you know my size? What style I like?" Blake asked.

Making sure she was stylish wasn't high on our priority list, but I had a feeling it mattered a lot to Blake. The cheap department store clothes we'd purchased wouldn't meet her standard, but they'd get the job done. *She probably won't like gym shoes.* I'd only seen her wearing heels. I glanced at her black leather, knee-high boots—*why are knee-high boots so damn sexy?*—the heels had to be at least two-an-a-half inches.

Why were women so worried about being short? I liked the way she had to tilt her head to make eye contact with her striking cobalt eyes. I loved how I could shield her entire body with mine, protecting her from almost any threat just by stepping in front of her.

"The clothes won't be what you're used to, but," I stopped myself before I said something stupid about not needing to look good or be in fashion where we were going.

"But what?" Blake asked.

"But you'll be comfortable for the next couple of days," Jamie saved me.

Meg and Emily shooed me away so they could look at the clothes with Blake.

I listened as they comforted her while they sorted through Jay's purchases. Emily made a game of it, rating his taste. When Blake said she liked some of the outfits, I made eye contact with Meg and smiled. She hadn't told Blake I was the one who provided her size and color preferences. And she wouldn't, unless Blake asked again.

I hoped she wouldn't. I didn't want Blake knowing every outfit she'd worn in the last few days was seared into my mind.

Chapter 26

Blake

"What do you mean, AJ told you my size and what I like to wear?" I asked after Meg finally told me how they did such a good job shopping for someone they didn't know. AJ had moved to the office with the others, so they couldn't hear us.

"He's noticed everything about you," Meg answered. Then rushed to add, "He's observant, like all the guys at SSI."

Is that guilt I detect in her voice?

I accepted her answer because it made sense; as a private investigator, he'd notice things others didn't.

Every guy should take PI classes or lessons, *or whatever it is they do to learn their skills.* It'd make girls everywhere very happy indeed because nothing was more annoying than changing something, like cutting or dying your hair, and your boyfriend not noticing.

"For food, we got a variety," Emily changed the subject. "But if there's something specific you want, just let me know and Jack can bring it when he relieves Jay tomorrow."

I sagged on the couch. *This is really fucking real.* I clutched the cute pink turtleneck to my chest. *I'm going into hiding.* Meg and Emily exchanged looks, but waited for me to speak. Having been through some rough shit themselves, they probably understood how overwhelmed I felt.

"Thank you," I finally said. "For everything you've done for me."

"You're welcome," they answered together.

"I know you'd rather do your class work, but I'd be happy to lend you a book or two if you want something fun to read," Emily offered.

"That's okay, I have books on my…"

Laptop. The laptop I can't bring with me. The laptop that is more like an extension of my body than a tool.

The tears filling my eyes overflowed when I squeezed them shut. I curled forward and rested my elbows on my knees, hiding my face in my hands.

Please let this be a bad dream.

A hand rubbed small circles between my shoulder blades.

I looked over just as Meg said, "It'll be okay. The guys are close to figuring this out, so it shouldn't be for long before this is all over."

Her words were empty platitudes, but I was desperate and latched on to them like a drowning kid to a life preserver.

I sniffled and nodded. The whole situation was hard to accept.

I was about to be a millionaire, so it'd make sense for someone to kidnap me after I have access to my money. But they were threatening my father through me, which made no sense.

But it did. Threatening me was a sure way to get my father to do whatever they wanted. Had they threatened me before? Had he been forced to help criminals to protect me?

I feel so alone. There was no one I could talk to, not even my dad. *I can try.*

Without thinking, I reached into my back pocket for my phone. Right, it wasn't there. I sighed and asked, "Have you talked to my dad? How is he doing?" He had to be a nervous wreck with everything going on.

"John talked to him earlier and we're sending him regular updates so he knows you're safe," Meg answered me.

"He must be so worried." He hadn't been himself since all this started, so I knew the fear and stress were getting to him. Thanks to SSI, I couldn't help but wondering if there was guilt in the mix too.

"Let's get all this put away in your room," Emily said after a few minutes of silence. "Then we'll have some more tea and ice cream."

Wine sounded better, but I didn't think they'd approve of me asking for it.

"Maybe we can sneak a shot of whiskey in the tea," Meg whispered. "The boys don't have to know." She winked.

Who winks anymore? Laughing for the first time in days, I stood and wiped the tears off my cheeks with the back of my hands. "That sounds like a plan."

Emily, Meg, and I carried the bags to the spare bedroom, where Emily pulled a suitcase out of the closet for me to borrow. "Can't have you lugging your things around in plastic bags."

Tears of gratitude filled my eyes but I blinked them away. I didn't want to cry anymore, not even tears of gratitude.

Meg worked at SSI so I could convince myself she was just doing her job by being so nice, but Emily didn't. She was doing this out of the goodness of her heart. I had a feeling Meg was too.

There's no way sneaking whiskey into a cup of tea is in her job description.

Their generosity was almost too much to handle, bringing more unwanted tears to my eyes.

Needing to think about something else, I asked, "Where's AJ sleeping?" My eyes shifted to the full size bed. Not that I expected them to tell me we had to share it, but my mind went there anyway.

"He has to run home." I turned fast enough to lose my balance, causing Meg to add, "Don't worry, he'll be back. He just needs to pack a bag and get his truck."

"I wasn't worried." I lied. When had I become so attached to AJ? *I'm not. I'm just clinging to him because he's familiar.*

"If he sleeps at all, it'll be on the couch." Meg said, ignoring my dismissal.

"And Jamie and Jay live here, so at least one of them will be awake throughout the night," Emily added.

She didn't mention Jack and Meg, which made sense. I couldn't imagine all of them needing to stay here.

"Jaden lives with you?" It was easier to talk about that than my fear.

Emily answered, "For now, he just got home from the Marines and didn't want to live with his parents." I could understand that, it was why I lived on campus during the week despite living close to campus. "So we said he could crash here until he finds a place."

When I asked, "Is this his room?" Emily nodded. "I feel bad. Everyone's life is being disrupted because of me."

"Don't, this is shockingly normal for us," Meg said.

That couldn't be right. "It's normal for you to have clients sleeping in your spare room?" My shock filled the room.

Meg and Emily shared another look. I didn't like how often everyone here communicated without talking.

"Well, that part isn't normal," Emily said with a smirk.

What the hell does that mean? I didn't have time to ask.

"Let's go get that tea," Meg added before I could ask any more questions.

If it's not normal, why am I here?

Chapter 27

AJ

We talked in the office to give the girls some privacy. I wasn't comfortable leaving them alone, but Jamie had the feed to his security cameras pulled up. Without being asked, he'd turned the monitor so I could see it from where I stood near the open office door, ready to spring into action.

"Relax, Janerek. She needs time to decompress and your over-the-top protective hovering won't help," Jack said.

"Says the asshole who bit my head off when I joked about asking Meg out during the Wyatt Fundraiser."

"If I remember correctly, he wasn't being a protective asshole that night, he was being a jealous one," Jamie laughed.

"What am I missing?" Jay asked.

"Nothing," Jack said as I started telling the story. "Your brother had it bad for Meg, but refused to admit it."

Jamie coughed, "Mirror."

"What was that Sheppard?"

He smirked and cleared his throat, then over-annunciated, "Have you looked in a mirror lately?"

I hadn't. Nor did I intend to, not in the sense he meant. I had it bad for Blake, there was no point in denying it, but she'd never go for a guy like me. I couldn't tell them why, but she deserved so much better.

"Whatever," I said, flipping him the bird.

"So, is it an SSI thing to fall for the woman we have to protect?" Jay asked. That stupid, trademark Sheppard lop-sided grin on his face. The one they'd all inherited from John.

Jack defended himself. "I fell before Meg hired us." He pointed at Jamie. "But our by-the-book, straight as an arrow, big brother broke all the rules when he fell for Emily while we were protecting her from Asshat Craig." Jack used the nickname Ashley had given Emily's ex. We didn't talk about him much, not wanting to disrespect the dead, but he'd earned his name.

Jamie scowled at Jack, but it didn't last long. He thought he'd never find love again after losing his first wife and counted his blessings every day for finding love a second time. Of course, he was beyond overly protective of Emily, but she didn't seem to mind.

Jamie smiled; his love too big to hide behind a scowl. "No regrets."

"Me either," Jack said.

They all looked at me. "What?" I feigned indifference, refusing to give them more ammo to fire at me. If things could be different, if I could have what they had, I'd happily stand in front of the firing squad with a smile on my face.

But I couldn't, and their good-natured teasing hurt too much. Not that they understood my hesitancy. I'd never told anyone the extent of my father's abuse, or about my anger management issues. Unwilling to destroy their opinion of me, I'd never shared my full history or fears. *Better to let them think I'm the class clown who doesn't want to settle down.*

"She'd be lucky to have you," Jack said.

On the contrary. "Why Jackson, you're making me blush." I said in my best southern belle voice while fanning my face.

I was done with this conversation and needed to pack a bag and gear up my truck. "I'm running home to grab my shit. I'll be back soon." *Should I check on Blake first?*

"You know you don't need to come back tonight. You can stay home and get some rest," Jamie said. I half expected he said it just to force me to argue.

I glanced down the hall. "I'll be back in thirty," I huffed as I turned and walked out. "Lock the door behind me," I said without looking back. It took an enormous amount of effort not to walk to Blake's room first.

"Right behind you," Jack said, clapping my shoulder.

At the door, Jack asked if I was okay. What was I supposed to say? Professionally, I was okay to do the job—I'd snap every single neck in Texas to keep Blake safe. Personally, I was a nut job—it was killing me to be so close to Blake knowing she could never be mine.

"I'm here if you want to talk," he said as he held out his hand. When I took it, he pulled me into a hug.

"Don't go getting all girlie on me, Sheppard." I didn't bother telling myself he wouldn't notice the pain in my eyes. Jack noticed everything. It was a great quality in a PI, but I hated it when I was in his crosshairs.

"You know where I am." He didn't take the bait. "Hurry back. Blake's calmer when you're around."

I'd felt it, but refused to let myself believe it, so hearing Jack say it was like a knife through my heart. *It's only because I'm familiar.*

Memories of my father beating my mother, beating me, filled my dreams. But the worst was when my father's face morphed into mine as he, as I, hit Blake.

Things weren't much better when I was awake. I'd get up, talk to Jamie or Jay, hit the head, then walk the inside perimeter of the house, stopping to peek in Blake's room. I needed sleep to be effective at my job, so after a few minutes of annoying whoever was up, I'd go back to the couch and try again. Eventually, I'd drift off and the cycle would start all over again.

During one of my self-appointed rounds, I stood in the doorway and watched Blake sleep. She was curled up in a tiny ball with the blanket tucked up to her chin. *My Sleeping Beauty.*

Meg chose well when she gave Blake the call sign Aurora. *I know way too fucking much about princesses for a man without kids.* Shaking my head, I went back to the couch.

When I woke up around four-thirty, I stayed up. The plan was to get on the road by seven, so I expected Blake to sleep in for another hour.

"Coffee's brewing," Jamie said when I walked back to the kitchen.

"Thanks. Mind if I shower real quick?"

"Towels are in the closet."

"Thanks. I'll make breakfast when I'm done."

Jamie nodded and lifted his coffee mug.

I ran the water as hot as I could get it, hoping to burn away my feelings. When that didn't work, I switched to the other extreme. The shock of the arctic blast didn't work either.

Fuck. My life was easier when I didn't have to worry about feelings. Feeling things brought back the fears and memories I'd trapped in steel boxes in the deepest recesses of my mind. Feelings that had me longing for a future with someone. No, not someone; Blake.

Bastard. It wasn't enough he'd stolen my childhood, but he'd destroyed my chances for a happy future.

I stepped out of the bathroom, rubbing a towel over my head to dry my hair, and bumped into Blake.

"Sorry," Blake whispered without looking at me.

"It's my fault. I should have been watching where I was going." I stepped aside. "It's all yours."

"Thanks." she bit her lower lip as she turned away.

Damn, that's fucking sexy. So were the rainbow pajamas hugging her ass and breasts.

Double Fuck. I adjusted myself, dropping the towel to hide the movement in my pants, and marched to the kitchen.

"You okay?" Jamie asked. *One of these days, I'll smack one of those grins off one of their faces.*

"Fine. Blake's up."

"I heard." Jamie chuckled as he noticed me hiding my still noticeable erection. He smiled and joked around a lot more now that he was happily in love.

Something I can never have. I practically barked, "I'll make breakfast."

"Suit yourself," Jamie said around a laugh.

God, I fucking hate how easily these guys read me. To be fair, I'd loved how close we were until they realized I had it bad for Blake. Now they were thorns in my side, using that knowledge to goad me.

The same way I did with Jack? And Jamie? And Doug? Karma's a bitch.

By six, everyone was in the kitchen, where I'd set out a buffet of scrambled eggs, bacon, sausage, yogurt, and fresh fruit.

Not wanting any surprises, we were watching the video feeds from Jamie's and the safe house. Getting the motion sensor sensitivity right was tricky, and the ones at the safe house were paranoia level sensitive, which meant we got a lot of alerts because of the local wildlife.

Better too sensitive than not sensitive enough.

Chapter 28

Blake

After breakfast, John, Doug, and Jaden escorted us to the safe house. I thought three cars were excessive, but they didn't.

My heart raced while AJ and I waited in his truck for the other guys to check the small, run-down farmhouse. In the middle of fucking nowhere west of Dallas.

As John walked out of the house, I couldn't help but replay his greeting earlier at Jamie's. John's calm, fatherly tone when he told me he was updating my father regularly almost brought on a fresh round of tears. Especially when he relayed my father's message, quoting him without hesitation. "I love you. Please be good. This will all be over before you know it."

It was already too late to be over before I knew it. *I wish it had never started.*

A loud noise caused me to jump in my seat and scream.

"It's okay. It was just Jay tapping on the hood," AJ reassured me.

It sounded a lot louder than a tap, but I didn't trust my voice enough to say it.

"You ready?" AJ asked.

"Do I have a choice?" I asked. "Sorry." AJ didn't deserve my snark.

He nodded.

John opened my door and offered me a hand down. I wasn't usually one to accept a man's help getting in or out of a car, but AJ's truck was huge and I was short.

"Thank you."

AJ grabbed our bags while Doug and Jay carried in everything else.

"Do you guys own this house?" I sounded judgmental, but it had seen better days. The exterior needed a coat of paint, the windows were beyond dirty, and the lawn hadn't been tended in a long time.

"No, Maxwell used her FBI contacts to get us a loaner from the US Marshalls. We usually use motels," John said as he held the door for us.

"I could have stayed at a hotel?" The inside wasn't much better than the outside. It was small, sparsely furnished, and completely devoid of charm. Not to mention, dark. Shades and curtains covered all the windows.

"Motels, not hotels," John corrected me.

"You're not missing out," Doug said. "We use random motels off the beaten path. They're run down and shady."

This place wasn't?

"Are there cameras inside?" I asked, knowing there was a ton on the exterior.

"Only in the public spaces," Doug answered. "Not in the bedrooms and bathrooms, and there's no audio."

That was a relief. I didn't think I could deal with a complete lack of privacy on top of everything else.

"I'll show you to your room," AJ said from behind me.

I nodded and followed him as he walked down a short hall to the left of the living space.

"You can choose whichever of these two bedrooms you'd prefer," AJ indicated the bedrooms on either side of the hall.

"What's that one?" I asked, pointing to the closed door at the end.

"The master, but we can't use it."

"Why not?" *The master probably has a private bath.*

"The FBI said so." AJ shrugged. "Take your pick."

I looked inside both rooms and couldn't see a difference, so I picked the one on the right. AJ insisted on carrying my bag in for me. He dropped my suitcase—*Emily's not mine*—on the bed.

"There's only one bathroom, so we'll have to share."

"Okay." I looked around, grateful I'd never had to live like this. *Maybe it felt less depressing when people lived here.*

The frameless full bed was pushed against the far wall and covered with a faded quilt. The scratched night stand beside it didn't match the dresser at the end of the bed. The closet was the smallest I'd ever seen, and that was saying something—our dorm rooms had tiny closets.

The idea of unpacking was more than I could handle, so I went to the kitchen where the guys were putting away the last of the groceries.

"Let us know if there's anything special you want to eat, and we'll have Jack bring it when he relieves Jaden later today," John said.

"Thanks. Can I ask you a question?" My voice trembled as I asked.

"Sure." John answered, heading for the living room.

Grateful for the privacy, I followed him. I looked over my shoulder, making sure no one had followed.

"Do you think my father…" John waited patiently as I struggled to finish. "Is he involved with the people threatening me?" I couldn't say guilty, or dirty, or on the take.

"I don't know." John's tone took on that kind, fatherly tone again. "I know it's not the answer you want to hear, but it's the only one I have. We're investigating every angle."

Which means they're investigating my father, though he didn't say it. My emotions flip-flopped between grateful for the kindness and frustrated by the half-truths.

Even though he hadn't said it, I felt the need to defend my father. "You probably won't believe me, but he's innocent. He'd never do anything illegal."

I didn't sound as strong as I had when I defended him the night before. *Is my conviction waning?*

"For your sake, I hope that's true." Empathy radiated from his eyes. He held out his arm and escorted me back to the kitchen.

Apparently, the conversation was over.

Doug was wiping down the table, stirring up a dense cloud of dust, which made me sneeze.

"Bless you," three different voices called out.

"Thanks." I sneezed again. "Can I open a window?" I didn't think I could live with the dust and the musty smell filling the house.

"Unfortunately, no, they're nailed shut."

Nailed shut? That had to violate some housing code or something. "What if there's a fire and we have to get out?"

"You break the glass."

I didn't appreciate Jaden's condescending tone. He might be used to this kind of thing, but I wasn't.

"Jaden," his father's tone invoked an apology.

"What happened?" AJ asked, walking in to the kitchen.

"Nothing," Jaden answered.

"Jaden was being less than polite." Doug didn't hesitate to throw him under that bus.

AJ growled at Jaden, who raised his eyebrows and chuckled.

Men.

I grabbed a bottle of water and went back to my room to grab one of the books Emily let me borrow, then tried to get comfortable on the lumpy couch. *You'd think they could've found a better place to stay.* I'd happily dish out more cash for a five-star hotel. Knowing they'd tell me no; I didn't bring it up.

I got as comfortable as I could and opened the book. Before long, the cozy mystery transported me to a fictitious English village filled with magic and mystery.

I was a few chapters in when John and Doug left. Three cars suddenly made sense. Jaden and AJ each had one, and John and Doug needed one to get home.

"Holler if you need anything," Jaden said before closing and locking the door. He had keys so he could come in to use the bathroom and get food, as needed.

AJ sat in one of the mismatched recliners and opened a book. *He reads?* Probably a thriller or mystery. Looking down at my novel, I realized I had zero room to judge.

I usually played background music when I studied or read, but hadn't needed it before the guys left. Their chatter had filled the void, but now the house was eerily quiet.

Without thinking, I reached for my phone. *Right.* Annoyance rushed to the surface—I didn't have my phone or my laptop. I didn't have any of the luxuries I'd always taken for granted.

"You okay?" AJ asked over the top of his book.

"It's too quiet," I admitted.

"We could talk, or I could turn on the TV."

I didn't want to watch the tiny, probably black and white, ancient looking, TV.

"AJ, if I ask you a question, will you be completely honest with me?"

He paused, weighing his options. His dark eyes bore into my soul while I waited. "I'll be as honest as I can be," he finally said, putting his book face down, creating a tent on the table between us.

Which means he'll give me the party line and I won't learn anything.

I gathered my courage to deal with whatever answer he gave me.

"Does SSI really think my father is involved with whoever is threatening me?"

AJ hesitated a second before answering. "This will be hard for you to hear, but I don't want to lie to you." He ran his hands through his dark hair, making it stand up in places. "Even though I could get in trouble."

This can't be good. I nodded and waited for the hammer to fall.

"Blake, there's a lot of circumstantial evidence suggesting your father is involved with criminals, including the one trying to hurt you."

The room turned blurry as I shook my head back and forth. I thought I was ready to hear what he had to say, but I was wrong. I wanted to shout, Take it back!

Instead, I argued, "I don't believe you. He wouldn't do that. He'd never do anything to hurt me."

"We don't think so either, but we think they're using you to get to him," AJ said.

Could it be true? Could he have connections to criminals?

"I'm sorry, Blake."

Sorry? Was that supposed to make me feel better? Because it didn't. My mind went into overdrive trying to think of something that could explain it all away.

"I bet they offered him a bribe and are threatening him because he refused to take it." That made sense, fitting what I believed about my father.

"Maybe," was all AJ said.

A glance at my watch revealed it barely lunch time. *It's going to be a long day.* I got up and went to the kitchen to make myself something to eat. I found sliced ham and turkey, a variety of sliced cheeses, and mustard in the fridge. When I pulled away from the refrigerator, I felt AJ's presence before I saw him.

"Want a sandwich?" I didn't really want company, but I didn't want to be rude either.

"Sure. I'll grab plates and the bread."

We each made our own sandwiches. Mine was a couple of slices of turkey and a slice of provolone. He made two, one ham and swiss, the other turkey and provolone. Both thick and slathered with mayo and mustard. I gained ten pounds just looking at them.

Not that he has to worry about it. AJ was solid muscle and probably worked out every day. I wasn't shallow enough to be attracted to someone based solely on their looks, but that didn't mean I couldn't appreciate a ridiculously good looking man when I saw one.

"You want chips?" he asked, breaking me out of my stupor. *Please tell me I'm not blushing.* "Thanks."

We ate in silence, which AJ disrupted as soon as we finished. "Blake, can I ask you a few questions?"

Something in his tone made me nervous. I bit my thumbnail before answering. "I guess."

"How well do you know your step-mother?"

"Not well. I know she's a gold-digger who married my father for his money and she's pissed he didn't inherit my grandfather's." I didn't mention I had. *He probably already knows.*

He nodded. "What happens to your inheritance if you die before you turn twenty-five? Would it go to your father?"

Yup, he knows. Maybe SSI had it all wrong, and it was Priscilla who was involved with the people threatening me, not my dad.

"Do you think she's behind this?" I asked.

"We don't know. We're looking at every angle."

There it is, the party line.

Before I could accuse him of avoiding my question, he asked another. "Did you know your parents are having money problems?"

"What?" I asked. My father had assured me they weren't. Sure, Priscilla whined about daddy supporting me, but that was because she was greedy, not because he couldn't afford it. I folded and unfolded my napkin until it fell apart. It couldn't be true; my father would never lie to me. *But what if?*

"If it's true, I'd happily give my dad my inheritance to make this all go away, but…"

"But you can't, not yet," AJ finished for me.

Did everyone at SSI know I'd inherit my grandfather's fortune on my twenty-fifth birthday? Is that why they were so nice to me? It wouldn't surprise me. Most people were nice once they learned I'd be worth almost enough millions to qualify as a billionaire.

"Blake?"

"What?" I mumbled. I didn't want to talk about it anymore.

"You didn't know, did you?"

"I don't think it's true," I argued without conviction. Memories flashed through my mind. Individually, they meant nothing, but together they added up to one giant red flag.

"I assure you it is, and unfortunately, having money problems is a strong motive to make questionable decisions."

Questionable decisions? My head snapped up to look at him, ready to argue again, but the honesty, and empathy, in his eyes stopped me dead in my tracks.

He's telling the truth.

"Why didn't he tell me?" I buried my face in my hands and cried.

If he'd just told me, I could have helped and none of this would have happened. I wouldn't be locked up in the stupid house with no way to call him. What if they get pissed they can't get to me and go after him? Would they kill him? What would I do then?

I felt the comfort from AJ's large, warm hand on my forearm a moment before he answered. "I can't answer for him, but it's safe to assume he didn't want to embarrass himself by asking his daughter to bail him out of debt."

When he put it like that, it made sense. Daddy was a proud man, and he'd never ask me for help. He wouldn't want me to see him as anything less than the man I'd loved and worshipped my whole life.

But would it really be so bad? Surely, it wouldn't be worse than this? *He must be so worried.* If only I could call him and tell him I was okay and offer to give him what he needed.

"Is my dad doing okay?" I asked.

"As far as I know, he's fine." Something about the tone of his voice, and the guarded expression in his eyes, felt off.

What isn't he telling me now?

Chapter 29

AJ

I wasn't lying when I said Davenport was worried about her, but I didn't tell her everything. I couldn't—I'd already told her too much. Upsetting the guys at SSI didn't worry me; they'd understand and forgive me. But I wasn't sure Blake could handle any more surprises.

So I didn't tell her Davenport was being less than helpful and deflecting our questions like the politician he was. Shrugging off the questions about his financial issues. Refusing to talk to us about who could be behind the threat. Defending his questionable choices as a DA. Declining all our suggestions to keep him safe.

However, he continued to insist we do whatever was necessary to keep Blake safe. Regardless of what he'd done, might still be doing, there was no doubt he loved his daughter. The only subject he would talk to us about.

"What aren't you telling me?"

"We're still investigating, so there are a lot of unanswered questions." *Great, now I sound like a fucking politician.* At least it wasn't a lie.

"Great. Another non-answer, just what I need." She rolled her eyes. "I'm going to my room."

Damn it. That hadn't gone well. Not that I'd expected it to, but I had hoped maybe. I wanted her to talk to me, not shut down and run away.

I messaged Jack on the SSI secure phone and told him what little I'd learned. Blake was ignorant of her father's questionable practices and his money woes.

Then I messaged Jay to ask if he wanted a sandwich.

After swapping places for a few minutes so he could eat and take a leak, I sat back down to read. A crime thriller probably wasn't the best choice given the circumstances, but it was all I'd packed.

I must have fallen asleep because my book thunked on the floor when a scream caused me to jump out of the chair.

Blake!

I ran to her room and charged in without knocking, gun drawn.

She sat on the bed, eyes distant with silent tears streaming down her cheeks. When I invaded her space, crashing the door into the wall, she jumped and yelped. I saw her eyes widen when she saw my gun, then she buried her face in her knees, covered her head, and rocked back and forth.

I scanned the room, verifying no one was inside, before holstering my gun.

The bed sagged as I sat down beside her and rubbed her back. "What happened?"

She lifted her head and sniffled. *I wish I had tissues for her.* "Nothing, I just had a bad dream." She pulled away from me. "You didn't need to come charging in here ready to shoot the place up."

Not expecting her anger, I stood up and walked back to the door.

Before I left, I turned back and said, "I'm sorry if I scared you, but I won't apologize for responding to your scream."

She turned away and curled up in a ball instead of answering me.

"I'm leaving the door cracked. Please don't latch it," I said. I wanted to be able to check on her without disturbing her.

No answer. I sighed and did a sweep of the house, for my sanity, before going back to the living room.

When I got up a few hours later to use the bathroom, I checked on Blake. I could hear her muffled crying, so I knocked softly before pushing the door open with my knuckles. I asked from the doorway, "Blake, do you want to talk about it?"

"You don't have to pretend you care," she said around sniffles. "My father isn't paying you to be nice."

What the actual fuck. Where did that come from?

"Blake, I'm not pretending." I took a few cautious steps into the room.

"Nobody cares. I bet my friends haven't even noticed I'm not around." She didn't bother to move while answering me.

Why does she think that? I chalked it up to the stress of the situation and being isolated.

I was sure they'd noticed. Paige seemed okay, at least when Fuckface wasn't around. I was sure he'd noticed when he had to pay for his own lunch, or some other selfish reason. Not that I'd ever tell her that. I had to believe she had better friends, ones I hadn't met.

"I'm sure they have," I said, keeping my voice soft.

"They don't even like me. Not really." She sniffled.

Where had all this come from? I'd expected her to be upset about her dream, or being locked up in a safe house, but not this. *At least she's talking to me.*

"What makes you think that?"

"They can't. They don't even know the real me." She sniffled. "They just like me for my money." She rolled onto her back and leaned up on her elbows.

I hated seeing her puffy, bloodshot eyes and wished there was something I could do to take her pain away. I'd suffer a thousand deaths if it'd guarantee she'd never have a reason to cry again.

"Why don't they know the real you?" I asked.

"It doesn't matter. You don't really care."

"I do care, Blake." *More than I can ever tell you.* I repeated the question.

"They only know the me I'm supposed to show them."

The image of the perfect politician's daughter couldn't be easy to maintain.

"Hang on one second, okay?" I asked. When her eyes rounded in shock before lowering in disappointment, I added, "I'll be right back."

I sprinted out of the room and returned with a box of tissues and a bottle of water.

"Here you go."

This time, the expression in her eyes was shock and gratitude.

"Thank you."

"Why do you hide who you are?" I'd seen glimpses of the real Blake, and I liked her better.

Loved her, even.

"I've been told all my life who I should be, how I should act, what I should wear." She ran her hand through her hair, exposing the strip of pink. "I got in trouble when I dyed my hair, even though it's mostly hidden."

It sounded ridiculous to me that her parents would be upset about a little hair dye, especially since it was barely visible. I'd noticed she always exposed the stripe at school, but hadn't seen how she wore her hair at home. Thinking back, her pink stripe wasn't visible in the office.

I understood her feeling like she had to hide a part of herself, I'd lived it.

Wanting to lighten the mood, I said, "I kind of like it. It's playful."

She was quiet for a minute before saying, "Thank you." She turned to stare at the blinds covering the window, as if she could see the field beyond.

We sat in silence for a few minutes; her staring out the window lost in her thoughts; me watching her while lost in mine.

I understood how it felt to not live up to someone's expectations. My father had reminded me regularly, with his fists, that I wasn't good enough and never would be.

Understanding the conversation had ended, I didn't push. The sun was setting, and I was getting hungry so I asked, "Want me to cook some burgers?"

"That sounds good." She gave me a weak smile, and when she lifted her eyes to mine, the only emotion I saw was gratitude.

My heart did this weird little thing where it felt like it jumped out of my chest. But I had to ignore it. Blake was grateful I offered to cook, not confessing her love. And certainly not asking for me to confess my love for her.

This job is going to be the death of me.

Chapter 30

Blake

I misjudged him. The thought struck me again. Sure, he was violent when he was protecting me, but he'd been nothing but nice, and kind, and compassionate since then.

I drank half the water he'd given me before going to the bathroom to wash my face, wishing I had time to shower. A long, hot shower would help me relax. *Maybe after dinner.* But now I needed to eat.

The smell of ground beef filled my nose and made my stomach rumble as I walked into the kitchen. "Smells good in here."

"Thanks."

AJ looked a lot less menacing while flipping burgers in the kitchen. *What is it about a man in the kitchen that's so sexy?*

There was no denying AJ looked sexy with his shirt sleeves rolled up and his cargo pants hugging his muscular thighs.

"How do you like your burgers?"

Shit, did he see me staring? "I, um, medium rare, please."

"Good." He nodded like there was a right answer. "They're almost done. Grab a plate and dress your buns."

Did he just look down at my ass and smile? Must be my imagination. There was no way he'd be interested in a curvy girl like me. Plus, we lived in two very different worlds. Though at the moment I was jealous, because AJ got to be himself in his world and I had to be the woman my father expected me to be in mine.

We talked about trivial things while we ate AJ's perfectly cooked burgers. The sharp cheddar and crisp bacon made the heart attack on a bun a drool worthy meal. *I should have said two when he asked me how many I wanted.* But, if it wasn't proper etiquette or lady like behavior to eat one juicy burger like a man starved, it'd be downright scandalous to scarf down two.

I balanced the meal with carrot sticks. They weren't as tasty as fries, or AJ's chips, but at least I felt less guilty.

"What TV shows do you like?"

"I don't watch much TV." *That sounded snobbish.* I explained, "I try not to watch too much TV because I'm always worried I'll lose track of time. I'm always dying to know what happens next, but I can't afford to binge watch an entire season." I shrugged.

AJ had a weird look on his face; one I couldn't interpret. Feeling like I'd shut the conversation down, I added, "But I like watching movies."

He nodded. "We can do that. I'll even let you pick."

"Even if it's a rom-com?" I teased.

AJ stared into my eyes for a minute before chuckling.

"What's so funny?" *Is he laughing at me?*

"Nothing. I just thought you were teasing me."

I was. His response was perfectly normal. My reaction wasn't. "Sorry, I…" I wasn't sure why I over-reacted, so my apology fell short.

"It's okay." He smiled. "And a rom-com is fine. We could use something light and funny."

I offered to clean the kitchen since he'd cooked, but AJ insisted I go to the living room and pick out a movie.

Dad had a full staff, so I'd rarely ever had to cook or clean for myself at home, and we always ate out at school, so it should have felt perfectly natural to let AJ do all the work.

But it didn't; it felt wrong. *And I don't like it.*

I tried to argue, but AJ put his giant foot down and crossed his large, muscular arms in front of his wide, solid chest.

When I put my small hands on my wide, curvy hips in response and stood my ground—he grinned.

It was lopsided, so only the right dimple appeared. *I really shouldn't be staring at his lips.* Heat flooded my cheeks.

"Go," he ordered, unfurling his arms and pointing to the living room.

I wanted to argue and release some of my frustration, but something told me it'd be a bad idea. How many rom-coms had I seen where the two main characters didn't get along right up until they kissed each other mid-fight?

I worried my lower lip between my teeth. No way was I letting that happen.

So why am I still staring at his lips?

"Fine." I huffed and stomped away. I wasn't irritated with AJ; he hadn't done anything wrong. I was irritated at myself for being attracted to AJ's muscles and strength, for staring at his stupid lips, and for dreaming about kissing that stupid grin off his face.

Chapter 31

AJ

If Blake hadn't given in and turned away when she did, I might have lost what little control I had and swallowed up the distance between us so I could taste her lower lip.

She looked so damn sexy working that plump red lip between her teeth, that I had to beat back imagines of carrying her curvy body to the bedroom.

Can't think like that. Focus.

Thank God she hadn't looked down because there was nothing I could do to hide the evidence of how turned on I was without drawing attention to it. Splashing cold water on my face before washing the dishes didn't help, so I thought about my parents. Not only was the thought a mood-killer, but it reminded me of all the reasons I couldn't kiss Blake.

What if I couldn't control my temper? I knew from experience bruises weren't the only wounds abuse left behind. In fact, my father was so good at keeping up the appearance of being a loving father to the outside world that I didn't have any physical scars.

My father started hitting me when I was a defenseless kid. Initially, my mom tried to stop him, but gave up after taking one too many beatings of her own. He was the reason I worked so hard to bulk up and train in Brazilian Ju Jitsu after he left us high and dry when I was a teenager. He was the reason I'd sworn off love.

What if I'm just like him?

My back pocket vibrated, pulling me out of my unpleasant stroll down memory lane.

"Janerek."

"How are things going?" Jack asked.

"Quiet." He didn't need to know what was going on in my head.

"Good to hear. How's Aurora holding up?"

"Struggling, but she's stronger than she realizes, so I think she'll be okay."

"Anything I should relay to her father?"

"Tell him he's an asshole for forcing her into a mold instead of letting her blossom into the woman she wants to be," I said before I could censor myself.

"I think I'll leave that out when I talk to him, but I'm glad she's opening up to you." I could hear the amusement in Jack's voice.

I thought about making a joke, but figured it'd only fuel the fire. "Thanks."

"I'll be outside, ETA fifteen, if you need me."

"Copy that." I disconnected the call.

I left the clean dishes in the strainer to air dry, figuring I could put them away later. *It'll give me something to do when I can't sleep.*

Blake was still scrolling when I walked into the living room.

"Can't decide?"

"I decided, but I'm waiting for you to start." Her small smile reached her eyes, lighting up her face.

I pretended my heart didn't skip a beat as I walked to the reclining chair closest to Blake. Sitting next to her on the couch would have been a thousand times better, but I wouldn't do it without an invitation.

"Ready?" she asked.

"Ready."

Blake only lasted about thirty minutes before falling asleep. I blamed the movie for making me think her soft snores were cute. Rom-coms weren't my jam, so I spent more time watching her sleep than I did watching the movie. *She looks so peaceful.*

And beautiful.

A soft smile played on her slightly parted lips, giving her an angelic appearance. Gone was the fear of being threatened. Gone was the stress of trying to please everyone. Gone was the anger at having her world turned upside down.

Because I was staring, I saw when her lips turned down and her hand twitched. The soft, angelic features twisted into fear. She started whimpering before I had time to take the two steps needed to reach the couch and sit down beside her.

Should I wake her?

Her head rolled back and forth as more whimpers escaped her lips.

I couldn't let her suffer. Not wanting to freak her out, I gently shook her shoulders. "Blake, wake up. It's only a dream."

She screamed as she jerked awake; her eyes the size of saucers.

My heart shredded as I watched her head whip from side to side, fear radiating off her as she tried to get her bearings with unfocused eyes.

When I find the guy responsible for this, I'll tear his fucking head off his fucking body with my bare fucking hands.

As I unclenched my back teeth, I lifted her chin until she looked at me. "Blake, sweetheart, it's okay. You're okay. It was just a dream." I did a remarkable impression of sounding like someone who didn't want to commit murder.

Her desperation-filled eyes locked on mine, her chest wasn't moving.

Shit.

"Blake, sweetheart, I need you to breathe," I begged as I held her shoulders, offering what little comfort I could.

Her eyes found mine. "AJ?" her hopeful voice squeaked as she sucked in air.

Thank God. "It's me, I'm here.

"Where am I?" Her eyes swept the lackluster room before staring blankly at the rom-com still playing on the TV.

"You're in the safe house."

Her body shook with her deep inhale. She turned her head slowly and looked at me before exhaling with a sob.

"It's okay." I took her hand and gently tugged her towards me, wrapping the other arm around her shoulders as I pulled her into my chest.

She didn't hesitate to curl into me.

I can't risk loving her, but I can comfort her.

Holding her tight against my chest, I let her cry.

And protect her.

Her tears soaked through my thin t-shirt, warming my skin while chilling my soul. I held her tighter, supporting her the only way I knew how.

"I'm right here, Sweetheart, and I swear to you, I won't let anyone hurt you." I made a vow I knew I shouldn't. Nothing was guaranteed in our line of work.

"It's okay, let it all out," I whispered into her hair before kissing the top of her head.

Sweetheart?

Kissing her.

I was truly, completely, one-hundred percent, absolutely fucked.

Chapter 32

Blake

I sighed and relaxed in AJ's arms. I didn't understand why, but his embrace comforted me.

Oh my God, I'm slobbering all over him. Without moving out of the comfort and safety of AJ's arms, I sniffled and wiped my nose on my sleeve in the most inelegant fashion. If only Priscilla could see me now.

Does it matter if I'm lady-like while locked away in a safe house?

Did AJ call me sweetheart? Why? I was no one special. At least not without my inheritance.

"I'm sorry," I said as I pulled away and wiped at the tears on my cheek. There was no doubt in my mind I looked like crap.

"No need to apologize." AJ's touch was butterfly soft when he wiped a tear off my cheek. "Want to tell me about your nightmare?"

"That's okay; I'm sure you don't want to hear about my stupid dreams." I wanted to curl up in his powerful arms and feel safe again, not relive my nightmare.

A finger under my chin turned my head until I looked into AJ's intense dark eyes. "You're wrong. I want to hear about your dream, stupid or not." He swept my bangs across my forehead. "I want to hear everything you're willing to tell me," he whispered.

"You, um, I, um…" It wasn't the first time AJ's touch short-circuited my brain.

He chuckled and handed me a box of tissues. "I'll get you some water, then you can tell me about it."

I sagged as the couch rebounded from his weight after he stood up.

I really misjudged him. AJ was supportive and kind. Safe and warm.

He handed me a bottle of water and turned towards the recliner.

"You can sit here." I scooted over so he'd have plenty of room.

His eyes darted from me to the couch and back again before he moved. He sat at the far end, creating a gaping space between us.

Missing the warmth and comfort of his body, I willed him to sit closer.

Oh. My. God. I'm attracted to him.

Not physically, I mean, I was, but I liked him too.

It didn't matter if AJ was the complete opposite of every guy I'd ever dated, and totally not my usual type. My last boyfriend was good looking. More cute than handsome. He was tall, like AJ, but thin. *His idea of being supportive was asking why I worried about my grades when I'd be rich soon.*

People expected me to live off my inheritance, but my mother would roll over in her grave if I did that. No, I'd earn my degree and work to support myself.

Maybe that's why it hadn't worked out with any of them. *None of them were half the man AJ is.*

Was I really the type of woman who wanted to be with a guy who oozed toxic masculinity?

"Want to tell me what's going on in that pretty little head of yours?" he asked.

I'd been so lost in my head thinking about AJ, I'd forgotten he was sitting a few feet away.

Masculine, one hundred percent.

Toxic, not at all.

"Nothing." I chugged my water to hide my embarrassment.

AJ patiently coaxed the details of my nightmare out of me. Not that it was hard; I wanted to talk to him.

It wasn't long before I yawned more than I talked.

"Let's get you to bed."

When AJ stood and offered me a hand, I happily put my hand in his and let him help me stand.

He walked me to my room but didn't come in. "I'm right next door if you need me."

"Okay." I nodded. I could still feel his eyes on me as I walked into the room. "Thank you, AJ. Good night."

"Good night, Blake." AJ pulled the door closed; but it didn't latch.

After changing and cleaning up, I crawled into bed and hugged the second pillow, wishing I was home in my own bed.

I tossed and turned most of the night, not getting more than a few hours of fitful sleep at a time. I finally gave up as the sun rose over the horizon, and dragged myself out of bed. Maybe a hot shower would help me feel better.

And coffee. Lots and lots of coffee.

Chapter 33

AJ

I'd tossed and turned through most of the night. In an attempt to calm my mind, I walked the interior anytime I woke up, checking on Blake each time. From the sound of it, she hadn't slept well either.

Needing to disrupt the freight train of negative thoughts plowing through my mind, I called Jack.

"Sheppard. Everything okay?"

I couldn't blame him for his concern; it was three am. "Yeah, I couldn't sleep, so I thought I'd see if you needed anything?" I lied.

"I could use a bathroom break," he answered. "And some coffee."

"I'll start a pot and throw some shoes on. Meet you at the door in three."

"Sounds good."

We'd agreed to switch places after ten minutes, so I took advantage of the space and walked around the front of the house to really stretch my legs and work off my nervous energy. Jack took advantage of the modern plumbing.

The blast of cool, fresh air did me good because I fell back asleep easily after my walk.

I woke up two hours later and didn't bother going back to sleep. Instead, I did some bodyweight exercises after checking the house again.

After a quick shower, I brewed a fresh pot of coffee and started breakfast. I prepped everything I'd need to make omelets and cleaned up the living room. I couldn't do much else without waking Blake, so I read until she woke up.

I gave up reading when I heard the water running. *Fucking thin walls.* Fantasizing about her small, curvy body in the shower, suds running down her silky smooth skin, was the last thing I needed.

I forced myself to walk through the entire house in my mind, trying to remember every detail of every room.

When Blake joined me in the kitchen, her hair was still damp. *Don't think about the fantasy. Don't think about the fantasy.*

"Thanks for making coffee."

"You're welcome. Want an omelet?" I asked, as if I wasn't just envisioning her naked.

She nodded as she poured and doctored her coffee.

I let her enjoy her coffee for a few minutes while I started the sausage links on the stove. I'd cook the omelet after the links were done.

"Did you sleep okay?" I asked, knowing she'd slept no better than I had but wanting to start a conversation.

"Not really. I'm guessing you didn't either; I heard you get up a few times during the night."

"Sorry if I woke you."

"It wasn't you."

I heated a second cast iron pan and coated it in butter to sauté the cut veggies before adding the egg mix. I scrambled in some cream cheese to make them extra creamy before letting them cook. After flipping the omelet, I added a generous helping of cheddar jack cheese.

"Here you go." I set her plate in front of her.

Her eyes rounded. "That's a lot of food." Her laughter was music to my ears.

"You don't have to eat it all, but you'll need the energy after not sleeping well."

While we ate, I got a message from John asking me to call him. Not wanting to be rude and walk away during breakfast, I said I'd call in ten.

This time, when Blake volunteered to clean up, I let her. "If you'll excuse me, I have to call John." I didn't miss the flash of concern that crossed her face before she nodded and turned towards the sink.

"I'll be right back."

I dialed John's cell as I walked to my room, shutting the door behind me to lessen the risk of Blake overhearing me.

"Janerek, how are things going?" He greeted me with a question.

"As well as it can, sir. Aurora's struggling, but doing her best to adjust."

"Good. St. Charles is on his way to relieve Jack." It was weird having him refer to Dean by his last name, but it was his standard procedure during missions. The only exception was his sons, to avoid confusion.

"Copy that. Any updates?" John hadn't called to tell me Dean was on his way.

"We've uncovered evidence of Davenport's corruption." *Shit.* This would kill Blake.

"I need you to push her a little harder for informa-"

"She's not involved." I cut him off, practically barking.

"Calm down, I'm not saying she is." He paused, waiting to see if I had anything else to say. I didn't. "She may have noticed things that could help without realizing it."

"If you have evidence, why do you need Blake's help?" It seemed cruel to question her about her father's misdeeds if I didn't need to.

"Because the evidence doesn't help us narrow down who's threatening Blake." John sounded like a cop, which wasn't surprising given he'd spent most of his adult life in uniform.

Identifying the threat, not convicting Davenport, was our priority. I ground my back teeth. "What should ask about?" I hated adding this to her already overflowing pile of stress.

"Ask about behavior changes, visitors who may have seemed abnormal or given her the creeps, more late night meetings than usual, that kind of stuff. Like I said, we don't think Blake is involved, but anything she might have observed could help."

"Copy that."

"I can ask Jack to stick around if you're not comfortable questioning her."

Hell no. Jack was a good guy, but there was no way I was going to make it seem like we were ganging up on her.

"I'll handle it." I hung up on my boss without waiting for a reply.

I took a few deep breaths to steel my resolve before walking back to the kitchen.

I refilled my coffee, wishing I had some whiskey to take the edge off.

"Thanks for cleaning up," I said, interrupted her reading.

"Everything okay?" Her voice trembled ever so slightly.

"Yeah, but I need to ask you a few questions."

She sighed and put her book down.

Blake alternated between irritation, anger, and shock as she answered my questions. Huffing out answers without thinking, then apologizing.

She admitting to noticing her father had seemed more stressed than usual lately, but had chalked it up to Priscilla's constant whining.

"A lot of the people who visit him give me the creeps. They're old politicians who like to grope women and think they can get away with murder," she said, exasperation thick in her voice.

"What about non-politicians?" I pushed.

"None that stand out. I was only there on weekends, so I didn't see much." She looked ashamed when she said, "To be honest, I always checked out during Daddy's events, so I barely remember anyone I met."

"No shame in that."

Because she lived on campus during the week, she couldn't really speak to changes or abnormalities in his schedule.

"Blake, I'm sorry I had to ask. We're trying to put some pieces together." It wasn't exactly the truth, but it wasn't a complete lie, either. *I still hate myself.*

"You found something, didn't you?"

I twirled my coffee cup in my hand. I didn't want to lie, and she was smart, smarter than me, so there was no sense in playing word games to disguise the truth.

"They have, though I don't know what it is. It sounds like it's-"

She cut me off. "He's innocent. He has to be."

"I know you don't want to hear this, but there's a good chance he's committed a few crimes."

"No." She stood up and slammed her cup on the table, causing coffee to spill over the rim. "I don't believe it. I won't." She started crying. "My father is a good man."

"Blake, please-"

She cut me off. "Please what? Listen? Why, so you can tell me what crimes you think he's committed." She crossed her arms but didn't give me time to answer. "You think you know everything, but you don't. You know nothing about my father."

We know a few things. But she wasn't in the right frame of mind to hear any of it.

She turned and ran to her room, leaving me struggling with what to do. I wanted to talk to her, help her see the truth, and then hold her and make everything better. *But I'm the last person she wants to see right now.*

Swearing into my cup, I fought back the urge to follow her.

Instead, I called John and relayed the few things she'd been able to tell me. Without names or specifics, it wouldn't help much.

Then I walked the interior of the house, stopping to listen at Blake's door. It was quiet, so I continued walking.

I grabbed my book and sat on the couch, positioning myself so I could see the hall. And Blake's bedroom door.

Chapter 34

Blake

I threw myself on my bed, buried my face in my pillow, and cried.

He couldn't be corrupt. Even after talking to AJ the night before, and hearing they had circumstantial evidence against him, I refused to believe he was on the wrong side of the law.

Not my dad. He was a good, law-abiding guy. A good father. A respected District Attorney.

He was the type of dad who always found time to spend with me, no matter how busy he was. He was the type of husband who brought my mom flowers, just because, and always told her she was beautiful.

He was the type of man other men looked up to. Honest. Generous. Successful.

Sure, he wasn't perfect. He worked a lot of late nights, more so after we lost my mom to cancer, but that was to be expected. He still came home most nights and had dinner with me before retiring to his office. With us, after he married Priscilla.

She complained he was never home, but she was prone to exaggerating.

In the last year, she'd complained a lot about money. I'd thought it was because she didn't like Daddy spending money on me, but maybe there was more to it. Had she spent them into debt with her extravagant shopping sprees, luxury vacations, and 'upgrading' the interior of the house? Her words, not mine.

I loved the house as it was—every room held memories of my mother.

I never understood why my father married her. It wasn't for love, that's for sure. He only bought her flowers for the obligatory holidays and only told her she looked nice when guests were around. *Or when she fishes for compliments.* He showed her off at dinner parties and political events, but rarely did anything fun with her. She was nothing like my mom; and I could tell he didn't love her.

Priscilla was probably the one doing stupid illegal things, not my dad.

I was still struggling to believe he was in financial trouble, even though AJ said it was true. He may have had an investment or two not do well, but we weren't hurting for money. No matter how much Priscilla carried on about it. *She's just a greedy bitch who wants my grandfather's money.*

When I'd told AJ that a lot of my father's guests gave me the creeps, I wasn't lying.

I thought back to a recent dinner party. It was a formal event, and my attendance had been required. Daddy loved showing off his honor roll, law-student daughter, and bragged about my desire to work for a not-for-profit.

"Thank you, Daddy." I said, desperately wanting to get away from the man he was introducing me to. He was the kind of guy who made your skin crawl with nothing but a look.

Men like him were the reason I didn't want to get into politics like my dad.

"Such a waste to push paperwork for a not-for-profit company when you could make a fortune working with your father," the guy said while swirling the expensive bourbon in his glass.

"Blake doesn't need the money." I'm sure he said it to get the guy off my back, but it had the reverse effect.

"That's right, you're set to inherit a fortune. No need to work at all." I vomited a little in my mouth as he spoke. "You should find yourself a handsome man and settle down, start a family."

I held back the shiver of disgust that wanted to run from my head to my toes. I held back my snarky responses too, knowing my father would get mad, and excused myself.

As I was escaping the room, I overheard, "It'd be a shame if he goes back on his word. I'd hate to have to enforce our agreement." The hair on the back of my neck stood up.

I didn't know who they were talking about, but it didn't matter. I didn't want to hear anymore.

Pretending I hadn't heard anything, I rushed to the stairs and up to my room. My father's dinner parties were rarely fun for me, but that one had been downright awful.

I snapped back to the present and sat up on my bed. That party was a week before I got the note.

Were they talking about my father?

I convinced myself I didn't need to tell AJ since I didn't know who the men were, or if they were even talking about my dad. *No point in making things worse.*

Needing to wash my face, I left my room and went to the bathroom. I pretended not to see AJ reading until he lifted his eyes over the paperback.

When I finished in the bathroom, I returned to my room without saying a word.

Chapter 35

AJ

The urge to check on Blake had me going stir crazy, but I wanted to respect her privacy while she processed everything. At least that's what I told myself. In truth, I didn't want to see the accusation in her eyes. She was in a shoot the messenger mindset and unfortunately, I was the messenger.

Knowing she couldn't call or text anyone, or even numb herself with social media, I got up and walked to her door at least a dozen times.

Each time I stopped and listened, but never knocked. *Coward.*

I called Jack for an update, hoping he'd found something positive I could share with Blake. People don't shoot messengers who bring good news. But there wasn't. There wasn't anything negative to add either, so that was good.

Blake still hadn't come out of her room by the time lunch came around, so I worked up the courage to knock. Not wanting to startle her, I rapped a finger on the door softly. Nothing. I knocked again, this time a little louder.

"Go away!"

"I'm making lunch. Can you come out and eat?"

"I'm not hungry," she announced through the door.

I doubted it was true and considered begging, but let it go instead. She'd come out when she was ready.

"I'll be in the kitchen if you change your mind." I waited to see if she'd respond—she didn't.

I made myself a sandwich and ate alone in the kitchen. The ham and cheese could have been cardboard for how little I noticed the taste.

Blake giving me the silent treatment was killing me. No, not her silence, her pain. And shutting herself away to hide it from me.

We weren't friends, but I'd thought we'd made progress. *She just started trusting me.*

I worked out again, wishing I could go a few rounds in the ring with Doug. I read, I watched TV. Nothing kept my mind off of Blake for more than a few seconds, so I called Jack. Again.

"Dude, what's going on?" he said after making sure everything was okay.

"She shut herself in her bedroom after I questioned her and she won't come out." I rushed to get it out before I lost my nerve.

There was a hard pause before Jack responded, "Is there a problem, something we need to worry about?"

I bit back my reflexive, angry response as I scratched the stubble on my cheek, I hadn't trimmed my beard in days and it showed.

"No." I finally admitted. The problem was she wouldn't let me help her, but how was I supposed to say that to Jack?

"Want to tell me what's going on?"

"I want to help her, but she won't talk to me." It was as much as I would admit in the moment.

"You know, when I fucked things up with Meg, I recall a wise man telling me to give her time."

I was that wise man, well, one of several, who told him to give her time. But he was in love with her, and everyone knew it. I hadn't told anyone I'd fallen for Blake. Hell, I was barely willing to acknowledge it myself.

"It's not like that," I lied, knowing he wouldn't believe me.

"You keep telling yourself that," he said around a laugh. "My advice stays the same. She'll come around after she's had time to process."

I hope so. Her silence was driving me insane.

"I'll be there in a few hours; we can talk more then."

"Thanks." I disconnected the call. If I couldn't talk to him over the phone, I wouldn't be able to do it in person. Unlike Jack, I hadn't grown up with caring parents and three siblings who loved me. While he learned how to talk about his problems, I learned how to hide mine.

Not for the first time, I envied Jack's relationship with his family. His upbringing helped him become a good man and a great husband. Things I'd never be.

I spent my whole life dismissing the idea of marriage, knowing I could end up being like my father. But Blake fucking Davenport had pierced my heart the instant I set eyes on that damn photo and, for the first time in my life, I wanted more. I wanted a future. With her.

I prowled up and down the hall as I tortured myself with visions of the future I could never have. *I need to hit something.* Ten minutes with a heavy bag would help me release my pent up stress, but there was nothing in the safe house sturdy enough to hit.

Deciding to be productive, I went to the kitchen and started prepping for dinner. I peeled and cut potatoes, wondering if Blake liked roasted garlic mashed potatoes.

I turned on the oven before separating a few cloves of garlic from the bulb and smearing them with olive oil. Focusing harder than required, I trimmed and seasoned the chicken breasts and put them back in the fridge to rest while I waited for the oven to heat up.

"Here goes nothing," I said to the pot of potatoes as I turned the burner on.

"What?" she called through the door after I knocked.

"Just wanted to let you know I'm making dinner; it'll be ready in thirty minutes."

I hate long pauses.

Assuming she was ignoring me, I turned to walk away. Before I lifted my foot, I heard, "Okay, I'll be out in a minute."

It was a small victory, but I'd take it.

Chapter 36

Blake

I waited until I was sure AJ had walked away before going to the bathroom to wash my face. Again. I'd been crying off and on all day and my cheeks were dry from the salt.

Red lines filled the whites of my eyes; the surrounding skin was puffy and swollen. No amount of washing could fix that.

I don't want him to see me like this. Not that I was overly vain, but still.

My stomach rumbled, mad at me for not eating since breakfast. Squaring my shoulders, I told myself I could face him as I walked down the hall.

My stomach didn't just rumble when the smell of roasted garlic and sautéing chicken hit my nose, it growled like a starving wolf.

I can do this. I can act like a civil human being and pretend my eyes don't look like I've been crying all day. I had to because there was no telling what my body would do if I didn't feed it.

"It smells good in here." *Nothing to see here, folks, just polite conversation.*

AJ turned at the sound of my voice. His eyes roamed up and down, pausing on my face. I saw something flicker in his eyes, but it was gone before I could identify it.

"Thanks. I hope you like chicken and garlic mashed potatoes," he said.

"I do. Anything I can do to help?" I asked. It felt like the right thing to do, even if my heart wasn't in it.

"Want to set the table while I finish up?"

"Sure."

So far, so good, but in a few minutes, we'd be sitting across from one another. And just because he hadn't said anything yet, didn't mean he wouldn't.

AJ plated our meals and set them on the table before taking his seat.

Hoping to hide my eyes, I avoided making eye contact.

"Dig in," he said, picking up his fork. "I wasn't sure if you'd like as much garlic as I do, so I went light."

"Thanks, it looks delicious." AJ's idea of light garlic was enough to make it the predominate scent.

The seasoned chicken looked fancy for a safe house meal, so I tried it first. It was so good, I involuntarily moaned with pleasure.

"I'll take that as a sign of approval." He chuckled.

"So good," I confirmed.

I tried the potatoes next. The texture was melt-in-my-mouth creamy goodness, and the garlic level was perfect.

"So good," I admitted. "If this is light garlic, how much do you usually add?"

Safe, polite conversation. I can do that without crying.

"Twice what's in there." He grinned. "You'd think I was afraid of vampires." He laughed.

I couldn't quite bring myself to laugh with him, but I did crack a smile.

The food was delicious, but I only ate about half before I was full. AJ broke the silence when he noticed me pushing the food around my plate.

"Blake, you don't have to force yourself to finish if you're done."

"Thanks."

He put his fork down. "Blake." He waited, but I didn't look up. "Blake, please look at me."

I gave in and lifted my head. The empathy I saw in his eyes wasn't what I'd expected. *How does he keep doing that? Surprising me at every turn?*

"I know this is hard, but I want you to know I'm here if you want to talk."

"Thanks, but I'm fine." I wasn't, but I couldn't talk to him about any of this.

While we cleaned up, I asked AJ if he'd always wanted to be a PI. It gave me a chance to get to know him a little, while alleviating the uncomfortable silence.

"Not really. I wasn't sure what I wanted to do after leaving the Army."

"How'd you end up at Sheppard & Sons?"

"I was doing building security in Florida, but hated it. When Jack told me SSI was looking to hire a full-time bodyguard and private investigator, I booked the next flight to Texas and never looked back."

"I can't imagine leaving my family behind like that."

If I hadn't been standing so close, I might have missed his jaw clenching. I didn't know what had upset him and was afraid to ask.

"Was it hard to become a PI?" I moved back to the original topic.

"No, but it took me a while to earn my bachelor's degree. Luckily, my time at SSI while I earned my degree counted as my on-the-job training; I got my license last year."

We talked for a few more minutes before I went back to my room. I still felt bad for not eating more of the dinner he'd worked so hard on, but I couldn't stomach it.

I picked up the book, but my mind wouldn't let me concentrate, and before long, I was crying again.

I'd never felt so alone. My friends were probably at the library getting ready for mid-terms while I was locked away in hiding because my father might be a criminal.

Did any of them know what was happening? Did they care?

They had their own problems and wouldn't worry about me missing a study session. It didn't matter that I usually organized them. Or sprung for pizza during late night study sessions. Or picked up the tab at the bar after exams were over.

Did they even like me, or just my bank account?

I wasn't sure how long I cried before I heard the door creak after a quick knock.

"Blake, can I come in?" AJ asked softly from the doorway.

I sniffled before answering, "Yeah." Not wanting him to see my tear-stained face for a second time, I didn't turn over.

The bed sagged behind me.

"Want to talk about it?" he asked.

Sniffle. No, I didn't want to admit to the man who was surrounded by loving and supportive friends that I was crying my eyes out because I didn't think my friends really liked me.

No, I didn't want to tell the strong, gorgeous man who was being paid to protect me because I'm rich that I didn't think anyone would care about me if I was poor.

"Blake? Do you want me to leave?"

My arm moved without my permission, reaching for AJ. "No."

"Can you turn over and talk to me?"

I did him one better, turning over and sitting up.

The light from the hall was enough for me to see the soft expression on his face as he leaned back on the headboard.

Resisting the urge to lean into him, I hugged my knees to my chest.

"Can I ask you a question?"

"Anything," he answered.

"Why are you being so nice to me?" I avoided looking at his face. "I mean, I know you have to be nice to me because my dad is paying you, but you're being nicer than required."

His chest lifted as he sucked in a big breath. It sank as his exhaled breath whistled out.

"Blake, look at me."

He reached out one hand, holding me captive as I watched his long, muscular finger reach for my face. *Good Lord, he has muscles everywhere.* He tilted my head up, so I had no choice but to look into his eyes.

My breath caught in my throat at the depth of emotion I saw there.

"We need to get a few things straight. I'm not being nice because I have to. Being friendly isn't a requirement for me to do my job."

"Then why?"

"I..." He ran his hand over the stubble on his jaw. "You deserve some kindness in your life."

I could see the war in his eyes. *What's he hiding from me now?*

"What makes you think I don't have kindness in my life?"

"I've seen how some of your friends treat you, and I wouldn't call it kind." He sighed.

"Paige isn't so bad."

"Maybe, but what's up with Danny?"

I'd asked myself that more than a few times.

"He befriended Paige. I ignore a lot of his shit for her sake." Before Danny, Paige and I were a lot closer. If it weren't for her, I would have already ended my friendship with him.

"Are they dating?"

I laughed at that. "No. He's never asked her out. Though he's tried to manipulate me into a date a time or two."

"Wait, what? How does one manipulate someone into a date?" He sounded skeptical.

"He'd ask if I wanted 'company' to different events. I took him up on it once, but he kept calling it a date. It took weeks of me reminding him it wasn't before he finally stopped." I shrugged. "I never accepted again."

"He's a piece of work."

AJ wasn't entirely wrong. I tried to be a good friend to Danny, but he was selfish, which made it hard.

"Most of my other friends are really just acquaintances. People I know from school or friends of the family." I thought about it. "Not even that anymore, Priscilla wants them all to herself."

"She's the epitome of the 'wicked step-mother' archetype." AJ chuckled.

I laughed so I wouldn't cry. He was right, and I wanted to hate him for saying it. For seeing it. Seeing me.

Instead, I felt drawn to him.

What would it be like to kiss him?

I released my legs and changed my position, so I was on my knees and sitting on my heels. I stared into AJ's dark eyes, looking for answers.

His gaze flicked to my lips, my breasts, my hips, and then back up. His desire was unmistakable, but there was something else. Doubt. Hesitation. There were probably rules about getting involved with a client.

I leaned forward, balancing myself on my hands. Could I do this? *Can I lean forward and kiss him?*

Emotion warred in AJ's unblinking eyes as he held his breath.

I'll tell him it's okay. I won't let him get in trouble.

I put a hand on his shoulder and closed the last bit of distance between us.

Before our lips touched, AJ turned his head away and gently pushed me back on my heels.

Oh my fucking God. I totally misread the situation. *I'm such an idiot.* A guy like him would never be attracted to a woman like me. *I bet he has a string of gym-going gun-toting women on speed dial.*

"I'm sorry, I shouldn't have," I whispered as I inched away from him, shifting so I could hug my knees again.

"Blake-"

"No, I get it. You're not attracted to me. It's fine." *I will not cry.*

"Hell no, that's not it."

What? "Then why? Is it because you don't like me?"

"I do." AJ leaned forward and held one of my hands in both of his. "I don't just like you, Blake. I love you. But I can't let this happen."

Wait, what?

He loves me? That makes zero sense.

Before I could voice my confusion, he continued, "I don't want you to do something you'll regret tomorrow."

I shook my head back and forth. "Blake, the only reason

you want to kiss me right now is because you're scared and overwhelmed."

"Right. Whatever. Being scared doesn't make you want to kiss someone." It was hard to keep the hurt out of my voice. *But could it be true?*

"Actually, it can," AJ said.

I barely heard his explanation because I was too busy thinking about what he'd just said.

My plan to ask him about his declaration in a calm, rational manner flew out the window when I blurted out, "Did you just say you love me?"

He stopped mid-word, his jaw hanging open.

"Why?" I openly stared as he slowly closed his mouth and gently shook his head back and forth.

"I don't know. I can't explain it, but from the moment I looked into your eyes that first day in the office…" He paused. "No, I felt it the instant I looked at your picture. It was like you reached out and grabbed my heart. It doesn't make sense. I just know what I felt."

He looked as confused as I felt.

"You fell in love with me? Before meeting me? Before knowing me?" I couldn't keep the snarky disbelief out of my voice.

"Sounds crazy, right? But it's true. They say the eyes are the window to the soul, and the Blake I see when I look in your eyes is not the same Blake everyone else sees."

He sees the real me, not the mask.

"But you deserve so much better."

I shook my head no. *I'm a hot mess.*

"Trust me, I have no delusions I could ever be good enough for you." He looked at my lips. "And kissing you, knowing I can't have you, would destroy me."

AJ swung his legs over the side of the bed and stood up. The bed suddenly felt too big.

"AJ?" I had no idea how to ask him to stay.

He turned and waited, but I couldn't find the words or the courage to tell him what I wanted.

Chapter 37

AJ

"Try to get some rest." I'd foolishly bared my soul and would have to live with the consequences. It would've been so much easier keeping my distance if she'd been the spoiled brat I'd expected.

Still reeling from the shock of her initiating a kiss, I went to the bathroom to douse my face in ice-cold water. Sad eyes stared back at me in the mirror.

I'd hurt her when I turned away from her kiss, but what else could I do? I was confident the only reason she wanted to kiss me was because we were locked away together. That, and kissing her would kill me.

No, tasting one heavenly kiss, then being denied her sweet lips for the rest of my life would kill me.

If I was a better man, I'd ask to be re-assigned and let someone else stay here with her. *But I'm not, and I can't.* As hard as it was to be with her every day, every hour, every minute, knowing I couldn't be the man she needed or wanted, it'd be impossible to be anywhere else.

I had to stay if I wanted to maintain my sanity.

Needing to work off some energy, I cleaned the kitchen. Then I called Jack, offering to relieve him so he could use the restroom and grab a snack.

Once he was back in his car, he called. He greeted me with, "You look like hell."

"Fuck you, Sheppard." Leave it to my best friend to kick me when I was down. Not that he knew what had happened, but still.

"She's under your skin, isn't she?"

I chugged the last of my water instead of answering. She had been from day one, and he knew it.

"Be patient. She'll eventually see the teddy bear behind the ogre." He'd laughed his ass off when I told him what she'd called me. "I'm right outside if you want to talk."

"Thanks." I couldn't imagine a scenario in which I'd open up to Jack more than I just had. I trusted him with my life, but couldn't bring myself to share my darkest secret with my best friend. *Which says more about me than him.*

Jack would have my back if I shared my past with him. He wouldn't hold my father's sins against me, but I wasn't a talk about my feelings kind of guy. And I didn't want him looking at me differently, wondering when I'd lose control. I hadn't yet. But what if one day I lost control?

"Try to get some rest. You're no good to anyone if you're dead on your feet."

"Yes, sir." I feigned sarcasm I didn't feel.

I walked the interior perimeter again before taking a cold shower. The torture of the ice-cold drops pelting my skin was the punishment I needed to force my mind back to the task at hand.

Protecting Blake.

Once in bed, I counted the flowers on the wallpaper to bore myself to sleep. Eventually, it worked.

My eyes couldn't have been closed for more than a few minutes before a blood-curdling scream pierced the night.

I was out of bed and across the hall before my mind registered that I was moving. I pulled Blake's trembling body into my arms before I finished exhaling my next breath.

"It's okay. I got you," I whispered into her hair as I held her, rubbing my hands up and down her back.

Footsteps in the hall had me on my feet and aiming the gun I didn't remember grabbing at the door.

"It's Jack," he called out before stepping into the doorway.

He must have been in the house. I put my gun on the nightstand and sat back down, pulling Blake back into my arms. "It's okay. You're safe."

Jack waited for me to make eye contact before mouthing, "You good?"

When I nodded, he did the same and left quietly.

I was okay.

But Blake wasn't.

"Blake," I stopped myself from calling her sweetheart, "tell me what happened in your dream."

She talked to my chest as I held her. "I was being hunted and every time I thought I found somewhere to hide they found me and they tried to hurt me and I couldn't run fast enough to get away but then I would and I'd try to hide but they'd find me." Her run-on re-telling ended with a sob.

"Shhh, it's okay. I got you," I whispered before kissing the top of her head. "Can you tell me what they looked like?"

It was possible the phantoms in her dreams were the people threatening her. There was always a chance, no matter how slim, that she'd picked up on something subconsciously, and it was coming out in her nightmares.

She sniffled. "Their faces were blurry." She sniffled again. "I'm sorry."

"No need to apologize," I whispered.

After a few minutes, her breathing returned to normal as she melted in my arm, her muscles relaxing.

I reached behind me for the water on the nightstand. "Here, think you can take a few sips for me?" I untwisted the cap and held the bottle out to her.

She nodded and took it. Her eyes tracked from my now empty hand, up my arm and across my shoulder. Her eyes opened wide as she looked at my ink-covered chest.

She reached out and traced the outline of the geometric pattern over my heart. "Did it hurt?"

Not half as much as your touch does, knowing you can never be mine. Great, I've turned into a fucking poet.

"Not too much."

I was in blissful agony as she continued tracing the lines, but I wouldn't have stopped her if my life depended on it. Her eyes followed the lazy path of her fingertip, as if she was using my body art to calm her mind.

I suffered in silence until she brushed over my nipple, causing me to inhale a sharp breath. *Do not get an erection!* My body didn't respond to the command, so I begged, *please don't get an erection.* That didn't work either, so I forced images of battle-ravaged villages into my mind to kill the mood quickly.

"Did I hurt you?" her small voice asked as she stared into my eyes.

The side of my mouth lifted. "No, you didn't hurt me," I answered as I laced her fingers in mine, putting an end to the sweet torture of her touch.

"Oh."

Her eyes gave away her recognition before her voice did. "Oh," she repeated with more energy.

"Feeling better?" I played with her small fingers, liking the feeling of her soft skin on mine.

"A little."

"Want to try going back to sleep, or would you rather watch a movie?"

She looked at the door, contemplating. "I should try to go back to sleep."

"Okay." I let go of her hand and started to move off the bed. "I'll leave-"

"Will you stay with me until I fall asleep?"

The fear and hesitation in her voice were more than I could bear.

I'd do anything for her. Suffer anything for her.

I hadn't even kissed her, but Blake Davenport had ruined me for all other women.

"Of course." I sat and reclined against the headboard. "Come here."

I wasn't sure whose sigh was bigger when she curled into my side.

Without thinking, I reached for my phone to put on some white noise to help her sleep. *Shit.* I'd left my phone in my room when Blake screamed. It wasn't a big deal that I didn't have it to lull her to sleep, but that phone was our only means of contact, and not having it close by made me twitchy.

"What's wrong?" she asked, lifting her head.

"I was going to put on some white noise, but I left my phone in the other room."

"Do you want to go get it?"

I did. "Do you mind? I'll be right back."

She pushed herself off my chest and sat up, her eyes drifting to the nightstand. "You brought your gun, but not your phone?" She didn't sound as freaked out as I would've expected, given her previous reactions to seeing my gun.

"I acted on instinct when I heard you scream. A gun can stop the bad guy, a phone can't," I answered as I got off the bed. Knowing she still wasn't comfortable with it, I brought my gun with me.

"I'm going to the bathroom," Blake's voice carried into my room as I grabbed my phone and holster. She might not be comfortable with my gun in the room, but there was no way in hell I'd be caught in a gun fight without it. I tossed on a clean t-shirt before waiting in the hall.

Chapter 38

Blake

The first thing I noticed when I stepped out of the bathroom was that AJ had, much to my disappointment, put on a t-shirt. I could no longer see the ink covering his chest and back in separate but interwoven, intricate geometric patterns. My fingers itched to trace the hypnotizing blend of thick and thin black lines. *I wonder if there's a story behind them.*

The second thing I noticed was his gun, or more specifically, my lack of fear. It had scared me earlier. No. The nightmare, and the crash when AJ burst through my door, had scared me. But not the gun itself.

I feel safe with him. I trust him.

I wasn't sure he'd get back in bed when he returned to my room, but I wanted him to. I wanted to fall asleep, curled up in his arms, and let him keep my nightmares away.

AJ leaned against the door frame. "Want me back where I was?"

My nod was enough. He put his phone and gun on the nightstand and reclined into the same position. When he opened his arm, I didn't hesitate to snuggle up, resting my head on his chest.

"Thank you," I whispered into his soft t-shirt, wishing I could feel the warmth of his skin without it.

"You're welcome." He made lazy circles on my shoulder with his thumb. "Sorry I can't play white noise or music to help you fall asleep." He apologized again for the limitations of his burner phone.

"It's okay." I yawned. "Sorry, I'm so needy."

"Blake," he said, lifting my chin and looking deep into my eyes. "You're not needy. We all need help once in a while, and what you're going through is a lot."

"Thanks." Propping myself up on an elbow so I could see him, I said, "I misjudged you." Finally acknowledging my mistake.

He grinned before asking, "Yeah, how so?"

"You're not a big, dumb ogre." I laughed, recalling what I'd called him after he'd stopped Danny.

"Are you sure?" he asked, laughing.

"Well, you're big, no denying that." I let my eyes skate over his broad chest. "But you're not dumb and you're definitely not an ogre."

His chest shook as he laughed.

"Unless there's such a thing as a nice ogre." I added, enjoying the sound of his laugh.

"I don't know much about ogres, but I believe they're generally mean and nasty."

Missing the physical connection, I put my hand back on his chest, moving my fingers in a lazy circle.

"Blake," AJ said, his voice deeper than it was a second ago. "While I enjoy the sweet torture of your touch, I'm going to have to ask you to stop doing that."

Sweet torture? I stilled my hand and looked up at him. "Right. Sorry."

AJ laid his free hand over mine. He held my gaze as I studied his eyes, trying to figure him out. He claimed he loved me, called my touch sweet torture, held me to comfort me, but he wouldn't kiss me because he thought he wasn't good enough.

"AJ?"

"Yes?"

"Why do you think you're not good enough for me?"

"I don't think. I know. You deserve the man of your dreams. Someone who fits your lifestyle. Someone well-dressed, smart, rich. Someone your father would approve of."

Did that describe the man of my dreams? Not really, but having my father's approval was important to me. It always had been. So, like the good girl I was, I'd dated men he approved of. *I'm not nearly as strong or independent as I thought I was.*

None of the men my father approved of made me feel half of what AJ did.

What do I feel for AJ? I wasn't sure, but I knew how I felt when I was with him—safe, comfortable, seen. The answer was no; he hadn't described the man of my dreams. I dreamed of finding someone like the heroes I'd read about.

Never in a million years would I have anticipated needing one.

"I used to want that. At least that's what I told myself. It's what my father wanted for me, expected from me; and I wanted to please him." *God, I sound pathetic.* I'd always believed I was confident in who I was, what I wanted. But I wasn't. I was merely comfortable in my role.

Emotions flashed across AJ's face too fast to read. Hope, maybe. But I couldn't be sure. Sadness, for sure, because it was still there. But why?

"You deserve someone gentler, kinder," he paused, "less angry." He brushed my cheek with the back of his fingers; his touch was the softest, most reverent I'd ever felt.

Gentler? Kinder? No one had been kinder to me than AJ. Sure, they were nice on a surface level, but none of them would have held me the way he did, *the way he is.* They wouldn't put my needs first, or stop me from kissing them because they didn't want me to regret it in the morning.

"You're wrong. You're one of the gentlest, kindest men I've ever met." I said, poking his rock-hard chest to emphasize each word.

"Blake," my name sounded like a prayer on his lips.

"I mean it. You've been kinder to me these last few days than anyone else my whole life." Except my mom and dad, but that was a given. Parents had to be kind and gentle with their kids.

Chapter 39

AJ

I wanted to believe her, but there was so much she didn't know. Desperately needing to change the topic, I asked about her mother.

Blake squinted her eyes at me, as if debating whether she should call me out. Luckily, she didn't.

"My mom was amazing. She would read to me, play with me in the backyard, and make my lunches, even after my dad hired a cook." Blake's eyes radiated love and sadness as she painted a picture of her mother. "She was short like me, so she kept a stool in the kitchen. I always stood on it when I helped her."

"Do you look like her?" I asked, loving how her eyes lit up with joy as she shared the memories.

"Mostly. I have my dad's eyes, but my other features are from my mom. Though she got the skinny genes, and I got my dad's not-so-skinny genes." Self doubt filled her eyes as she circled her midsection and hips with the wave of a hand.

No way I'd let that take root. Blake was beautiful, with curves in all the right places. "Don't do that." I took her hand. "You're beautiful."

She bit her lower lip, making me think things I had no right thinking.

"Thank you," she said shyly. After an awkward pause, she asked, "What about you, which parent to do you look like?"

I flinched internally at the thought. I was the spitting image of my father, only three inches taller. Not that he knew that little fact, having left before I reached my full height. Too bad, because I was a hell of a lot stronger by then, too.

If he'd stayed, I would have forced him to stop hitting us. At least I'd like to think I would have. *He beat obedience into me more times than I care to remember.*

"I take after my father's side of the family." It was all I'd admit.

"What about your mom?"

She was beautiful once, but in most of my memories, she appeared small, weak, timid. He'd made her that way. She was always there to help me clean off the blood, but she was afraid to stand up to him.

"She was taller than you," I said, resorting to my default setting and making a joke out of my answer.

I didn't like the awkward silence, but didn't know what to say.

"AJ, why do you think you're not a good man?" she asked, returning to the topic I'd been trying to avoid.

How do I make her understand I'm dangerous?

"Have you forgotten about me tackling your friend and that innocent guy asking for a signature?" I was laying it on pretty thick, having done neither, hoping she'd remember how violent I could be. "I'm a violent man." I hardened my heart as I looked her in the eyes. "And you hate violence."

I could see the wheels turning in her head as she thought about it.

"You're not violent. You were doing your job," she said, throwing me a curve ball.

When'd she change her mind? I released her as I sat up. This wasn't going the way I'd expected, and I needed to create distance.

"I was, but I could have been less physical with them," I argued, using her words. Not that I believed them; I'd used the force necessary to get the job done.

"AJ." She put her hand on my arm. "Why are you trying so hard to convince me you're a bad person?"

Because I need you to stop looking at me like that. Like you could love me back.

"There's so much you don't know." I didn't believe I was a bad person, but I'd inherited my father's anger issues and didn't trust myself to not lose my temper and hurt the people I cared about.

"Tell me." She sat up and crossed her legs. "Please? I want to understand."

I opened my mouth to repeat the same generic reasons and excuses, the ones I gave everyone, if I gave them at all, but what came out was the truth.

"I have anger issues. I always have, and while I'm better at managing it, I can't risk losing control and hurting you." Saying it out loud felt like the final nail being hammered into the coffin of my future. I barely recognized my voice as I confessed, "I'm afraid I'll be like my father, and you deserve better than that."

Sympathy filled her eyes. *Not fear?*

"Did he hit you?"

I'd never admitted it to anyone before, but with Blake, the truth flowed from me like floodwaters rolling down a mountain.

"Yes," I answered without making eye contact. "He beat me and my mom."

And just like that, I'd told Blake, who I'd known less than a week, more than I'd ever told my best friend.

Blake's small hand grabbed my chin and forced me to look at her. "I'm so sorry, Andrew."

I waited for the usual anger to rise.

"Say it again."

"I'm sorry–"

"No, my name."

"Andrew?"

I nodded.

My first name on her lips, the name I shared with my father, the one I refused to use after he abandoned us, felt like a bandage on my wounded soul.

"Thank you." The words weren't nearly potent enough, but they were all I had.

We sat in silence for a moment before Blake asked, "Why didn't your mom help you?"

"She couldn't, not without incurring his wrath."

"Do you ever talk to her?"

That was a loaded question. On the surface, sure, I called her for the usual holidays, but we never shared more than pleasantries. I considered filtering the truth, or making a joke, but Blake's hand on my arm was like a truth serum.

"Not really. I wish I could say I've forgiven her for letting the abuse continue, but I'm not quite there yet."

"She was a victim, too." Her soft words brought tears to my eyes.

I nodded. Logically, I knew that. Emotionally was a different story.

Blake continued to ask and with each gentle touch, each sympathetic tear, each word of encouragement, I found it easier to open up and share my history.

"I'm sorry you don't have a family," she said.

"The Army gave me a brotherhood, which is pretty close." It wasn't the same, but she let it slide. The Sheppards offered me acceptance and support. They'd even invited me to holiday dinners; not that I'd ever accepted. Not wanting to feel like an intruder, I usually volunteered for holiday shifts so everyone else could enjoy the time off with their families.

I'm such an idiot. I'd been denying myself a loving family for years.

"AJ?"

"The Sheppards are my family. Though I've neglected the relationship."

We talked for over an hour before I could no longer ignore Blake's exhaustion.

"Let's get some sleep."

As Blake nodded, with the most adorable yawn, I slipped my feet under the blankets, slid to my back, and held my arm open. I felt lighter than I had in years. Decades, even.

Blake didn't need a verbal invitation to shimmy onto her side and curl up against me. Her head on my chest, her hand over my heart. Holding Blake felt right; it settled something inside me. Made the world feel right, even though I knew I could never have her.

Home.

I wrapped my arms around her, creating a cocoon of safety for both of us. A physical one for her. An emotional one for me.

I felt her head lift a second before I felt her lips on my chest. "You're a good man, Andrew Janerek." Her warm breath tickled my skin as her words warmed my heart.

Resisting the temptation to kiss her lips, to claim her, I settled for kissing the top of her head.

My need for Blake Edith Davenport was so much more than physical desire.

And there was nothing I wanted more in the world than to be the man she believed I was.

Chapter 40

Blake

I felt his absence before opening my eyes and seeing the empty space beside me. Not bothering to cover my mouth, I stretched like a cat and released a very unladylike yawn. *Take that Cilla.* Remembering AJ comparing her to a wicked step-mother brought a smile to my lips.

I regretted waiting so long to get to know him. But I'd been too caught up in my fear and anger to try.

My bladder complained, so I reluctantly dragged myself out of bed instead of reliving the night before. After my brief visit to the bathroom, I padded into the hallway. When I heard grunts coming from AJ's room, I stopped.

It'd be rude to spy on him. I turned away, but my curiosity won and I peeked around the doorframe.

My brain shut down the instant it registered the image my eyes sent it.

AJ, in nothing but boxer briefs, doing pushups. The grunts were his count coming out in huffs each time his thick, corded, sweaty arms lifted him off the floor.

He was focused on the floor in front of him, so I allowed myself to gawk like a wanton woman. The light reflected off his glistening back, highlighting his dragon tattoo, as he lifted himself up and lowered himself back down.

I let my eyes drift down his back, to his ass. His snug black boxers outlined every muscle leading down to his thick thighs, covered in dark hair. A scar on the side of his left thigh, just above the knee, stopped my appraisal.

"Is that a bullet hole?" *Shit.* My hand shot to my mouth.

AJ turned his head, his dimple deepening as he grinned.

"Morning." He stood and faced me. "Like what you see?" he asked, his voice raspy.

He knew I was watching.

Heat flooded my cheeks, and I forgot to breathe. But I didn't look away. I couldn't. He was magnificent. I didn't even bother telling myself I wasn't attracted to his giant muscles or gorgeous looks.

"Yeah, I, um," *was just drooling over your hot body,* "I just noticed the scar on your leg." I pointed, like maybe he didn't remember where it was. Clearly my brain had left the building.

He glanced down. "Yes, it's from a bullet." He turned his leg so I could see it better, flexing his thigh as he did. I was sure he did it just to see how deep my blush would get.

The answer was very deep. Embarrassingly deep. "Did it hurt?"

Did it hurt? Could I sound any dumber?

He laughed. "It did, though we were in the middle of a gunfight, so it wasn't too bad until the adrenaline wore off."

Sadness filled his eyes as they lost focus on the room.

"Andrew?" I wanted to ask why he looked so sad, but his head snapped up.

Anger replaced the sadness in his eyes for a split second before softening. "Sorry. It's been a long time since anyone has called me that and I'm still adjusting."

That didn't really explain anything, so I pushed. "Why?"

He sat with a sigh and invited me to join him with a pat on the bed. Heat radiated off his body, his rugged leather scent filling my nose. I forced my attention back to the subject.

"It was my father's name; he made me hate it."

I struggled to imagine hating a parent enough to change my name, but then I'd never had a parent hit me. I wanted to hug him, but he had more to say.

"When he left us, I wanted to destroy the connection to him."

"I'm so sorry you went through all that."

He turned and looked into my eyes, searching for something.

"Say it again," he said.

I don't know how, but I knew he meant his name. Staring deep into his eyes, I whispered, "Andrew."

His dark eyes bore into my soul as his head tilted ever so slightly to the side. I'd never held such intense eye contact with anyone before—it was unsettling.

I was about to look away when he said, "Thank you." *I didn't do anything.* "For giving me my name back," he whispered.

I didn't understand how I'd done it, but it didn't matter. The look in his eyes told me it meant the world to him.

Emotions whirled around in my head like I'd hit puree on a blender. Everything I'd believed about AJ, Andrew, was wrong.

He was kind, intelligent, protective, and complex.

AJ wasn't the opposite of what I wanted, he was everything I needed.

Chapter 41

AJ

I couldn't tell what was going on in Blake's mind, and I wasn't sure I wanted to know. I'd dumped a lot on her over the last twelve hours. *More than I've ever told anyone.* She'd need time to process it all. So would I.

"I'm hopping in the shower, then I'll make breakfast while you take yours."

Nodding, she stood up to leave. Before she reached the door, she turned and asked, "Which do you prefer?"

I bit back my default sarcastic response, raised my gaze to hers, and answered, my voice thick with emotion. "Andrew, but only from you."

Her smile lit up her face as she nodded. Then she left me alone with my tornado of thoughts and emotions.

Clean and dressed, I went to the kitchen to make breakfast. I was whisking the eggs when I heard what sounded like someone trying to pick the lock at the front door. *No text from Jack*. I drew my gun as I sprinted to the hall, positioning myself between Blake and the person coming in.

I lowered my gun when I saw Jack's face behind my sights. "What the fuck!" I holstered my gun. "You're supposed to message me if you're coming in, so I don't blow your fucking head off."

Panic radiated off Jack as he closed and locked the door.

Concern replaced my agitation. "What happened?"

"Meg hasn't shown up for work." *Fuck.* "And I can't reach her." His voice cracked as fear choked him. His eyes darted around, like he hoped to find her in the safe house living room.

"What can I do?" I couldn't do much from here, but I had to offer.

"Nothing. Jay will be here in ten, then I'm going back."

He paced the room, stopping occasionally to pull back the curtain on the door window, willing Jay to arrive sooner.

I glanced down the hall as the shower shut off, knowing I'd be acting the same way if I was in his shoes. No, I'd be less calm. Less patient.

When Jack's phone buzzed, he put it on speaker. "Janerek's with me."

"We got a message." It was John. "They have Cinderella." His flat tone disguising the fear I knew he felt.

Jack's knees buckled. I closed the distance and pulled him up before leading him to the nearest chair. "Breathe."

"Jack?" John asked.

"He's here. Give us a sec," I answered, prying the phone out of his hand. "You good?" I asked.

He nodded before saying, "Tell me."

"They want to exchange her for Aurora."

"No fucking way." I barked, my voice thick with venom. One look at Jack's face and I back-pedaled, softening my tone. "There has to be another way."

"We're working on it," John offered.

"What's it say?" Jack asked, reaching for his phone as he stood.

"We're sending a screen shot now," John said as a text popped up on Jack's phone. "Sharpe's tracing it, but it'll take him a while."

"Got it," Jack said.

John disconnected the call.

I had to concentrate to read the screen in Jack's shaking hands.

You have something we want.
We have something you want.
Let's make a trade.
Details to follow if you agree.

I didn't want to think about what would happen to Meg if we didn't agree. "It's not a lot to go on."

Jack's eyes never left the screen. "No." He pulled the phone in close and typed a reply to Jamie: tell them we agree.

I ripped the phone out of his hands before he could hit send and stepped out of reach. "No. No fucking way."

He stood. "We don't have a choice." Desperation filled his voice. I felt for him. I loved Meg like a sister, but I wouldn't sacrifice Blake. I couldn't.

"There's always a choice." I said, squaring off against my best friend. "We'll find another way."

"They have Meg," Jack pleaded, his voice thick with panic.

"I know, and we'll get her back. But I'm not risking Blake's life to do it."

"We'll keep her safe." He stepped forward, holding his hand out for his phone.

I stepped back. "You can't guarantee that."

"Janerek."

"Sheppard."

Jack glanced past me, causing me to look. Blake stood in the hall, her eyes darting back and forth between us.

"What's going on?"

Instinctively, I moved between Jack and Blake—protecting her from my best friend.

"The people after you took Meg." Jack didn't couch his words.

Her hands flew to her mouth. "Oh no."

"They want to exchange her for you."

Blake gasped as she stumbled back, bumping into the wall.

"Jack." I warned him.

"I'm just telling her the truth," he growled in response to my implied threat.

"It's not happening," I growled right back, crushing his phone in my clenched fist. Every muscle in my body tensed, ready to strike.

We'd had our differences before, but never come to blows. *If we don't agree on a solution, that could change today.*

Blake's soft footsteps the only sound as Jack and I stared each other down.

"Andrew," Blake whispered as she put her hand on my bicep.

Jack's eyes rounded in surprise—he'd seen me rip more than one person a new asshole for using my first name.

"Oh," he said, stepping back as he looked from Blake to me and back again.

I relaxed my shoulders, "Yeah."

And just like that, we were good. He understood how much Blake meant to me, and how far I'd go to protect her.

"What do we do?" Jack asked, resigned to the fact I loved Blake and wouldn't give in.

Before I could answer, Blake squared her shoulders and said, "You trade me."

"No!" I barked, causing her to flinch. "I'm sorry, I didn't mean to yell, but there's no way in hell I'm letting them get their hands on you."

"AJ, she's pregnant." Jack's terrified whisper cut me to the quick, weakening my resolve.

Meg's pregnant? Since when? No wonder Jack was losing his shit. I still wasn't willing to sacrifice Blake, but it explained why Jack was uncharacteristically willing to sacrifice a client.

"We can't," I begged. Blake was my everything.

Blake stepped in front of me, her eyes glistening with unshed tears. "You have to. I can't let them hurt Meg because of me."

"Blake." Her name fell from my lips like a prayer.

"I have to do this," she begged. "It's the right thing to do."

Cupping her face, I said, "I can't lose you." I didn't even have her yet, not really.

"You won't. You'll save me." She placed one small, trusting hand on mine. "I know you will."

Her trust was a balm to my soul. And a dagger to my heart. I wanted to promise her I would, but I refused to lie to her.

"I'll go to the pits of hell and battle Satan himself." *Not a lie.*

Her soft smile soothed my nerves. "They're after my money, not me. I'll just tell them I'll give them whatever they want, if they promise not to hurt me. You'll have plenty of time to rescue me."

So innocent. So trusting.

So wrong.

Blake turned twenty-five in six days. Six days too many for her to be in the hands of someone with a vendetta against her father.

"Blake," I begged.

"Jay's here," Jack interrupted.

"We have to do this," Blake answered.

I held Jack's phone out over Blake's shoulder. The second my hand was empty, I used it to trace the soft, beautiful edges of her face. Memorizing every inch as tears blurred my vision. I blinked them away as I lowered my forehead to hers.

I whispered, "I know, but I'm terrified of losing you."

I heard the knock and let Jack handle it.

A few seconds later, Jay's shocked, "Whoa," broke up the moment.

I lifted my head, willing laser beams to shoot out of my eyes.

He held up his hand. "Sorry, man." He turned to Jack. "Dad said you'd fill me in on why we're bringing Blake to the office."

I wrapped one arm around Blake's shoulders, pulling her in close. "It's not safe; they know where it is."

"It's the safest place we can be," Jack countered.

Fair point. The entire building was bulletproof, but it wouldn't matter if we didn't make it there.

I nodded at Jack over Blake's head.

"We leave in fifteen. Grab what you need while I fill Jay in," Jack ordered. His voice was less shaky now that we had a plan, but his composure wouldn't last long. Jack loved Meg with every fiber of his being and then some.

I'd watched him fall apart when the trafficker she'd testified against came back for revenge and kidnapped her. I helped him stack bodies outside the cabin as we shot our way to her. I stood beside him as he forced the guy to shift his gun from Meg's temple to his chest, giving Jamie a clean shot. Jack took two bullets for Meg that day.

He'd sworn he'd destroy heaven and hell to bring her home safe.

I made the same silent vow to Blake.

Chapter 42

Blake

What did I just do? The people after me took Meg, and I'd just volunteered to trade myself for her. *Because she's pregnant and it's the right thing to do.* And no matter how scared, terrified, I felt, I couldn't live with myself if I did nothing, and they hurt her.

I barely registered AJ following me down the hall and into my room.

Within seconds of my door closing, he pulled me into his arms and crushed me against his chest. My fingers barely touched when I wrapped my arms around him, savoring the emotion swirling between us until I had to come up for air.

I pulled back and made eye contact. The intensity almost knocked me off my feet. His love taking up space like a physical presence between us.

I stared back, wishing I could show him how I felt as effectively as he was showing me.

"I lo-"

"Don't. Please," he begged, his voice rough as he put a finger over my lips.

My nod was barely perceptible as I kissed his finger.

His eyes darted to my lips. Half a second later, every thought drained from my brain as his lips crashed into mine.

Our first kiss wasn't gentle. No, this was AJ releasing his fear, giving me his heart, and staking his claim. He banded one arm around my back, while his other hand fisted in my hair.

I gripped fistfuls of his shirt, deepening the kiss, begging for more. I poured every ounce of my love into the kiss, telling him what he needed to hear, but wouldn't let me say.

Time stood still.

My knees were weak by the time he ended the kiss. *Holy shit.* I'd never been kissed like that before. Hell, I didn't even know it was possible.

"Thank you," I stuttered as my legs struggled to hold me upright.

"Did you just thank me for kissing you?" he asked, chuckling as he slowly released me.

"No, I um, it was..." *so fucking amazing that I can't find the words.*

He looked at my lips and took mercy on me, saving me from further embarrassment. "Thank you for being so brave and putting yourself in danger to help Meg."

"How could I not? I can't let them hurt her." I turned and started packing so he wouldn't see the fear I'd momentarily forgotten about clawing its way back to the surface. "And I'm not brave."

"Yes, you are. Not many people would volunteer the way you just did."

I turned so he could see my fear, thinking it'd convince him I wasn't. "I'm terrified."

His soft smile didn't reach his eyes. "Mark Messier said, 'Bravery is not the absence of fear, but the action in the face of fear.' You, Sweetheart, are brave as fuck."

Sadly, his confidence didn't help me control the fear and anxiety building in my gut. I didn't know what they'd do to me while we waited for me to turn twenty-five so I could use my inheritance to pay my father's debts. *And where's my dad?* I hoped they hadn't hurt him, and would leave us alone once they had their money.

"We should hurry." I turned back and shoved what little I had into Emily's suitcase.

Chapter 43

AJ

It only took me a minute to toss my stuff into my duffle. Not worried about appearances, I tossed my vest on over my t-shirt and joined Jack and Jay.

The living room was a buzz of activity as we prepared to transport Blake. *So much can go wrong.* My heart drummed in my ears as I unpacked the vest Blake would use.

Pain flashed in Jack's eyes before he turned back to his rifle.

"We'll bring her home," I said to the back of his head.

His slight nod was the only indication he'd heard me. Jay looked at me and nodded, his normal smart-ass attitude gone now that we were in mission mode.

Blake gasped when she walked into the room and saw us preparing.

I jumped up and made sure she was okay.

"Yeah, I just wasn't expecting," she waved her hand towards the room, "all this."

"I should have warned you." I grabbed her bag and walked her to the couch.

"Are the rifles really necessary?" she asked, her fear of guns resurfacing.

"Yes," Jack and Jay answered together.

"Rifles are the best tool we have to get the job done." I picked up the vest. "Let me help you put this on."

The only evidence of Blake's inner freak-out was the white of her eyes doubling in size as she held her breath.

"Blake, I need you to breathe." I waited until she'd taken a few breaths before continuing. "The vest is a precaution; we're all wearing one."

Jay tapped on his chest to emphasize my point.

"But they don't know where I am." The fear in her voice ripped my heart into confetti-sized pieces. I wished I could make this all go away.

"We don't believe so, but won't risk it," Jack answered.

She looked at the vest in my hands and nodded. Jack and Jay stood up and slung their rifles, letting me know they were ready.

"Blake, this won't be like when I was protecting you at school. Jay will go out first and make sure the coast is clear. He'll hold the door to the sedan open while I walk you there. Jack will be behind us."

I hated scaring her as I delivered the information impersonally, but it was the only way. I had to keep my feelings separate from the job at hand. *My priority is keeping her safe, not worrying about her feelings.*

"Ready?"

"What about your truck?" she asked. I'd seen that look before—the need to focus on anything except her fear. "You can't leave it here."

"I'm not. Jack will drive it." I stood and extended my hand. "Ready?"

She swallowed hard before placing her shaking hand in mine. "I think so."

That's my girl. I leaned down and kissed her forehead before whispering, "I won't let anything happen to you."

I let go of her hand just long enough to sling my rifle, then gave the order, "Let's go."

We were safely in the cars and on the road in under three minutes. Jay drove in the front, with Jack behind us.

"You okay?" I asked, knowing she probably wasn't, but also knowing talking would help keep her mind off what was coming.

"I don't know." She stared out the window, her hands compulsively pulling at her designer purse strap.

"Tell me what you're thinking."

"You'll think I'm pathetic."

How could I, given what she was about to risk for Meg? "I assure you, I won't."

"I'm scared, but not as scared as I think I should be." She turned to me. "I should be terrified right?"

God knows I am. "Not necessarily. Why do you think you should be?"

She looked towards Jay's truck, then down at the vest covering her chest. "All this. You have a gun." I had two, plus my rifle. "They have rifles. And I don't know what'll happen."

"So why aren't you terrified?" I asked.

She turned towards me and laughed. Not a 'that was a great joke' laugh, but the type of laugh one releases when they're two seconds from losing their shit. "Because you have a gun, and they have rifles, and I know you won't let them hurt me."

That was the last thing I expected her to say.

I turned to her and met her eyes for a second. "Damn straight," I said, before turning my attention back to the road. I held out my hand and waited for her to take it.

Our relationship had changed in the last twelve hours. It happened without effort, without my consent, and against my wishes. *I kissed her.* What was I thinking?

It didn't matter; that kiss had rocked my world and I couldn't wait until I could do it again.

Blake Davenport had snuck in under my radar and taken root in my heart. *There's no going back now.*

When her fingers curled around mine, my heartbeat slowed to normal for the first time since drawing my gun on Jack. *She's mine to protect.* And I would, no matter what it took.

We rode in silence until my phone rang.

"Sierra Four. You're on speaker." Jack would know to be careful with his word choice.

"Copy. They sent instructions. Sierra One will update at Base Camp. Already notified Seven."

"Plans to keep Aurora safe?"

"Six is back. She and Five are working on it."

"Copy that," I said.

Jack disconnected the call. Maxwell being back was good news. One more warrior to help rescue Meg and Blake.

I squeezed Blake's hand to offer what little assurance I could.

"We're back to code names?" she asked.

Why does she sound annoyed?

We'd transitioned from casual to mission so many times it came easy to us. Switching to our call signs came with the mindset shift. *But Blake doesn't have our experience.*

"We're in mission mode."

Before I could explain, she said, "I don't like it."

A quick glance was all I needed to see the tears forming in her eyes. I squeezed her hand again. "I know, and I'm sorry, but we have to."

"Is it easier for you if it's impersonal?" she asked, her former attitude coming back. "Does it help to dehumanize us?"

"What? No." Nothing about this job was impersonal. Quite the opposite. "The call signs aren't to depersonalize or dehumanize anyone. It's a safety protocol."

"I don't like it," she repeated with a huff while pulling her hand away.

I left my hand on the center console, palm up, ready for her if she changed her mind. "Want me to tell you who's who, so it feels less impersonal?"

"Sure."

Wanting to eat up time, I gave a longer explanation than necessary. "Sierra is the military phonetic for the letter S."

"Sheppard," she said.

"Exactly. John, as the oldest and CEO of SSI, is Sierra One, Jamie signed on first so he's Sierra Two, and Jack is Sierra Three."

"So, Jaden should be Sierra Four, but didn't you just answer that way?"

"After Jack, we're numbered in the order we signed our contracts. I'm four, Doug is five, Maxwell is six, and Jay, the last one hired, is seven."

"I guess that makes sense."

"SSI is growing, and will hire more people sooner rather than later, and we're thinking of breaking into two teams." Not that she'd care, but I wanted to keep her talking, so she didn't have time to freak out.

"What team will you be on?" she said, sounding less irritated.

"I'm not sure. I'll probably stay on Sierra, given my history with Jack."

"Your history?" she asked as she placed her hand back in mine.

It was enough to make me momentarily forget how Jack and I met. I laced my fingers with hers and smiled.

Right, we served together in the Army.

I shared a few Army stories, killing time until we were five minutes from the office.

My phone rang.

"Sierra Four, you're on speaker."

"Sierra Six and I will wait in back and escort you in. Seven will park in front and watch the door. Three will follow you to the lot."

"Copy that."

Jamie ended the call.

I hated what we were about to do, but if it had to be done, there was no one I'd rather have at my back than the SSI team.

My family.

❧

I escorted Blake through the back door and directly up the stairs to the conference room. I didn't move fast enough to prevent my eyes from glancing at Meg's empty desk.

Maxwell was right behind us, and quickly joined Doug at the far end of the table. They were arranging a mountain of audio and surveillance equipment while Jack and Jamie focused on the maps and schematics projected on the big screen.

Jay and John walked in a few seconds afterwards.

Blake's grip tightened on my hand as the organized chaos overwhelmed her.

John's eyes darted to our joined hands before he made eye contact with me. We shared a nod before he greeted Blake.

He knows what's at stake.

"Thank you for coming in. We'll do everything in our power to see that you don't get hurt," he said, ushering her to a chair.

Blake stared at the large windows along the side of the room, now blacked out.

"Have a seat," John's tone held just enough command that she didn't argue.

"Can I take this off?" she asked, pointing at the vest.

I was about to say yes, knowing the windows were bulletproof, but looked to John for confirmation. After he nodded, I helped her take it off.

John was about to fill Blake in on everything they'd uncovered so far. Thinking they'd want privacy, I said, "I'll get to work."

"You should stay," John said.

Fuck, this is going to be bad. I sat beside Blake and waited for the hammer to fall.

"Blake, there's no easy way to say this, so I'm going to be direct."

She sat up straight and did her best to be brave, but I felt the panic pouring out of her. I reached for her hand.

"Dallas detectives found evidence that your father has been accepting bribes to dismiss cases." Blake choked on a gasp, but John didn't stop. "They issued a warrant for his arrest last night. When they went to the house to arrest him, he wasn't there."

Blake stopped breathing.

John looked at me over Blake's head. "No one has seen or heard from him since he left the office yesterday."

Blake's death grip on my hand was borderline painful.

"Warrant…" she let go of my hand as she spun to face me. "Did you know?"

"No." Though I'd figured it was only a matter of time given the circumstantial evidence piling up.

John continued, pulling Blake's attention back to him, "They know they can't get to you while we're protecting you, so they're going after the people we love. But they're mistaken if they think we'll make the exchange and walk away."

My, "That's not going to happen," was louder than Blake's, "But you have to."

John echoed my sentiment. "That won't happen, Blake. We're working on a plan to bring Meg home without sacrificing you."

"Thank you," we said at the same time.

"Will you be okay for a few minutes with Sammie?" John asked Blake.

She turned to me, her unspoken question thundering in my ears.

"Sammie's a Weatherford Police Officer who works here part time. You'll be okay."

Turning back to John, Blake said, "Okay."

I pulled Blake close and kissed the top of her head before standing up. "I'll be right here if you need me."

"Janerek."

"Yes, sir." I said, never taking my eyes off Blake as Sammie escorted her to the smaller conference room across the hall.

Jamie started talking as soon as I closed the door. "We think the warrant for Davenport's arrest made them panic; they're getting sloppy."

"Which means they're prone to making mistakes," John added.

"Like taking my wife," Jack growled.

"We'll get her back," I said, clapping his shoulder.

"Sharpe, Maxwell?" John asked.

"We've set up two trackers for Blake. One will be obvious and easy for them to find. The other will be well hidden and turned off," Maxwell answered.

"I'll turn it on remotely after they sweep for bugs," Doug said.

"If they don't sweep?" I asked.

"I'll turn it on before she gets in their car," Doug answered.

I didn't like it. "Too many things can go wrong." I studied the marked up map. "Where's the meet-up?" I asked.

"The first 'meeting' is here." Jamie pointed to an X on the map. "They're demanding we send one person with Blake to retrieve it and then bring her to exchange location," John said.

"I'll go," Jack and I said at the same time.

"She doesn't go anywhere without me," I growled at Jack.

Jack got in my face and growled right back, "They. Have. Meg."

"Stand down," John ordered.

I found myself in a confrontational stare-down with my best friend for the second time in less than six hours. We'd always had each other's backs, but this was different. The women we loved were in danger—neither of us would back down.

"Now!" John stepped between us and forced us apart. "You're friends. Act like it!" John eyed us both, then continued, "Janerek will accompany Blake-"

"What the fuck?" Jack yelled.

John put his hand up. "Janerek will be with Blake in the car, the rest of us will be nearby. We'll have eyes and ears on them the entire time."

"They said no comms," Jack said.

"They did, but we're ignoring it," John answered.

"What if they hurt Meg? Or the baby?"

"Meg's pregnant?" Maxwell, Doug, and Jay asked.

"She is." The fear in Jack's voice destroyed my anger.

"They won't," I said, ignoring the shock on their faces. "You heard Blake; they want her money. Hurting Meg serves no purpose now that we've agreed to the exchange." *God, it's killing me to talk about this as if my future happiness wasn't at risk.*

"They have to know we'll rain hell on them if they so much as chip her nail polish," Jay added.

"He's right," Jamie said. "They're not stupid, at least the decision makers aren't."

"You'd think they'd be smart enough to not take Meg," Doug chimed in.

"If that's the case, why do they think we'll let Blake go without a fight?" Maxwell asked. It was a valid question.

John looked at me. "Because they don't know AJ's in love with her," John answered, clapping my shoulder. "They think Blake's just a client, but she's family."

Emotion burned in my throat. *Family.*

"We'll bring them both home," Jamie added, looking at Jack.

"We will." Jack added, "We've faced worse together, Brother. And we'll lay waste to anyone who gets in our way."

"Ooh rah," Jay said, adding the only thing he needed to say.

"Fucking men," Maxwell said, this time without malice.

We all turned and looked at her.

She rolled her eyes before giving a deep, hearty, "Ooh rah. Now let's quit talking and save your women."

I was on board with that, but first, I'd have to watch the woman I loved walk into enemy territory.

I'd need Herculean strength to control my impulses and not kill every last fucker who showed up at the exchange site.

Chapter 44

Blake

Officer Campbell, who insisted I call her Sammie, tried making small talk to distract me, but it didn't work. I was too keyed up and couldn't stop thinking of all the things that might happen, and what they might do to me.

And about my father's involvement.

Alternating between tapping my feet and pacing around the small conference room did nothing to calm my nerves.

My father, the man I'd looked up to, the man who'd always made time for me, the man who'd encouraged and supported me my entire life, had a warrant out for his arrest.

Was he guilty? Maybe the evidence was wrong or planted. "It has to be a mistake." I said during a lap around the table.

"What's a mistake?" Sammie asked, disrupting my pacing.

"My father can't be guilty. He's a good man. A loving father."

Sammie watched me for a second before answering, "He can be both."

Could he? How could I think of him as a good man if he took bribes, helped criminals, violated his oath?

Betrayed me?

I didn't think I'd ever see him the same way again. He'd always told me to be honest, to do good in the world.

All the while, he was in bed with criminals.

Did AJ know? And for how long? I couldn't handle another man I loved and trusted lying to me.

"How long have you known my father was…" I couldn't bring myself to say the words out loud.

Sammie looked across the hall and into the large conference room. I couldn't be sure, but I had a feeling she was trying to figure out if AJ wanted her to answer me.

I might not have military or police experience, or a PI license, but I wasn't blind. If she was worried about what he'd say, the answer was obvious.

"You've known all along," I answered for her.

"We *suspected* early on, but didn't *know* until yesterday." Her emphasis on the words to differentiate them did nothing to lessen my anger.

They knew.

"Blake, I know you're angry, but no one at SSI wanted to upset you unnecessarily."

"He should've told me." It came out before I could stop it. I didn't want to admit the truth—Andrew Janerek's betrayal hurt almost as much as my father's.

I tried to read her expression, hoping it would reveal something, but her face was a blank page.

It shouldn't surprise me; she wouldn't rat him out. They worked together, and I was no one to her.

"I know this is hard, and I can't even begin to imagine what you must be feeling, but we're on your side."

What I'm feeling? Hurt. Scared. Frustrated. Betrayed.

I was feeling everything. So much so I couldn't land on just one to express.

Movement caught my eye as AJ left the other conference room. Two steps later, he was opening our door. His eyes locked on mine; the intensity was almost too much to bear.

"Can we have the room?" he asked.

"Of course," Sammie answered as she stood.

After she left, he closed the distance and wrapped his arms around me.

He pulled back when I stiffened. "What's wrong?"

"How could you not tell me about my father?" I failed to keep the hurt out of my voice.

"I told you there was circumstantial evidence pointing to his involvement. That was all we knew at the time."

He did tell me, reluctantly, just last night.

"You really didn't know about the warrant?" I asked.

"No, but I suspected it might happen. I wanted to believe in his innocence, for your sake." He held my hands. "I'm so sorry, Blake."

Not knowing what else to do, I hugged him and cried.

The man I worshipped, the man I wanted to be like, the man who shaped my choice of career, was a fraud. A criminal.

"I wish I didn't have to say it, but we have to get you ready." Judging by the raw emotion in his voice, his reluctance was stronger than his words suggested.

I stepped back and wiped my eyes. "Can I go to the bathroom first?" I wanted to wash my face and make sure my bladder was empty. I'd never tell anyone, but I was afraid my nerves might get the best of me, causing an embarrassing accident.

The room was a hive of activity as AJ led me to the back, where Doug and Maxwell were waiting.

"Hi Blake," Doug said when we got close.

"You remember Doug and Maxwell?" AJ said, instead of offering a formal introduction.

"I do. Hi, Doug, Hi, um, Maxwell." I felt weird calling her by her last name.

"You can call me Max," she offered. "Did AJ tell you the plan?"

"You're going to bug me."

"That's right," she said, picking up a vest. "We put a recording and tracking device in the vest."

"So I'll be wearing a wire? Won't that piss them off?"

"Yes, but they'll expect it," Doug offered, as if that was explanation enough.

AJ rubbed small circles on my back with his thumb, surprising me with his open display of affection.

"Won't they find it?" I asked, sounding a hell of a lot calmer than I felt.

"Yes, we're stroking their egos by meeting their expectations," Max said.

"The second one," Doug picked up something small and white off the table, "will be a hell of a lot harder to find."

"So they can't find it?" I asked, staring at the small device in his large hand. *Where does it go?*

"They can, if they sweep you with the right equipment after I turn it on. So, it's not impossible, but it is unlikely," Doug answered.

AJ's voice came over my head. "This better work."

"I'll do everything in my power to make sure it does," Doug said.

In an effort to calm my nerves, I forced myself to remember what AJ had told me about Doug. He was in the Air Force, and a tech geek. When he first started dating Beth, a grief-stricken widow, who'd lost her husband and son, kidnapped his soon-to-be stepson, Chase. He must have been terrified.

"I'll be nearby, but out-of-sight, and will turn it on after they toss the bugged vest and finish their initial search," Doug said.

"Search?" My voice shook as my fear revved up like a racecar on the starting line.

Maxwell answered, "They'll likely do a thorough search for weapons and devices."

AJ's hand tensed on my back.

"How thorough?" I asked, getting more worried by the second.

Maxwell looked at AJ, then continued, "Thorough enough to be invasive. I don't want to scare you, but I want you to be warned. It's likely they'll enjoy the search a lot more than they should."

"Meaning they'll grope me?" I shuddered.

"You don't have to do this," AJ said, his voice deep with concern. "Say the word and I'll call it off."

I looked at Jack; his ghost-white face boosted my courage.

"No, I can do it." I turned to him. "You'll come get me, right?"

"There isn't a force on this Earth that can stop me." His dark eyes stared into mine, willing me to believe him. To trust him.

I did.

Turning back around, I asked, "Where does that one go?" I pointed at the small one in Doug's hand.

"In your mouth. Max will help you." Doug handed her the device.

"Let's go to the bathroom so I can wash my hands. This may be a little unpleasant, but it'll be over in a second."

When AJ started to follow, I stopped, turned, and put my hand on his chest. "It's okay, Andrew. I'll be fine."

The low rumble of people talking in the room came to an abrupt stop with a collective gasp. Thinking I'd done something wrong, I looked around to see shock on every face.

"What'd I say?"

He put his hand over mine and held it to his chest; his heart thumping a mile a minute under it. He whispered, "No one calls me Andrew. Except you."

Right, he'd told me that.

He brushed my hair behind my ear before cupping my face and kissing me on the forehead. "Go."

My skin was still tingling from his kiss when Max and I got to the bathroom. She set the tracker, now back in its case, on the counter before washing her hands.

"I'll do my best not to hurt you, but it may be uncomfortable while I put it in place."

"Is there anything I need to do?"

"Relax your jaw like you're at the dentist," she said before pulling on blue medical gloves. "And try not to bite my fingers."

"Okay." I took a deep breath through my nose and forced my jaw to relax. I said, "Ready," before letting my mouth hang open.

Max talked me through each step as she put her hands in my mouth, gave me directions to make it easier, and attached the device to one of my molars. She was right; it was uncomfortable.

After she finished, she said, "Alright, that should do it. Try closing your mouth, but don't slam your teeth."

I did what she said.

"How's it feel?"

I ran my tongue over the small piece of plastic attached to the top and outside edge of my back tooth. "Weird." Suddenly, I had a million questions. "Will it fall off? What happens if they find it and try to remove it? Will they break my tooth?"

"Slow down." She put her hand on my shoulder. "It should stay on as long as you don't chew on that side, and don't clench your jaw."

Panic rose in my throat.

"Don't worry. We plan to get you before dinnertime."

Some of the tension left my shoulders, but my stomach didn't get the memo. It was full of butterflies. *More like killer bees.*

Max looked at the door, "I want to warn you, without AJ hearing."

My lungs forgot how to work as the bees in my stomach went crazy.

"I meant what I said about them being thorough in their search. I'm sure you noticed his reaction when I mentioned it." She waited for me to nod. "He'll probably have to watch them do it."

He wouldn't handle that well.

"What can I do?" I didn't want him doing something stupid, like getting himself killed, because he was mad some jerk was touching me.

"Try not to react."

That sounded impossible. "What do you mean?"

"Try not to flinch or show any emotion. AJ will blow a gasket if he thinks they're hurting you. They won't kill you, but they won't hesitate to kill him if he steps out of line."

I gasped, clutching the counter for support.

Max reached out to steady me, saying, "I'm sorry. I shouldn't have been so blunt."

"It's okay." I appreciated her directness, even if I didn't like the news. I straightened to my full five-foot-two and asked, "What else can I do?" *AJ can't die because of me.*

"Keep being brave," she said. "And comply as much as you can. Remember, they need you, so it's not in their best interest to hurt you."

Her words weren't as comforting as she seemed to think they were. "We won't be far behind you." She glanced at the door. "We should go back before Janerek busts down the door."

I laughed. It sounded ridiculous, given all that was going on, but it was all I could do. In the last twenty-four hours, I'd not only come to expect his protectiveness—I realized I liked it.

I feel safe with Andrew. "Let's go."

Back in the conference room, Doug tested the tracker before turning it back off. AJ and Max helped me back into my vest, making sure all the wires were hidden. Which seemed silly if they wanted them to be found.

"You okay?" Andrew asked.

"As okay as I can be," I answered with a soft smile, hoping to reassure him. I couldn't stop thinking about what Max said—don't let him see you react.

I don't know if I have it in me, but I'll do everything in my power to make sure AJ doesn't have a reason to get himself killed.

John issued orders as we filed into the lobby. Jamie and Jaden would leave first and watch us from nearby rooftops. Jack would ride with John and they'd follow us. Doug and Maxwell would drive together, making sure they stayed within remote control distance of me.

My life is an action movie. One I didn't want to see, let alone star in.

"AJ will drive you to the first site, where you'll get instructions on the meetup location. They'll expect our non-compliance, but we won't be too obvious."

"If we're only getting information, why does everyone have to go?" I asked.

"One, it may be a trap." I felt AJ's grip on my hand tighten. "If they think you're not well protected, they may try to take you." I looked at Jack, who was clenching his jaw and fists so tight I expected them to break. "Two, they probably won't give us a lot of time to get to the exchange site," Jamie said.

"The team needs to be ready to roll as soon as we have the location," John added.

"What happens if they grab me at the first site? Will they release Meg?"

Jack flinched. "Probably not," he said through gritted teeth.

"Then we can't let that happen," I said with a bravado I didn't feel.

Chapter 45

AJ

When everyone was ready, we filed out the back door. I opened the door to the sedan and helped a spaced-out Blake get in.

We kept chatter to a minimum over comms. It was non-existent in the car. I had a million and one things I wanted to say to Blake, but couldn't find a good way to say them.

Instead, I held her hand, tracing circles on the back of it with my thumb, trying to convey what I felt.

"Andrew?" Blake broke the silence.

I was still getting used to hearing my full name and not hating it. "Yeah?"

"Please don't get yourself killed," she whispered.

"What?" Where had that come from? I mean, I was glad she felt that way, but why'd she think I'd get myself killed?

"Max told me not to react to anything they do because you'll do something stupid and get yourself killed."

Fucking Maxwell.

"Blake, it's going to kill me to hand you over and watch them touch you, knowing I can't do anything."

"Just, don't do anything stupid, okay?"

I looked at her. *What the fuck do I say?* I couldn't make that promise, because as soon as the leash came off, I'd kill every single person who'd laid a hand on Blake.

"Blake."

"Andrew, listen to me. I already lost my father today." My head whipped towards her. Did she know something we didn't? No way. I heard mutterings over the comms; everyone wondered the same thing.

"I mean, I lost the man I thought he was. The only thing keeping me going right now is knowing I can help Meg." She clenched my hand as she whispered the next two words, "And you."

"I love you, Blake," I said it again because it was the only truth I could speak to her in that moment

It'd take an act of God to keep me from going full rampage and killing everyone standing between me and Blake when the time came.

Which meant taking risks that could get me killed. *It's worth it to save her.*

"Andrew, please be careful."

I squeezed her hand. "I will."

"Sierra Two in position," Jamie relayed over the comm. Soon after, everyone else checked in. Blake and I were three short minutes from the meeting spot.

When we got to the convenience store outside of town, I walked Blake to the woodpile and stood watch while she looked for the note.

They were watching. I could sense it, but I couldn't see them. "Anyone have eyes on the Tango?" I continued scanning as everyone responded in the negative.

Doesn't mean they aren't watching.

Blake found a handwritten note with an address and a time, nothing more.

Pocketing the note, I escorted Blake back to the car. I relayed the address as I plugged it into the GPS, knowing Maxwell would look it up and tell me what I needed to know.

We had just enough time to get there, but not enough for Jamie and Jay to set up their sniper nests in advance.

Fuck. I didn't like going in before our snipers were in place.

There was more chatter over comms during the short ride to the exchange location, an abandoned warehouse, as we developed a game plan on the fly.

The exchange would take place in the back lot, out of view from passing traffic, and most of SSI.

They'd chosen well; cutting off our back up while providing plenty of cover for theirs.

We'd be sitting ducks.

They won't kill her. They need her. Played on repeat in my head. Every so often I squeezed her hand as fear gripped my heart; she squeezed back every time.

Under different circumstances, it'd be cute, her trying to squeeze my hand as much as I was hers. But I was terrified, and probably hurting her.

I forced my hand to relax. "I'm sorry."

"It's okay. I'll be okay," she said.

She sounded like she was trying to convince herself more than me. I nodded, the knot in my throat making it hard to talk.

Everyone except Jamie and Jay found places to hide and wait. "Sierra Two and Seven are scouting locations. They'll take up position ASAP," John said. "Sierra Four, stall if you can."

"Copy that."

"What's happening?"

"Not everyone is ready yet. We have to buy some time." I didn't know how, but I'd figure it out.

Jack's voice sounded in my ear, "Drive around the building at a crawl, make a show of looking for their backup and snipers. They'll expect as much."

"I'll delay as long as I can." I didn't want to do this without backup anymore than he did.

"Be careful." I heard everything he wasn't saying. Blake's life wasn't the only one on the line if I fucked up.

"Sweetheart, I'm going to come across as mean and uncaring when this goes down." I swallowed hard, forcing down the fear. "Please know, it's only to keep myself sane and you safe."

She nodded as I lifted her hand and kissed it. Sixty seconds later, we turned into the parking lot and I let go. Slowing to a crawl, I made a big show out of craning my neck forward and looking at every window. I relayed the information without moving my lips. "Tango on each corner of the second floor, east side."

"What's a ta–"

I cut her off. "Shhh."

I turned into the back lot at a snail's pace, which wasn't as easy. "Tangos everywhere in the back. Blacked-out van, no plate, no sign of Cinderella. ETA on Two and Seven?"

"Nesting now," Jamie answered.

"In place," Jay said immediately after.

"Show time," I whispered.

"I'm scared," Blake confessed.

"So am I." Too many things could go wrong. "Take a deep breath, square your shoulders, and tell yourself you can do this."

"Is that what you're doing?"

Taking a deep breath, I squared my shoulders and said, "I can do this." I inhaled another lung inflating breath before saying, "Your turn."

When she finished, I put the car in park but left the engine running.

There was no turning back now. I'd have to watch her walk away.

Please, God, don't let me lose my temper and risk everyone's life. Take mine if you need to, but don't let me fuck this up.

"It's time," John's voice cut through my prayer. "Everyone in place?"

Jamie and Jay checked in. Followed by Doug and Maxwell.

I closed my eyes and sent up another prayer. "Sierra Four is ready." Opening my eyes, I turned to Blake. "Blake, I'm going to get out and walk around the back. Please wait for me to open your door." I reached over and released her seatbelt.

"I will." She stared into my eyes. "Please be careful."

"I will. No matter what you see, remember I love you."

Then I flipped the switch. My expression turned to stone as I got out of the car. This was a mission, just like the hundreds I did in the Army. Get in, do the job, get out. If I could stay mission focused, I could do this.

Easier said than done.

I scanned as I circled the car. Too many bad guys for me to handle on my own. I opened Blake's door and extended my hand to help her out. "Stay behind me." Not that it mattered; guns pointed at us from every direction.

I stopped when one of them opened the sliding door on the van and helped Meg get out. Her hands were tied, but she looked unharmed.

"Cinderella's okay." I wasn't sure I'd said it loud or clear enough until I heard Jack say, "Thank God."

"We've got your back, but try not to start a gunfight. You're grossly outnumbered," Jaden said.

"How do we know it's Blake?" one of them shouted at me.

"Ms. Davenport, take one step to your left," I ordered, sensing her movement but never taking my eyes off Meg.

"See for yourself," I shouted back.

"Blake Davenport, just the girl we wanted to see."

Every word oozed slime, making me want to rip out his tongue and choke him with it.

His days, no, his hours, are numbered.

"Come here, girl," he ordered.

"She doesn't go anywhere until I have Mrs. Sheppard."

"Look around you. You don't make the rules. I do." He swept his arms, pointing out his gang of armed lackeys.

"You won't risk killing Ms. Davenport in the crossfire." I sounded so cold, so detached. *Please let her remember this is just what I have to do.*

"You're right, but I see you've already helped me in that regard." He nodded at her bulletproof vest.

I itched to reach for her hand. Ignoring him, I called out, "Mrs. Sheppard?"

"I'm okay," she answered. She was looking around for Jack, fear showing through her bravado.

"They cross at the same time," I commanded.

"Fine, let's get this done." He signaled to the lackey holding Meg's arm. "Let her go." They didn't untie her hands.

"Blake, I need you to walk slowly towards Meg. Don't say anything when you pass. And please don't look back," I said without moving my lips.

"Okay." She sounded so small.

My fists could have turned coal to diamonds.

"Cinderella and Aurora are on the move," Jamie confirmed for all to hear.

I held my breath as I watched.

"Sierra Four, breathe."

The air felt like sandpaper on my throat, and daggers in my lungs. My gut screamed for me to run and grab them both as Blake and Meg passed each other. I could cover them while the team killed everyone else.

I watched Blake ignore Meg.

Meg returned the favor.

Every cell in my body vibrated with the need to act. I watched Blake hold her head high, as I counted off the seconds it took Meg to reach me.

I could have ground a diamond to dust with my back teeth as each second, each step, brought Meg closer to freedom and Blake closer to captivity.

My heart cleaved in two as Jamie gave the play-by-play as Blake reached her captors.

When Meg was only a few steps away, I shifted my focus. "Get in the car," I said, harsher than I should have.

"Where's J–"

"Now! Close the door and buckle up." I said, shifting my attention back to Blake.

"You have what you came for. Now get lost before we turn you into Swiss cheese."

Blake turned to me; the trust in her eyes was my undoing. "I can't leave her." I heard the panic in my hushed voice.

"You have to. We'll keep our eyes on her; as soon as they check her, Sierra Five will turn on the tracker."

My eyes stayed glued to Blake as I walked to the driver's door. I didn't need the updates Jaden was giving. "They've removed the vest. And found the tracker."

I hesitated behind the open door as one of the dead men walking leered at Blake while running his hands over every inch of her body.

When she flinched, I growled.

"You're risking my wife's life."

Jack's whispered growl was enough to snap me out of it. Not that Meg mattered more than Blake, but to save them both, I had to stick to the plan.

I'll come back for you, I promise.

In the few seconds it took for me to get behind the wheel and close the door, the fucker in charge put his hands on Blake and checked under her shirt and in her pants.

My knuckles blanched as I gripped the wheel.

"AJ?" I ignored Meg's question.

Blake held her head high and pretended she didn't care one bit about the asshole squeezing her breasts. *He's a dead man.*

"Sierra Four, it's time to go," John issued the order. It was the same tone I'd heard him use with Jack and Jamie. Firm, but compassionate.

"We're going," I growled as I put the car in reverse and slowly backed away.

"They're done searching," Jamie said. "They're tying her wrists."

I punched the steering wheel.

I finally asked Meg, "Are you okay?"

"I'm okay. They were assholes, but they didn't touch me."

"Thank God," Jack responded in my ear.

"Your husband is relieved," I said.

"I assume you guys have a plan."

Doug came over the comms before I could answer, so I nodded.

"Signal on Aurora is strong. We'll follow as soon as they move."

Thank God.

"Delivering Cinderella to the rendezvous point. Keep me posted."

So far, things were going as planned.

Which made me nervous. *Things never go as planned on a mission.*

Chapter 46

Blake

He's leaving. I knew he would, but that didn't make it any easier to watch. *You can do this*. My internal voice sounded a lot like the strong, protective, caring man who'd just gotten in his car.

I willed myself not to flinch as the overly enthusiastic guy frisking me made sure my boobs, butt and crotch were device free. Cringing internally, but refusing to give AJ a reason to come back, I didn't react. Holding my head high and back stiff, I endured the torment.

For the first time in my life, I embraced the idea that violence might be the answer. Listening to their taunts, I couldn't imagine there was anything I could say to keep these guys from stealing every dollar I had, and the millions I would have, then raping and killing me.

I blinked away my tears as AJ backed out of the lot, taking Meg to safety. *He'll come back for me.* He promised he would. *Dear God, please don't let him betray my trust.*

A second guy tied my hands together before the first guy said, "Get in the van," pointing at the open sliding door with his gun.

His gun scared me. No, it wasn't the gun that scared me; it was the guy holding it.

I rolled my tongue over the tracker. *Please let it work.* Max had warned me I'd have no way of knowing when they turned it on, so I'd have to trust them.

I do. I didn't understand why, and it didn't really matter. I trusted them, trusted Andrew, to find and rescue me.

Maybe it was because they were my only hope, and not trusting them meant giving up.

When the door slammed into place, I flinched in my seat. Panic set in when the locks clicked.

What if the tracker isn't working? What if Andrew can't find me? Where are these guys taking me? What will they do to me?

I fidgeted in my seat as my heart raced.

"Don't worry your pretty little head, Darlin, we won't hurt you," the guy who frisked me said.

"Why are you doing this?" I asked in a shaky voice. *Why did I ask?* I already knew what they wanted. Did I really want to start a conversation?

"Well, Darlin'," *God, I hate it when men call me that,* "Your daddy owes our boss, Mr. Roman, a lot of money, and you have a lot of money." His voice made my skin crawl as he confirmed what SSI had told me.

Not yet, I don't.

Remembering no one had seen my father since the day before, I asked, "What'd you do to my father?"

"To him? We didn't do anything to him. You'll see for yourself soon enough."

"You kidnapped him, too?"

"You've got it all wrong," he made eye-contact in the mirror, "he came to us."

What?

My world shattered as bile rose in my throat. I'd wanted to believe my father was innocent. That the evidence of his involvement was a set-up. That the warrant issued for his arrest was one big, ugly mistake. But how could I deny it now?

He's voluntarily working with these guys.

"Don't look so surprised. Your daddy's been helping us for a long time."

I didn't bother wiping away the silent tears tracking down my face. My father was a criminal. Everything I'd known, everything I'd believed, had been a lie. He wasn't a good guy, a lawful citizen, or an honest man.

And now, because of him, I'd been kidnapped. I didn't care if they took all my money, but thinking about what they'd do to me was terrifying.

Please, God, let Andrew find me.

"Get her a tissue," the driver ordered the guy next to me. "We don't want her all blotchy for her reunion with Daddy Dearest."

I stared out the windshield as the world passed by in a blur. Why did he do it? Was Priscilla guilty too? How long has this been going on?

Did my mom know? Somehow, that'd be the worst betrayal of all. A sob escaped my lips.

Someone shoved a tissue into my hands. Instead of using it to wipe my face or blow my nose, I tore off tiny strips and let them fall to the floor.

Breadcrumbs that couldn't leave a trail. and would never be seen.

I was wrong. I can't do this.

"It'll all be over soon, Darlin'. As soon as you turn twenty-five and pay off your daddy's debts, you'll be free to go."

Why didn't I believe him?

I lost track of time, but it didn't seem like it was more than fifteen minutes before we parked at an abandoned two-story farmhouse and they dragged me from the van.

When I stumbled, the driver grabbed my elbow and said, "Let's go." Then pushed me towards the door.

Empty fields surrounded us. The dirt road gave off dark desert highway vibes, despite being in farm country.

The half-dozen cars and trucks on the lawn hinted at a full house.

The nearest house wouldn't survive a strong gust of wind, so I couldn't imagine anyone living there. There was no one to witness them forcing me inside. *No one to hear me scream.*

We passed through a crowded dining room with half a dozen men playing cards and smoking cigarettes at the table. The thick, nasty smoke filled my lungs, causing me to cough.

They stopped playing to stare as I walked by. Several of them licked their lips as their eyes roamed up and down my body. One of them said, "I like a girl with meat on her bones. Gives me something to hold on to."

I couldn't have stopped my involuntary shiver if my life depended on it. The predatory look in his eyes made my skin crawl and my stomach heave.

I prayed. Please hurry Andrew.

A voice cut through the din coming from the kitchen. *Daddy.*

Chapter 47

Blake

My father's laugh cut through my heart like a hot knife through butter. How could he be here with these guys, laughing?

I channeled strength I didn't know I had while chanting, I will not cry, on a loop in my mind.

My father sat with his back to me, so I saw him before he saw me. One man leaned on the counter, but I didn't give him the time of day.

"Welcome, Blake." The guy sitting at the table tilted his head in my direction.

I glared holes in the back of my father's head instead of answering.

He stood up and turned. "Princess," he sounded far too cheerful as he reached for me.

"Don't," I said, holding my still bound wrists in front of me as I stepped back.

His face had a few bruises, like he'd gotten in a fistfight and lost. Did they do that to him? *Maybe they'd forced him to be here and then lied to me about it.* But I couldn't convince myself—he looked relaxed, and he'd been laughing. No, they may have hit him, but he wasn't a prisoner.

The driver stopped me from backing away more than a step.

"I know this looks bad, but it's not what you think," he said.

"So you didn't betray me?" I lifted my hands and shook them in front of his face. His eyes stayed glued to the ties binding my wrists as he stammered out an answer.

"What? Betray you? No." He was lying. The high pitch of his voice gave him away. "I'd never do anything to hurt you."

"But you did. You lied to me and you're corrupt." I poured my disappointment into every word.

"It's not like that."

The smirk on the other guy's face eliminated the last shred of doubt I had.

My anger flared, replacing my fear and disappointment. "If you're here against your will, why aren't you tied up?" I lifted my hands in front of his face again.

"Can you untie her, please?" he asked.

"Not yet." The guy at the table answered. He must be the man in charge. *Good to know.*

The man leaning against the counter laughed, sending shivers up my spine.

I turned towards him, focusing on his face for the first time. My eyes rounded as my breath caught in my throat—he was the guy I'd seen outside the coffee shop on the Friday of my father's dinner. The guy I'd convinced myself wasn't staring at me.

When I'd mentioned the situation to AJ, and told him how creeped out I'd felt, he told me to always trust my gut instinct in situations like that. Neither of us could have known how right he was.

"Can I have a moment alone with my daughter?" he asked.

"Sure thing." The guy at the table stood up, signaling for the other guy to follow him. "But don't do anything stupid, Stevo. I'll be right outside this door." He nodded to the driver, who backed away from me.

Stevo? What the fuck! My father had his own gangster nickname. Because that was the only word that came to mind when I thought about these guys.

I glanced behind me; the driver hovered just outside the doorway, acting like he wasn't listening. I couldn't see the other door to the large kitchen, but it wasn't hard to envision the other two guys doing the same thing.

We're not really alone.

"Princess, I'm sorry you got dragged into this."

"What exactly is this?" I gestured with both hands.

"I, here, sit, so you're more comfortable." He pulled out a chair for me.

I glared at the chair like it was responsible for all my problems. "No. Tell me why I'm here."

"I owe them money."

At least he had the decency to sound embarrassed. Not that it made me any less angry.

"I know that much. Why?"

None of this made sense. If they were bribing him, why'd he owe them money? I asked him as much.

"After your mom died, I was a wreck. I started gambling to numb the pain."

At least mom didn't know. I no longer recognized the man standing in front of me. Sure, he looked like my father, but the words coming out of his mouth didn't sound like the man I'd known all my life.

"Don't blame Mom." My voice could have frozen a lake.

"I don't. Gambling was an escape and winning felt good."

Was he a gambling addict?

"I was winning. A lot. Then I started losing, but I had it under control." He paused. "Until I didn't. I started chasing the next win." After a particularly heavy loss, which drained his savings, he'd stepped away.

"Most of my savings were gone when I married Priscilla, but I expected to inherit my father's fortune, so I figured everything would be okay."

How dare he blame everyone but himself? "Don't blame this on me or Grandpa." I wanted to cross my arms in front of me in a huff, but couldn't.

"I don't. But Priscilla demanded a certain lifestyle, one I'd promised to provide and couldn't. I went back to the table thinking I could earn some quick money and then quit for good. But I messed up."

He looked sad as he told me that after a big win, he'd doubled down with money he didn't have. And lost.

"Roman told me he'd erase half my debt if I dismissed charges against a colleague of his. I said no, told him I'd find the money. But I had no choice when he threatened to expose my gambling addiction."

"So you violated your oath? Committed a felony? How is that better?"

"I couldn't let them destroy my reputation and ruin the career I'd worked so hard for. And I didn't want my father finding out."

No wonder I hadn't seen the signs; I was away at college.

Is this why his relationship with his father deteriorated near the end? And how was committing a felony and betraying your family's trust better than a little embarrassment?

"He suspected I was in trouble. That's why he left everything to you."

"He knew you lost all your money," I said, more accusation than question.

"Yes. but I didn't find out he'd cut me out of his will until it was too late. After I'd already promised Roman I'd pay him back once I settled the estate."

But he couldn't, because Grandpa changed his will, leaving his fortune to me.

My father looked remorseful when he explained how Roman blackmailed him, saying he'd turn my father in if he didn't help another colleague.

"Instead of reducing my debt, he transferred money to my account, knowing it'd look like a bribe. He trapped me; I had to do his bidding."

I thought back to all those times Priscilla whined about money problems. "Does Priscilla know?"

"Not about the gambling, no. But she knows I'm in financial trouble."

Now he needs me to bail him out. I would've given him the money if he'd just asked, but he sold me out. I'm a prisoner until I turn twenty-five. *And God only knows what'll happen after I give them the money.*

"But you can help me," he practically begged.

So why hire SSI? Was it just for show? And how was he paying them?

"Why'd you hire a bodyguard?"

He clasped my hands as he said, "Because I wanted to protect you. I thought I could take care of things. You have to believe me. I never wanted this to happen, for you to get involved."

That I could believe. He'd always done his best to take care of me. In his own misguided way, he'd tried to protect me by hiding the truth.

"Did you know about the attack at school?" *Was he in on it?*

He claimed he didn't know until after it had happened. Though he admitted he found out from Crowley, not SSI.

When I asked, Dad explained Crowley was the guy he was talking to when I walked in. "He's Roman's right-hand man."

"They didn't realize I'd hired a bodyguard." He touched the bruises on his face. "That's when they threatened to kill me if I didn't bring you to them."

"But you told SSI to send me to a safe house instead?" I might be able to forgive him for fucking up so badly if I could trust he had nothing to do with the attack or the kidnappings.

"I did, but then I changed my mind. I told John I didn't think it was necessary."

What the hell! No one had shared that nugget of information with me.

"You would have brought me here," I whispered as the weight of my father's betrayal sank in. He would have handed me over to clear his debt.

My father was willing to risk my life to save his own.

That's why they had to take Meg—SSI had ignored my father and kept protecting me.

Andrew.

"You let them kidnap an innocent woman to get to me?" I gave up trying and accepted my father wasn't the man I thought he was, not anymore.

"They didn't give me a choice," he whined.

"There's always a choice," I said, turning my back on him.

And he'd been making the wrong ones for a long time.

Chapter 48

AJ

Seconds ticked by at a snail's pace as Meg and I waited for Jack and the others. As soon as Jack parked and got out of his car, Meg ran to him. He met her halfway and fell to his knees, burying his face in her belly as he hugged her.

My fear-fueled impatience paused as I watched Meg reassure Jack that she was okay. He stood as Jamie parked.

"Sierra Four to Sierra Six. Where is she?"

During the ride, Meg filled me in on the situation at the farmhouse they'd held her in. She didn't know where it was because they'd blindfolded her, but she told me what she could about the interior and the number of people.

We'd be busting in on a heavily armed group of twenty or more people.

And Steven Davenport. A man who was about to have a very bad day. If Jack didn't kill him for endangering Meg, I would for everything he'd done to Blake.

"Heading northeast, her signal is strong. Sending details now," Maxwell answered.

"We need to get moving," I called to the team.

Jack looked from me to Meg, indecision written all over his face. He needed to protect Meg, but he wanted to help save Blake.

"If you need to stay behind…" I needed him, but I couldn't blame him. If the roles were reversed, I didn't think I could leave Blake.

"No, we're helping," Meg answered.

"Meg." Jack begged. It'd kill him for her to be near the danger.

"You need to help AJ save Blake." She forced him to look at her. "They don't care about me anymore."

"It's too dangerous," he argued.

"You two get going. You'll need the extra time to set up your nests," John said to Jamie and Jay.

"Yes, sir," they answered as they got back in their trucks.

At least our snipers will be in place.

"How you holding up?" John asked, squeezing my shoulder, the same way he'd done with his sons whenever they needed his support. The act untangled a knot deep inside. I might not be blood, but he offered me the fatherly support I needed.

"Impatiently." I said before admitting, "It's killing me, not knowing what they're doing to her."

"They won't hurt her," Meg said.

I prayed she was right.

"Meg's coming with us," Jack said through gritted teeth. He looked at her. "And she'll stay in the car."

"I promise." She put her hand on her belly, already displaying protective mama-bear instincts.

"Let's go get your girl," Jack said.

"This is Sierra One. We're rolling out. Keep the updates coming," John said. He turned to me. "Grab your gear; you're riding with us."

I nodded before jogging to the sedan and grabbing my bag from the trunk. I locked the car before slipping my battle belt on and tossing my rifle in John's trunk.

"Let's go."

We received regular updates from Maxwell for the next ten minutes, providing us with the van's coordinates. I typed them into the GPS as John drove.

Jack sketched as Meg re-iterated what she'd told me about the layout of the house, at least the first floor, and the number of people inside.

It wasn't a blueprint, but it was better than going in blind. The biggest thing working in our favor was the acres of abandoned cornfields that would provide cover as we approached.

"Sierra Six for the team, Aurora is stationary. Sending coordinates."

"Copy that. Received," I answered.

I punched in the coordinates as soon as they came through.

"Coordinates received," Jamie and Jay answered immediately afterwards.

"Send ETA ASAP."

"Copy that." I checked the GPS. "ETA fifteen minutes," I replied.

"Sierra Two on site in ten," Jamie answered. Jaden had the same ETA.

I turned in my seat and showed Meg the terrain view on the map. "This it?"

She nodded. "The kitchen's in the back. I could see guys walking around with rifles through the windows."

"Thank you."

Doug sent coordinates for our command center. Jamie and Jay would meet them there and determine the best place to nest. Luckily, they didn't need to wait for us to get into position. This would be the first time we'd have two snipers.

Thank God, because we'll need them both.

The rest of the drive took forever as we started making plans. Jamie and Jay would take out as many of the guys outside the building as possible while the rest of us approached in two teams. John and Doug on one team, Jack, Maxwell, and me on the other.

Meg would hide in the back seat of the bulletproof sedan, out of sight.

I prayed more for Blake's safety in those few minutes than I'd ever prayed for anything else in my entire adult life.

Chapter 49

Blake

I wanted to believe my father when he said he didn't know they'd taken Meg until it was too late. I wanted to believe him when he promised me this would all be over once I paid them. I wanted to believe him when he said he'd get help and give up gambling.

But he'd lied too many times.

"Will you turn yourself in?" I asked, desperately wanting him to say he'd accept responsibility for everything he'd done and face the consequences.

He didn't. He hemmed and hawed until I got up and walked away.

I didn't go far because the driver blocked my path. *So much for an angry exit.* He pointed at the chair and told me to sit.

"Can you untie me? It's not like I can run away."

"Not unless the boss man says it's okay." He tilted his head towards the other door.

The 'boss man' walked back in as if saying his name had summoned him.

Figuring he'd know what I wanted, I held my hands out in front of me in a silent request.

"Untie her."

After they removed the ropes, I rubbed my sore, red wrists and sat back down. "Thank you."

Why am I thanking him?

"You see, Princess, I'm not so bad," the man my father called Crowley said.

The snake-like quality of his voice, and the way his eyes lingered on my chest, made my skin crawl. I resisted the urge to cover my chest with my arms.

Don't give them the satisfaction of seeing your fear. I reminded myself AJ would come for me and prayed it'd be sooner rather than later.

But doubt crept in with each passing minute. Could I trust him? I thought I could, but I'd always believed I could trust my father.

"You have a beautiful daughter, Stevo."

I couldn't hold back my shudder when he touched my cheek with his nicotine-stained fingers. I repressed my gag reflex as the scent of stale tobacco flooded my nose.

"You promised you wouldn't hurt her," my father said, sounding like he was begging.

Crowley laughed. "Oh, I won't hurt her." His hand slid down my neck and traced my collarbone. I jerked back and brought my hands up to cover myself.

I prayed AJ would get here soon, while giving my father a look that would make Medusa proud. *If only he'd turn to stone.*

"I'm so sorry," my father said before breaking eye contact and staring at the table.

"Want something to drink? Maybe something to take the edge off?"

"No." No way would I drink anything they gave me and risk being drugged. Remembering what SSI said about the guy who tried to attack me at school, I panicked and brought my hands to my arms.

What if they inject me with something?

One of his guys rushed in, concern written all over his face. "Something's going on outside."

He's here. I dug my nails into my arm to keep myself from smiling.

Andrew came.

Crowley turned to me, accusation in his eyes, before walking to the counter and picking up a radio on his way to the door. "Call everyone in," he said before pulling the curtain to the side and looking out.

I wanted to know what was happening, but there was no way in hell I'd ask.

"Fuck!" He turned to the table, his face blanching as he pulled a gun out of his waistband and waved it at us. "Get up."

Crowley, the driver, and two others rushed us upstairs and into a bedroom at the end of the hall. The first thing they did was close the thin curtains.

My heart beat against my ribs, and it wasn't because we'd just run up the stairs.

"You two, guard the door. Kill anyone who comes up the stairs," Crowley ordered. Leaving my father and me alone with him and the driver. Whose name I still didn't know.

Not that it matters.

They nodded before switching off the lights and stepping out. The door clicked shut behind them.

My heartbeat sped up to an impossible pace. My father didn't look like he was doing any better.

They shuffled us over to the far side of the room, putting us between themselves and the door.

"They'll have to shoot you to get to me," Crowley whispered in my ear.

There was nothing I could do to control my trembling as I stood in the dark room and waited.

Except pray.

Chapter 50

AJ

Jamie and Jay cleared the way for us, using deadly accuracy to remove the guards surrounding the building. The silencers on their rifles provided us with the tactical advantage we needed.

We took the front, while John and Doug moved to the back.

"Aurora and her father are being led upstairs, four tangos with them."

"This is Three, copy that," Jack said from behind me a second before John confirmed he'd also heard.

"Sierra One in place. Ready when you are."

"Sierra Four in place. On my mark."

"Aurora and her father are still upstairs," Jay confirmed before giving us the room's location.

Knowing they were on the second floor meant we could go in fast and hard.

I counted down from three.

On one, we kicked in both doors and started shooting at anyone holding a gun. Which was everyone. Jack and I moved in sync, clearing the front room with lethal speed while Maxwell covered the stairs. The non-stop percussion of gunfire filled the house, only interrupted by an occasional scream or one of our snipers updating us on tango positions.

They'd fucked with the wrong family, and were paying the ultimate price. The red haze lining my vision meant I didn't care they were just doing their jobs—their job was to harm innocent people, and it ended now.

John and Doug were just as merciless. This wasn't a small group of dumb guys doing bad things. This was a gang of enforcers and hitmen who were putting up one hell of a fight.

"Clear," I called out as we finished the last room.

"Clear," John called out a few seconds later. "Coming to you."

John and Doug joined us at the bottom of the stairs.

I signaled Maxwell to cover me. The instant she was in position, I headed up the stairs with Jack right behind me.

The two guys standing in the hall made it easy to verify what room they had Blake in. They lifted their guns.

In the space of a heartbeat, I pulled the trigger twice. So did Jack.

They fell before they could line up their sights.

I'm coming, Blake.

"I need an update."

"No movement," Jay answered.

John moved to the other side of the door, signaling he'd open it and watch the hall.

Doug, Jack and I would take the room, while Maxwell continued to cover the stairs. As soon as Jack squeezed up, I nodded. We were ready.

I took a deep breath and waited.

The door flew inward. We rushed in, flooding the room with light from our weapon-mounted flashlights.

Everything happened in the blink of an eye, despite moving in slow motion.

When I swung around to the far corner; my heart stopped.

Blake and her father were being held at gunpoint. The guy behind Blake was squatting so he could use her as a shield. Her body hid most of him.

Most, but not enough to save him.

She looked terrified, and I hated that there was nothing I could do to protect her from seeing what was coming next.

"It's over. Let them go," I ordered, my red dot steady on the space between his eyes. Jack and Doug had cleared the rest of the room, flipped on the lights, and spread out on either side of me.

The scumbag holding Blake dragged her with him when he stepped back. If I shot him, I'd save Blake, but the guy holding her father would probably kill him.

Will she blame me? Could I live with that?

"King's Tango in my crosshairs. Tell me when," Jay removed the problem when he confirmed he had a clean shot.

"There's nowhere to run," Jack said, giving them one last chance to survive the day.

It was more than they deserved.

"You won't shoot us. Not unless you want them to die, too."

Wrong.

In complete opposition to how I felt, my voice was calm and steady when I gave the order, "Send it."

The whites of his eyes rounded, and a fraction of a second later my bullet punched out his lights, forever.

Time sped back up as I rushed forward to catch Blake. Her eyes rolling back as the dead guy pulled her down with him.

Behind me, Jack and Doug helped her father.

Not bothering to so much as a glance at him, I checked Blake for injuries before picking her up. Knowing she wouldn't be unconscious for long, I cleared the hall and stairs in record time, ignoring the burn in my lungs as they filled with smoke from the gunfight.

I prayed Blake wouldn't wake up until after I got her outside. She didn't need to see the carnage or breathe the heavy metallic scent of fresh blood.

Voices relayed information, so I knew what was happening as I exited the house.

I split my focus between Blake's small, unconscious body in my arms and the chatter of assignments being handed out. John ordered Jaime and Jay to stay on over watch while he called 9-1-1.

Once we were outside in the cool afternoon breeze, Blake stirred.

I whispered platitudes in her ear as I sat down on the front steps, hoping to keep her calm as she came to. Jack must have called Meg because she rushed over to us with the first aid bag from John's car.

"Andrew?" Blake asked.

"Shhhh, it's okay. You're safe now."

"Where's my dad?" Her voice was rough from fear.

He was alive and unharmed. They'd frisked him and checked for injuries, and were bringing him out in zip ties.

"He's fine. You can see him in a few minutes." I stroked her hair as I held her head close to my shoulder.

"Did they hurt you?" I asked as I settled her on my lap and checked again for injuries.

"No, they just scared me." That much was obvious, as she trembled in my arms.

Blake said thank you when Meg handed her an open bottle of water, drinking half of it in one swig.

I couldn't stop touching her, reassuring myself she was alive and well.

She asked me if I was okay.

I was. "I'm good. Not even a scratch."

"And Jack?" Meg asked, fear in her eyes despite the attempt at bravery.

Jack answered over the comms, so I relayed the message. "He's okay."

"Sending Davenport out now," Doug's voice sounded in my ear.

When I told Blake, she hurried off my lap. Unwilling to lose contact, I stood and held her hand.

Not knowing what had happened between them in the farmhouse, I didn't know what to expect when she saw him.

Meg moved to stand on Blake's other side, where she'd be out of the way but able to offer support if needed. I nodded my appreciation before turning my attention back to my earpiece, waiting for them to announce they were at the door.

"They're coming out," I warned Blake.

Doug opened the door for Jack, who led a haggard-looking Davenport out the door. Jack watched for Blake's reaction, ready to remove Davenport if necessary.

Steve stuttered out an apology. Instead of accepting, she asked, "How could you?"

He blubbered out a lame excuse, stepping close as he did.

Jack's grip tightened, and Doug put his hand on Davenport's other shoulder.

I stepped between them, nudging Blake behind me.

"Back off," I growled.

Steve found some courage and challenged me. "I'm her father. Get out of my way."

After everything he'd put her through, I didn't give two shits if he was her father or not, I'd still take him down.

Jack and Doug pulled him back, creating distance between us.

Davenport leaned to the side so he could see Blake behind me and pleaded for forgiveness.

I turned my back on him and asked, "Do you want to talk to him?"

Blake shook her head softly back and forth. "No."

"Get him out of here," I ordered over my shoulder.

Maxwell took over escorting Steve so Jack could go to Meg, who was waiting patiently, but not calmly.

Maxwell and Doug took Davenport around the corner, out of Blake's sight.

"Dad?" The panic in Jack's voice caused me to turn.

John had bloodstains on his left arm.

"Did you get shot?" Meg asked, her voice a little too high to be considered calm or controlled.

"I'm okay, it's just a scratch," John answered. Jack and Meg rushed to his side to verify for themselves.

"Let me see," Meg demanded as she pushed up his sleeve.

Meg still didn't believe any of us when we said we had 'just a scratch' after Jack needed sixteen stitches for 'just a scratch' back when they first started dating. Or was it before they started dating? *It doesn't matter.*

You could've heard a pin drop as his other two sons, and the rest of the team, waited for verification.

"What is it with you Sheppard men?" Meg asked. "That's not a scratch."

"Meg, Honey, it's a graze," John reassured her.

She looked at Jack for confirmation. "He's right," Jack wrapped an arm around her, "It's nothing Doc G. can't fix."

We visited the doctor at the local clinic so often we were on a nickname basis with Dr. Greenfield.

A collective sigh of relief huffed over the comms.

Knowing John was okay, I turned my full attention back to Blake and pulled her into my arms.

Chapter 51

Blake

I felt bad about it, but I couldn't look at my father, let alone talk to him, when they brought him out. My heart had swelled with gratitude when AJ stepped between us to shield me.

From my father. *How fucked up is my life right now?*

AJ turned away when Meg asked John if he'd gotten shot, but not for long.

"Is he okay?" I asked from the warmth and safety of AJ's arms.

"He is, though Meg's not convinced." He leaned back and lifted my chin. His love radiated off him like a neon sign flashing in the night, knocking me off balance. Physically and emotionally.

I looked away and saw a man face down in the grass. *How many men did they kill to rescue me? And how had I not noticed them before now?*

It didn't matter. They were hardened criminals, and I didn't doubt for a second they'd take turns raping me before killing me. Crowley hadn't been subtle in the bedroom, telling me all the things he'd do to me before killing me. After taking all my money, of course.

I'd expected my father to say something, to at least try to help me. It's not like I thought he could really stop them, but he should have at least tried. *AJ would have.*

I was so wrong about so many things.

My father wasn't the man I thought he was. He was corrupt, and a coward.

Neither was Andrew Janerek, but in a good way.

My knees gave out as I remembered my fear of getting shot as Crowley dragged me to the floor.

"I got you," AJ said as he scooped me up.

"It's okay. I can walk."

"Please let me do this," he all but begged.

"Okay." Being in his arms felt too good to argue.

Sirens wailed in the distance as I wrapped my arms around his neck and let him carry me down the steps towards the cars.

I refused to release the death grip I had on his neck when he tried to put me down.

"Sweetheart, I need to put you down so I can take off my belt."

I forced myself to let go, embarrassed by my clinginess. *What happened to being an independent woman who didn't need an alpha man?*

Refusing to sound like I'd lost my grip on reality, I held back my laugh. The last few days had shown me, beyond the shadow of a doubt, that there were some things I needed an alpha man for.

Not just any man.

Andrew, no middle name, Janerek.

"Here, sit," he said as he helped me into the back seat.

I stared at all the things on his waist. Before I could identify half of what I was looking at, his rifle blocked my view. He moved it around, then took it off and handed it to someone.

I kept staring.

"Blake, are you okay?" he asked, tilting my face up, so I was looking at him instead of his war-ready belt.

I nodded, then shook my head and laughed. "What's all that?" I asked, hiding my fear and anxiety behind the question.

AJ asked, "You really want to know?"

I wasn't sure, but I needed something to focus on.

"Rifle magazines, pistol magazines, and a tourniquet." He pointed to each thing as he identified it.

"Oh." What else could I say? I'd seen people wear things like it in the movies but never in person. *It looks a lot scarier up close and personal.*

"You okay?"

Knowing he was asking about my reaction to everything that had happened, not his belt, I took a second to think about it.

Am I okay?

"I think so." I stood up, so it was easier to see his face. Okay was a stretch, but I'd get there, eventually.

How easy it'd been for me to say violence was never the answer when I'd never been in danger. It was the scariest, hardest lesson I'd ever learned.

But now I understand—sometimes violence is the only answer.

When he wrapped his arms around me and squeezed, I yelped.

"Sorry," he said, pushing me away by my shoulders. "Give me a sec."

I stepped back and watched him strip off his belt. Once again, he handed it off to someone, I couldn't say who because I never took my eyes off AJ. The sirens wailed louder; the cops would be here any minute.

Then I'd have to give them my statement. *Tell them my father is a criminal.* Tears flooded my eyes.

When AJ opened his arms, I rushed back in and planted my face in his sweaty chest and inhaled.

My nose wrinkled involuntarily. He didn't smell like the same sweaty man I sat next to on his bed.

"Andrew, were you nervous?" He'd seemed so calm.

"Nervous? Nah," I felt his chest shake with a chuckle, "I was scared shitless."

I pulled back and looked into his dark eyes. He'd seemed so calm when he rushed into the bedroom. There were a million things I wanted to say, but a parade of flashing lights and wailing sirens made it impossible.

There was only one thing I wouldn't wait to say, "Thank you for saving me, Andrew."

Chapter 52

AJ

I kissed her forehead before pulling her close again. *The cops will hate us for the mess we created.* They'd be arresting anyone still alive, inventorying guns, and identifying dead bodies for hours. Per SSI standard operating procedure, we let John handle the lion's share of communication with the local LEOs. It was easier for everyone if we only had one point of contact, and his thirty years of experience in the Parker County Sherriff's Department made him the perfect point man.

The officers questioned Meg and Blake first, then everyone from SSI, including Jamie and Jay, who'd joined us.

I had a feeling Blake's vice-like grip on my hand as she answered questions was the only thing preventing her from breaking down. My suspicions were confirmed when she fell apart three seconds after the officer turned away. I caught her as her knees buckled.

"It'll be okay." I stroked her back as I held her head against my chest. "You're safe. It's over."

She didn't have the strength to walk, so I carried her back to the car to wait. Jack and Meg soon joined us.

Slowly but surely, so did the rest of the team.

It took hours, and we were all dead on our feet by the time John walked over with the Sergeant in charge and a detective.

The members of SSI stood to greet them.

"You're free to go. We'll be in touch if we have any more questions," the Sergeant said.

Thank God, we were all exhausted and starving.

"I suppose we should thank you for taking out half of the Roman syndicate, but..."

"But you're pissed you have to clean up our mess and deal with the paperwork," John filled in when the detective paused.

"Something like that." They shook John's hand and nodded to the rest of us before turning away.

"Let's go home." John didn't have to say it twice. I climbed into the back seat with Blake and pulled her onto my lap.

I heard Jack say, "He's a goner," before the door closed, and flipped him off through the window.

The car was quiet on the ride home until John broke the silence to let us know Mary, Emily, and Beth would have food waiting at the office.

Blake seemed surprised, but I wasn't. *She'll understand once she gets to know them.*

"Mary is the Mama Bear of SSI and won't be able to rest until we're all back, safe and sound," John offered. "Emily and Beth are a lot like her."

So is Meg. But Blake had already seen her in action.

The only sound for the rest of the ride was Blake's soft sniffles and my whispered words of comfort.

It'll take some time for her to process everything she's been through. And I'd be there every step of the way.

Mary met us at the back door, holding it open while we filed in. Her eyes sparkled as her lips curved up when she saw my arm around Blake. She patted me on the arm as I passed. "Let me know if there's anything I can do."

"Thank you."

Mary Sheppard was the type of mother I wished I'd had. The kind who would wreak havoc to protect her family and smile softly while tending their wounds. Strong and caring, she was a pro at giving tough love, and an expert at lending a sympathetic ear.

Blake needed someone like Mary in her life. *So do I.*

Beth and Emily fawned over Doug and Jamie, respectively, when they came in. Mary was checking on Jaden and Maxwell until John walked in and she saw the blood on his arm.

"John?" the concern in her voice was palpable as color drained from her face.

"It's only a graze." She must have looked doubtful, because he quickly added, "I swear. You can ask Meg."

Mary didn't bother verifying before hugging him. When she pulled back, she said, "I'm taking you to see Dr. Greenfield first thing in the morning."

Recognizing a losing argument when he heard one, John nodded.

After a few minutes, the chaos was replaced with a low steady hum of activity as the team hauled in our gear. Jack took care of mine so I could stay with Blake, who was curled up in my lap.

John released Dean, Sammie, and Eric, who'd been protecting the Sheppard women, but invited them to stay for food.

Blake stayed in my lap, quietly observing the entire time. Before long before she dozed off.

My poor girl was exhausted. When she woke up with a start, I calmed her back down. When she whispered she had to pee, I reluctantly let go, though I insisted on walking her to the bathroom.

It was then I noticed Ashley, and the wicked grin on her face.

As soon as Blake shut the door, Ashley said, "I never thought I'd see the day."

"Hey, Ashley." I looked back at the bathroom door.

"Cupid's arrow found you." She laughed. "Seriously, dude, I'm happy for you."

"Thanks. She's…" My words trailed off.

"She must be pretty damn special if she's taken you off the market," she said.

"She is." I felt Blake's presence before I heard her say, "Andrew?"

I reached back for Blake's hand.

Ashley's eyebrows shot up, but she held her tongue. Thank God, because, like me, Ashley's default sense of humor was sarcasm, and I didn't think it'd go over well.

Without guilt, I introduced them. "Blake, this is my friend Ashley. Ashley, this is Blake."

Blake eyed Ashley up and down before extending her hand. "Hi."

"Hi Blake. You're a very lucky woman," Ashley said. "I can't wait to get to know you better."

Blake visibly relaxed. "Thank you," she answered while squeezing my hand.

"Later Janerek. Blake, I hope to see you at one of our girls' nights," Ashley said before joining Emily and Jamie.

It warmed my heart, knowing they'd accepted Blake into the fold without hesitation.

A wave of panic washed over me. *What am I doing? What if I end up like my dad?*

Mary interrupted my thoughts before they spiraled, informing Blake and me it was our turn to get checked out.

"I'm fine, really, Mrs. Sheppard," Blake said.

"Humor me. I'll feel better when I've seen with my own two eyes that everyone is okay." Mary's request was a lot like one of John's, in that it wasn't.

"Best to comply. She won't take no for an answer." I nudged Blake towards the couch.

"That's right. This mother hen needs to know her chicks are uninjured."

I thanked God for the family I'd found at SSI. I wasn't one of Mary's cubs, but she never failed to include me in her mothering.

It didn't take long for Mary to confirm we weren't physically hurt, so she used her time with us to support Blake, telling me to add her number to Blake's phone, in case she needed anything.

"Thank you, Mrs. Sheppard."

"None of that, you're family now, call me Mary."

Tears filled Blake's eyes as she thanked Mary again. I blinked a few times and turned away to hide the evidence of my own emotions.

And looked right at John.

He smiled and lifted his head in acknowledgement. He was no stranger to the effect Mary had on people.

A few minutes after walking away and talking to Beth, Mary announced, "Food is upstairs in the conference room." She laughed as everyone stampeded up the stairs.

Blake didn't move, so neither did I.

"You should eat," I whispered. I didn't think she'd eaten anything today.

"I'm not sure I can," she said.

"Want me to bring something down so you can try?"

She glanced at the second floor landing. The noise from the room drifted towards us.

"Maybe in a few minutes."

I couldn't blame her; it'd be a madhouse until everyone settled down to eat.

We'd just stood up when Jack and Meg came down carrying two plates each.

"We thought we'd save you from the circus," Jack said as he handed me a heaping plate.

"I wasn't sure what you'd like, so I got you a little of everything," Meg said, handing a plate to Blake. Unlike mine, which was mostly meat and potatoes, hers had salad and vegetables too.

Gratitude filled my heart, as mashed potatoes and pot roast filled my stomach.

When Blake said my potatoes were better, I fell a little deeper in love.

Chapter 53

Blake

When Meg handed me a plate, my emotions got the better of me. I thanked her and sat back down, staring at the plate in my lap as tears blurred my vision before spilling down my cheeks.

It wasn't just Meg's generosity. It was everything. Mary's kindness. The stress of the day. AJ's gentleness. My father's guilt.

Losing my life as I knew it.

What am I going to do now?

AJ's hand on my back brought me back. "Sorry," I mumbled.

"No need to apologize. You've been through hell today," Jack said.

"We'll leave you alone," Meg said, standing up.

"No, it's okay." I wanted them to stay, hoping the company would keep my mind off my father while we ate.

I didn't think I was hungry until I took my first bite and realized I wasn't just hungry—I was ravenous.

We enjoyed our food in silence for a few minutes, too busy eating to talk.

When I finished my meat and started pushing the salad around, AJ offered me some of his. When I hesitated, he held his plate over mine and pushed more meat onto it.

"Thanks." I blushed.

"Anytime, I'm just glad you're not a vegetarian." AJ laughed.

"Me too." *It feels good to laugh.*

When the guys got up to throw our plates away, I took advantage of the time alone with Meg to apologize.

"You have nothing to apologize for. None of this is your fault," she replied.

"I know, but I still feel bad. Like I should've known what my father was doing." I still found it hard to believe he'd been corrupt under my nose.

"How could you have known?" Meg said.

"I don't know, but I feel like I missed so many signs." I sighed, the weight of everything pulling on my shoulders. "He's not the man I thought he was."

"I know it's hard to hear right now, but despite everything he's done, I truly believe he loves you."

Maybe he did, but that didn't erase the horrible things he'd done, or caused to be done. Thankfully, they hadn't hurt her or her baby. I wouldn't have been as lucky if SSI hadn't saved me.

"Let's go get some dessert," Meg said, hooking my arm through hers. "Beth said Chase insisted we needed ice cream, so Beth, Emily, and Ashley created a sundae bar."

Ashley was the woman I saw hugging AJ. Did they have a thing? "Who's Ashley with?"

"No one, at least that I know of. She's Emily's best friend."

"Her and AJ, did they?"

Meg's hesitation was answer enough.

"They did," I answered for her. How long were they together? How close were they? Would she steal him from me?

Steal him from me? I wasn't even sure he was mine, or I was his.

He acted like we were, but we hadn't talked about it yet.

And I wasn't sure I wanted someone claiming me like a Neanderthal.

Who am I kidding? That was the old, misinformed Blake talking. *I'd be happy if he called me his woman.*

If there was one thing I'd learned, the 'claiming' wasn't about possession or control, it was about pride and love. I saw it with Jack and Meg, Jamie and Emily, Doug and Beth, and to some degree, with John and Mary.

"You really should talk to AJ about it," Meg said.

Jack and AJ came back.

"We're getting ice cream sundaes," Meg announced. "Want to come with us?"

"Hell, yeah," Jack and AJ answered together before following us up the stairs.

I wasn't sure I was ready for the crowd in the conference room, but I wasn't ready to be alone yet, either.

Ice cream covered in chocolate and caramel with a mountain of whipped cream sounds like heaven.

The crowded conference room buzzed with comfortable friendship. The relaxed vibe was exactly what I needed. One end of the table was covered in large serving dishes with a few scraps of food left in each. I chuckled quietly at the small, still half-full salad container. I wasn't the only one who preferred meat.

Emily, Ashley, and Beth were at the other end of the table, organizing the ice cream bar.

"When did they have time to organize all this?" I asked, a hint of awe in my voice.

"I'm not sure, but Mary and Beth have a lot of contacts in Weatherford, and they aren't afraid to use them." AJ chuckled, leaving me to wonder what other marvels they could pull off on short notice.

Jack added, "One nice thing about living in a small town; when we ask for help, we get it in spades." He swept his arms wide.

"We were just going to call you up," Beth said. "Didn't want you missing out on dessert." She spread her arms over the colorful display in front of her.

"Thank you."

"Dig in." Beth announced to the group before stepping back.

"You first," Doug said. A round of "Ladies first" followed.

It was impossible not to see the love in the men's eyes when they looked at their wives.

I had it all wrong.

Everything these guys did was to honor the women they loved, not dominate them. They didn't want to control them; they wanted to support and protect them.

Not because they're weak, but because they're important.

I was still getting used to the idea that men could be strong, masculine, and protective without needing to diminish the women in their lives. *Why had I ever believed it?* I wasn't sure, but I no longer did.

Nothing could have prevented the smile that pulled at my lips when I turned to AJ and saw the same look in his eyes.

So different from the rich, powerful, controlling men in my father's political circle.

So different from the selfish, spoiled, petty boys I met at college.

I got in line to make myself a sundae, and enjoyed the distraction of the company and the sweet, creamy goodness.

Chapter 54

AJ

The guys cleaned the conference room after everyone finished eating, arguing it was the least we could do. Meg and Blake argued they hadn't helped set up, so they should help clean.

"Max is helping," Meg argued. Meg was always looking for ways to connect with Max, who kept a professional distance, and bring her into the family fold. So far, Max had declined offers to join the girls' monthly craft and booze night, which included Meg, Mary, Beth, Emily and her mom, Anne, and sometimes Ashley. And soon Blake, if she accepted their offer.

"Because I'm on the team," Maxwell said.

"You both had terrible days, go relax for a few minutes," Jack ordered.

Blake, following Meg's lead, kissed me and said thank you before leaving.

I stared as Blake walked out the door, fighting the urge to follow her.

She'll be safe downstairs. Sammie was still here, and the doors were locked, and the windows were bulletproof glass.

And we'd killed the men who'd threatened her.

What if there's more? We killed a lot of men, but not the head of the organization. Would he come for her?

"Janerek, you okay?" John disrupted my thoughts.

I nodded without taking my eyes off the door.

"She'll be okay," Jack clapped my shoulder.

Reluctantly, I turned and got to work. We functioned like a well-oiled machine and got the job done in record time.

As we finished up, John asked, "Have you told Blake she can't go home?"

"Not yet. I wanted to give her a breather before dumping more shit on her."

"If she isn't comfortable staying at your place, she's welcome to stay with us," Jack offered.

Doug laughed as I shot Jack a scathing look.

Which caused Jack to chuckle and add, "You both are."

"Will you be able to leave her alone anytime soon?" Doug asked.

"Could you?" My question was the answer. We were a lot alike, not just Doug and I, all of us.

"No. I hovered so much I drove Beth crazy after we found Chase."

"I was so damn scared of losing Emily that I slept outside her house for a week after the hospital released her," Jamie laughed as he said it.

"I watched so many rom-coms while Meg was healing; I swear I could write one," Jack admitted, causing us all to groan. Meg loved all things romance. Turns out, so did Emily, making Jack and Jamie grateful the two of them got along so well.

Jay rolled his eyes and made a whip cracking sound while mimicking the movement.

"Just you wait, Jay. Someday it'll happen to you," John said.

His 'fuck no' was so ice cold and filled with conviction I'd swear the temperature in the room dropped.

I wasn't the only one who felt it.

Someone had hurt Jay. Bad.

"I'm taking the trash out." Jay said, picking up the three bags and marching out of the room.

Maxwell stared at Jay as he walked out, her profiler gears spinning.

"Damn," Jamie said.

"Yeah," Jack agreed.

John didn't have to say anything; his sad expression was enough.

Even I hadn't had that level of anger or conviction when I swore off relationships.

Funny how one five-foot-two curvy blond with a whole lot of sass had changed everything for me. A stupid grin split my face. I needed to hold her like a fish needed water.

Now.

"I gotta go." Ignoring their laughter, I raced out of the room and down the stairs.

As soon as I got downstairs, I hugged Blake before asking her to follow me to my office.

I closed the door and sat in one of our guest chairs before pulling her into my lap.

Thinking it'd be easier to tell her she couldn't go home if she volunteered to stay with me first, I asked, "Blake, would you stay with me tonight?"

Asked? I practically begged. She couldn't go home, but that didn't mean she'd want to stay with me.

"I, um, I'm not sure. I should probably go home."

I was afraid she'd say that.

"Unfortunately, that's not an option. I'm sorry, but the police haven't released the house, so you can't go home yet."

Her shoulders curled in as she closed her eyes and inhaled a shaky breath.

Rubbing small circles on her back, I offered what little comfort I could. "It'll be over soon."

"Will it?" Doubt and disappointment vied for top billing in her expression.

"Not everything, but they'll be done with the house soon."

I didn't like the idea of her being anywhere but with me, but I had to let her make up her own mind. It felt like an eternity before she asked, "You're sure you don't mind?"

"Sure?" I laughed softly and brushed her bangs to the side. "Blake, I'd insist, and carry you home with me if I didn't think it'd piss you off."

She didn't quite laugh, but she smiled as she said okay.

Tension fell from my shoulders as relief washed over me.

If she'd chosen a friend's house or staying at her dorm, I would've gone crazy and pulled a play from Jamie's playbook—and camped outside her door.

We talked for a few minutes before a soft knock interrupted us.

"Come in," I called out, pulling Blake close when she tried to stand up. I should have released her, but my arms didn't get the message.

"Sorry to interrupt," Jack came in, carrying Blake's backpack. " I wanted to return these before you leave."

This time, I let her get up.

"Thank you." She immediately reached into her bag for her phone. When she turned it on, it chimed non-stop for what seemed like forever.

Jack asked quietly, "You good for tonight?"

Blake's shoulders sagged as messages continued to chime in.

"She's staying with me, but I don't think it'll be a good night," I answered. Blake looked even more defeated as she started scrolling through her messages.

"Let me know if you need anything. The rest of the team said to tell you the same."

"Thanks, man." We shook hands before hugging it out with a solid clap on each other's back.

After Jack left, I walked up behind Blake and wrapped my arms around her. "You don't have to read them tonight."

She turned in my arms. "Priscilla is blaming me because she's locked out of the house," she wept into my chest.

I pried her phone out of her shaking hands. "Why don't you wait until tomorrow to read the rest?" She'd had enough stress and trauma for one day.

I felt her nod into my chest. "Can we go home?" she asked.

Home. Hearing her refer to leaving with me as going home was music to my ears.

Chapter 55

Blake

I thanked everyone again as we said our goodbyes. Their support and generosity was in stark contrast to the blame and anger from Priscilla. She blamed me for the police kicking her out of the house, for their joint accounts being frozen, and for my father going to jail.

How is any of this my fault?

AJ seemed to understand I wasn't in the mood to talk. After asking if I needed to stop for anything, he turned on the radio to fill the silence.

My jaw dropped when he pulled in front of a small yellow house. *I would have guessed a small studio man cave.* The light over the door was enough for me to see landscaped flowerbeds on either side of the door.

AJ raced around the car to open my door and help me out. Usually I'd think it was too much, but I was so damned tired I could barely stand, let alone argue.

"Let's get you inside," he said, grabbing my bags.

"Your house is cute. So not what I was expecting."

"It's not really mine. I rent it," he said, "but thanks."

That made more sense. I couldn't imagine him spending a lot of time tending flowers. Cutting down trees, sure, but not pruning roses.

The inside was even cuter than the outside, with pale yellow striped wallpaper and dark wood built-in bookshelves. He'd adjusted the center shelves to hold his TV and gaming console.

"I'll give you the penny tour." He chuckled and put our bags down. "The two bedrooms are off to the right, but one is being turned into an office. The only bath is just around the corner. This is the living room, the dining room, and the kitchen is there." He pointed to corners in the open space. "Not that you can't see most of it from here." He grinned, making his dimples pop.

"Only one bed?" I asked, my voice hitching up an octave. *Really? That's what I want to worry about?*

"Yeah, but I'll sleep on the couch."

The couch in question was soft, black leather, with a recliner at one end. It looked comfortable, but it wasn't big enough for AJ's long body.

"Oh." I wasn't sure if I was more relieved, or less. We'd shared a bed last night, and it was the best sleep I'd had in a long time.

"Let's get you settled."

His apartment was cleaner than I'd imagined for a bachelor pad. The space was cluttered, like he didn't have time, or the space, to put everything away, but it wasn't dirty. An American flag decorated one wall, but there wasn't much else.

"Sorry, it's a bit messy. I don't usually have people over."

"It's okay," I said, my cheeks heating from embarrassment. Who was I to judge? The dorm room I shared with Paige always looked like a hurricane had blown through it.

AJ carried my bags to his bedroom and set them down. "I'll get clean sheets and make the bed."

"Thanks." His room had closets along one wall, a king-size bed, and one bedside table. *He sleeps on the right side of the bed.* Was it weird for him to be on the left side when he slept with me at the safe house?

While he went to get sheets, I pulled out my phone and looked through my messages. I skipped the ones from Priscilla, knowing they contained nothing but anger and hatred.

I also ignored the messages from curious acquaintances. *They can wait.*

Paige had sent non-stop messages asking if I was okay. Her messages grew more desperate the longer I didn't answer. At some point, she'd reached out to my father.

He must have lied, because her tone changed from worried to hurt.

Does she know the truth yet? I was sure it had to be all over the news by now. *I'll call tomorrow and apologize.*

Danny sent a bunch of texts too, but unlike Paige, he wasn't concerned when I didn't reply. He took it as a personal insult that I was 'ignoring' him.

"Blake?" AJ said, rushing to my side, one hand going around my back and the other wiping away the tears I hadn't felt. "Want to talk about it?"

Putting my phone down, I shook my head back and forth. Needing comfort, I curled into him and gave up the fight. Fear, anger, and sadness flooded my system—each taking its turn at the top of the list. All making me sob uncontrollably.

AJ soothed me with soft sounds and gentle touches until I finally stopped crying. His kiss on the top of my head was a gentle reminder of how much he loved me.

"I shouldn't have read my texts," I admitted. "You remember Danny?"

"I do," he sounded like he wanted to say more, but didn't.

"He's mad at me for not answering his texts and emails after the situation."

"Mad? Not worried?" His voice was borderline growling.

I nodded.

"He's a selfish ass, Blake," he said. "Don't let him get to you."

"It's not just him." I sniffled. "It's, it's everything." Another sob broke free. I wiped away my tears as we sat in silence.

"Want me to draw you a bath?"

A bath sounded amazing. I nodded and whispered, "Thank you."

He stood up, bent down, and kissed my forehead. "I'll be right back."

I grabbed some clean clothes from the suitcase I was still borrowing and walked to the bathroom.

AJ tested the water as it filled the tub, creating a mountain of bubbles.

"You have bubble bath?" Disbelief filled my voice.

"No, sorry, I had to use shampoo." He laughed.

I laughed with him. It was hard to reconcile the man I'd seen shoot someone earlier today with the man apologizing for using shampoo to give me bubbles for my bath.

"Andrew." I waited until he turned back towards me. "Thank you."

"You're welcome. Let me know if the temperature is too hot. I take scalding showers, so it's hard for me to judge."

I leaned over and put my hand in the running water and immediately jerked it back.

AJ took my hand and kissed my fingers. "Sorry, I'll adjust it."

Once the tub was full, AJ apologized for not having any candles, and asked if I needed anything before leaving me to relax.

I wasn't prepared for AJ's scent to envelop me as I eased myself into the bubbles. A quick glance at the shampoo bottle explained why—his shampoo was also his body wash.

Tension left my body as I sank under the bubbles, letting AJ's warm leather scent surround me like a warm hug.

A knock at the door made me yelp and sit up too quickly, splashing water everywhere.

"Are you okay?" AJ asked through the door. His voice cut through the fog in my mind.

"Yeah, I must have dozed off," I called through the door, wondering how long I'd been asleep in the tub. "You startled me when you knocked." Long enough for the bubbles to pop and the water to cool off.

"Sorry about that."

"It's okay. I'll be right out."

After drying off and getting dressed in cute PJ shorts and a matching tank, I joined AJ in the kitchen. The first thing he did was hand me a glass of water and two aspirin.

"Thank you." I drained half the glass. "Sorry, I keep freaking out on you."

"Blake, please don't apologize. You've been through hell. I'd be worried if you weren't 'freaking out', your words not mine, a little bit."

His words brought more tears to my eyes. *God, I'm a wreck.*

"Come on, let's get you to bed," he said, standing up and extending his hand. "Let me know if you want more blankets."

He'd put at least two on the bed with an extra one folded at the foot, so I didn't think I would unless he turned the air conditioner on.

"I'll be on the couch if you need me."

Not wanting to be alone, I looked at the bed and fidgeted.

"I'd be happy to stay with you until you fall asleep, or longer. If you want."

I wanted to be strong and independent.

I needed AJ's strong arms around me, helping me feel safe.

I nodded, then gathered my courage and said the words out loud. "I'd like for you to stay." Looking at the floor, I admitted. "Longer."

I'm no less strong or independent for wanting comfort.

AJ stepped close and lifted my chin, forcing me to tilt my head so I could look in his eyes, before saying, "It'd be my pleasure."

His rough voice sent shivers down my spine.

He helped me get in bed before promising to come right back.

I fidgeted with the blanket while I waited, a thousand and one thoughts floating through my mind.

My entire life had been turned upside down, and I had no idea what tomorrow would bring, but tonight I wanted to pretend nothing had happened.

The bed dipping startled me. I must have fallen asleep.

AJ sat on the edge of the bed and put his gun in the nightstand. I waited for the anticipated fear, but it didn't come.

When he tucked his feet under the blanket and stretched out on his back beside me, I curled up next to him.

I thought it'd be impossible to fall asleep, but the combination of AJ's steady heartbeat, his hand caressing my arm, and his warm body smelling like he'd just stepped out of the shower, I was lulled to sleep in no time.

Chapter 56

AJ

I woke up in a cold sweat; the image of Crowley holding a gun to Blake's head lingering.

My heart pounded, and my mind raged.

"Andrew?" Blake asked, her voice thick with sleep.

She snuggled up close and nuzzled her head into my chest, soothing my fear and calming my anger.

She's safe.

I pulled her closer and kissed the top of her head.

"Are you okay?" she asked.

Rather than lie, I avoided the question. "Sorry I woke you."

She pushed off my chest and propped herself up on an elbow, before turning my face towards her.

"Your heart is racing." I heard the repeated question in her statement.

"Just a bad dream." An understatement if ever there was one.

As my eyes adjusted to the dim light in the room, I saw the concern in hers.

I brushed her cheek with the back of my hand. "I thought I was going to lose you," I whispered. Unaccustomed to sharing my fears or showing my vulnerable side, I kept it simple.

"But you didn't. You saved me." She leaned down and brushed her lips across mine.

"Blake." I said her name as if it held the answer to my heart's desire.

"Andrew, I love you." It was the first time she'd said the words I'd longed for but didn't deserve. The vulnerability in her beautiful blue eyes was more than I could stand.

I wanted her more than I wanted my next breath, but how could I be with her? The rage I'd felt tearing through that house was something she should never have to witness. But she had. She had to watch me shoot someone without hesitation. Without remorse.

I'd kill a thousand men to protect her—but who'll protect her from me?

"Andrew?"

"Blake, you have no idea how much I love you." I looked at the ceiling while gathering my strength, hating the part of me that made my next words necessary. "But I'm not right for you. I want you more than life itself, but I can't risk being the one who hurts you."

"You think you're like your father?" Doubt filled her voice.

I nodded. "Yes."

"Are you a drunk?" she asked.

"No."

"Have you ever hit a woman?" Her voice was stronger.

"No."

"A child?"

My eyes rounded. "No, never."

"Then you're not like him," she stated, sounding like she was making a closing argument in front of a jury.

"How can you be so sure?" I wanted to believe her, but she couldn't see the anger that often burned just below the surface.

"I trust you." Those three words were the most precious gift she could give me, but I didn't deserve them.

I forced the next words around the lump in my throat. "But you shouldn't."

I could tell from the look in her eyes, she wasn't convinced.

She crawled out of bed, stood up, and crossed her arms. "Damn it, Andrew, you don't get to decide for me."

I sat up and faced her, planting my bare feet on the floor.

"You watched me kill a man." There was no way she could dismiss what she'd seen.

I saw determination flash in her eyes before she let loose. "Do you go around shooting random people? Do you yell at old ladies who drive too slow? Do you steal candy from babies?" She yelled the questions as she paced in front of me.

"What? No. I..."

"No," she said softly, putting her hands on my knees and leaning in close. "You did what you had to do to save me."

It was true; everything I did was to save her.

"AJ, you've been violent when you needed to be, but you aren't a violent man. You've been nothing but kind and gentle with me." She laughed. "You drew me a bubble bath and apologized for having to use shampoo to make it happen. Would your father have ever done something like that?"

I cupped her face. 'I love you so much it hurts."

"I love you, too," she said, her eyes never leaving mine. "Now, will you please shut up and kiss me?"

I answered by pressing my lips to hers.

The kiss started soft; but when she sighed and parted her lips, I claimed her mouth.

Something in Blake broke free. Her kisses turning desperate, needy, demanding as she straddled my lap.

The kiss burned her name on every cell in my body, staking her claim.

I'll never be the same. And that was probably a good thing.

I rolled her onto her back.

"Andrew, make love to me."

"Are you sure?" Why did I ask?

Because I'm not my father. And I needed to be sure.

"More than sure. Please?" she begged, her hands sliding down my back and slipping under my t-shirt.

Wanting more of her hands on my skin, I leaned up and pulled off the offending shirt. I tossed it across the room before leaning down to kiss her. Her moan just about did me in.

My hands were on either side of her, dying to touch her. I planned to take my time, making sure she felt how much I loved her in every touch. I kissed her forehead, the tip of her cute nose, and her soft lips before trailing kisses down her neck.

Supporting my weight on one elbow, I trailed the back of my hand down her side, barely touching her full breast. Seeing her arch into my touch while a moan escaped her lips was more than I could stand.

"This has to go," I said, my voice raspy as I tugged at her tank top.

I poured every ounce of my heart and soul into making love to Blake.

Every kiss was a promised to love, cherish, and protect her until my dying day.

Later that morning, I woke with the sun, feeling lighter and happier than I had in, well, forever. And it was all because of the sassy blond curled up next to me, with her head resting on my chest.

She looked peaceful. Happy.

My chest puffed with pride. *I put that smile there.*

Not wanting to disturb her, I eased out of her grasp and off the bed. Immediately missing her touch, I regretted my choice.

I slipped on a pair of grey sweatpants and headed to the bathroom.

After cleaning up, I went to the kitchen to brew coffee. Today would be a long day for Blake, dealing with the aftermath of everything that had happened. But I'd be at her side, helping her every step of the way, if she'd let me.

We'll need a good breakfast. I didn't cook fancy meals like Doug, but I made a killer omelet.

I chopped up tomatoes and peppers and whisked the eggs while the bacon fried. Before long, the smell of coffee and bacon made my stomach rumble.

I was on my second cup of coffee when I heard Blake in the hallway.

My body reacted to seeing her in my t-shirt, making me contemplate postponing breakfast.

"Good morning, Beautiful." It didn't matter that she was rubbing sleep from her eyes and yawning.

"Morning," she said. Her expression relaxing as she closed the distance. "It smells good in here." She stopped in front of me, suddenly shy.

"Thanks. Want a coffee, or a hug?"

"Both, but the hug first."

Ignoring the sizzling bacon, I held Blake until she was ready to let go.

Chapter 57

Blake

"When do you think I can go to the house?" I asked.

"I'm not sure. I'll call and get an update."

"Thank you." I finished my coffee but before I could get up to refill it, AJ turned towards the counter and reached for the carafe.

"Here you go," he said, grinning at me. "What?"

"Must be nice to have such long arms." Arms I was currently staring at and maybe even drooling over. We hadn't talked about last night, though I figured we probably should.

That and a million other things.

"A perk of being tall," he laughed, "though I'm not that tall for a guy."

"You're tall compared to me," I said with a smile. *Not like it's much of a challenge.*

He raised an eyebrow. "Everyone is tall compared to you."

"Not everyone," I feigned offense.

I added a spoonful of sugar and a generous pour of half and half to my coffee.

AJ watched me, but I could tell he wasn't concerned about my coffee drinking habits.

"How are you holding up?" He reached across the table with those impossibly long arms and put his hand over mine.

"I'm not sure." After thinking about it, I said, "I'm mostly putting off thinking about it."

AJ wove his fingers with mine. "It'll take time, but it'll be okay. I'll be here every step of the way, if you want me to be."

I wasn't sure how to answer. Would he be here on a professional or personal level, or maybe some combination of both?

He brushed his thumb over the back of my hand, causing me to look up.

"If you want, we can put everything off until tomorrow and spend all day in bed."

His grin, and those damn dimples, did wicked things to my insides. I felt myself blush as memories of the night we'd shared flashed through my mind. AJ was the most generous lover I'd ever had; his gentle touch, demanding kisses, and powerful... I cut off the thought, because now my cheeks weren't the only part of my body that was over-heating.

I laughed to cover my embarrassment. "As tempting as that sounds, I can't. I have too much to do."

AJ couldn't have known what I was thinking, but he was probably in the ballpark. He shook his head and chuckled before saying, "Your choice. Let's list the things you have to do and make a game plan."

I listed the things that immediately came to mind: talking to the family attorney, my attorney, picking up some stuff from the house, and finding a place to stay.

I groaned. "Midterms start today." I needed to call my professors ASAP to ask if I could make up the work and exams I'd missed. Otherwise, I'd have to withdraw and retake my classes in the fall. Panic set in again. If I didn't graduate in May, I'd lose my internship.

"I'm sure they'll understand and work something out with you," he offered.

"Do you think I can check on my father?" I assumed he was still in jail. The judge wouldn't be around to set bail until nine, and it was barely past seven.

Crap, AJ would need to leave soon. "What time do you have to leave for work?" I couldn't hide the anxiety in my shaky voice.

"I don't. John gave me the day off, so I'm all yours," he said. "I'll call the county jail and ask how your father is doing. Do you want to see him, if I can arrange it?"

I stared at my coffee, hoping it'd give me the answer. I wanted to make sure he was okay, but the pain of his betrayal was still too strong for me to want to talk to him.

Am I a bad daughter for not wanting to see him?

"You don't need to do anything you don't want to do. That includes deciding right now."

His ability to see to me so clearly still caught me off guard. "Okay. Thanks. I think I'll wait to see him." He deserved so much more than my clumsy words, but I was struggling to hold myself together.

"Let's tackle the things you can do from here first," AJ ignored my awkwardness. "Email your professors and ask if they'll meet with you."

His suggestion was perfect; it allowed me to tackle my list without having to deal with the heavier problems first.

I emailed my professors. The family lawyer wouldn't be in his office until nine, so I called and left a voice mail. Then I did the same for my attorney. Knowing I'd need help navigating the legal mess my father left, I wanted to talk to them right away. While I did that, AJ called John. Unlike my attorneys, John was already in his office and working.

"Will do. Thanks, John," AJ said before disconnecting the call and sitting back down. "John called the Sherriff's office. He doesn't think the judge will grant bail."

"They think he's a flight risk?" I asked, already knowing the answer.

"I'm sorry."

"It's okay. I expected as much," I answered, sounding calmer than I felt. "What about the house?"

"The FBI and police should finish today or tomorrow at the latest." He hesitated before continuing, "I should warn you; they ransacked the place looking for evidence."

My life is a fucking nightmare right now. "Even my room?" My voice squeaked.

"I'm sorry." He didn't offer more than that. He didn't need to.

"It's not like I want to stay there." Priscilla would be unbearable. "And I don't need to. I can stay in my dorm-"

AJ's low growl interrupted me.

"What? It's not like I can stay here." I didn't think AJ would want me intruding on his space for more than a night or two. *Do I want to stay if he asks?* I did.

"Why the hell not?" He asked, sounding mad, but looking hurt.

I scanned his face, looking for clues before asking, "You want me to stay?"

"Of course I do." His tone had the quality of a kid rolling his eyes while saying, well duh. "I'm sorry. I thought it was obvious." He reached for my hands. "Let me be perfectly clear. I want you to stay here with me." He smiled, adding, "Please."

I smiled back. *I should invite him to my birthday party.*

"Shit." I said, tearing my hands away.

AJ was on his feet and circling the table in a flash. "What's wrong?"

"I just remembered my birthday party." I fought back tears as anxiety washed over me. Now that I remembered, a thousand and one new things I needed to add to my list flashed through my mind.

AJ squatted beside me and turned me so I was facing him. "It's okay. I got you. Breathe in, nice and slow. And out."

I felt stupid for panicking, but my emotional reserves were depleted.

He waited until my breathing returned to normal, then hugged me. "Okay, first things first; when is the party?"

My twenty-fifth birthday party was Friday night at the Sussex Country Club. The guest list was a who's who of Dallas politicians and its wealthiest players, and a few of my friends. I'd have to cancel the reservation, the caterers, the musicians, and contact all the guests.

"Did your father hire a party planner?" AJ asked.

I blinked up at him. In my panic, I'd completely forgotten.

"He did." Tension drained from my shoulders; I only had to make one call. Scratch that, send one email. *I want to talk to as few people as possible today.*

In four days, I'd have access to my trust fund, making me a millionaire. I'd never hurt for money, but it still felt weird knowing I'd be rich in my own right.

Chapter 58

Blake

AJ insisted on driving me to campus so I could meet with the two professors who'd agreed to see me. After the meetings, I'd pack up my dorm room. I emailed Paige, so she wouldn't be surprised or think something was wrong, and asked if we could meet for coffee.

She said she'd meet me in our room as soon as her exam was over, then apologized for being a crappy friend.

As we parked, I asked, "Will it be okay if Paige and I go out for coffee?" Then got annoyed at myself for asking.

AJ chuckled. "Of course. Want me to stick close or give you space?"

I didn't want to admit how shaken up I still felt, so I said, "There's no reason you can't get a coffee and wait inside."

"Done." He flashed his killer dimples in my direction before getting out of the truck.

The professors I met with agreed to let me make up the work I'd missed, including the midterms. Hopefully, the other two would give me extensions to turn in my papers.

At my dorm, AJ insisted on lugging the empty boxes up to my room. We were almost done packing when Paige came in, stopping short and gasping when she saw AJ.

"Hi, Paige," he said before turning to me. "I'll be in the hall if you need me." He slipped out, closing the door behind him.

I closed the distance and hugged Paige. I hadn't realized just how much I missed her until I saw her again.

"I didn't think you still needed a bodyguard." It sounded more like a question than a statement.

"I don't. He's here as my…" *Is he my boyfriend?* I mean, I slept with him and he'd told me he loved me, and I'd be staying with him, but we hadn't actually talked about it. About 'us'.

"You slept with him!" she screeched.

I put my hand over her mouth. Was I that obvious? I felt the heat rise in my cheeks as I studied the box on the floor near my feet. I wasn't prone to discussing my sex life, but Paige was more open than me.

She turned towards the door as if she could see him through it.

I whispered, "I did." I wouldn't share more than that.

She turned back to me, a gleam in her eyes. "He might be a big dumb ogre." She used my words. "But he's hot. Was it good?"

My cheeks felt like they might spontaneously combust. I wouldn't answer her question, so I defended him instead.

"He's not dumb." It was my turn to look at him through the closed door. I paused and thought about everything he'd done over the last few days. "He's actually really sweet."

Knowing I wouldn't kiss and tell, she stopped teasing me and asked, "How are you holding up, really?"

I plopped on my bed and sighed. That was the million dollar question. "I'm not really sure. I'm pissed at my dad, and scared more people will come after me. And I'm freaking out about school." I sighed. "Everything's a fucking mess right now."

Paige sat and put her arm around me. "I'm sorry, Bee." She used the nickname she'd given me at the start of freshman year, but stopped using because Danny didn't like it. "I haven't been a great friend, but that changes now. Whatever you need, okay?"

"Thanks." I hugged her, happy my best friend was back. She sounded more like the Paige she was before Danny worked his way into our group.

When I asked about him, Paige told me they'd parted ways. "I'm sorry. I know he's your friend, but I couldn't take it anymore. No one should have to walk on eggshells to hang out with a friend."

"Seriously, I only put up with him because I thought you liked him."

We had a good laugh and agreed we didn't need Danny in our life anymore.

"Let's call in tall, dark, and handsome, and get you packed up." She looked around. "Are you moving back home?"

"No, I, uh, I'm staying with Andrew."

"Good for you." She hugged me again. "You know, Bee, despite everything, you look happy."

I felt happy. Because of AJ. Andrew, no middle name, Janerek. The big, dumb ogre who'd snuck in and stolen my heart.

Paige opened the door and ushered AJ back in. He gave Paige a nod before turning all his attention to me, his muscles relaxing as he scanned my face.

"I'm bummed you're stealing my roommate," Paige said to AJ. She put her hands on her hips. "You better be good to her."

I appreciated her effort on my behalf, but it was comical watching her try to intimidate AJ.

"I promise." He smiled, unfazed by her scrutiny.

"Good," Paige said with a quick nod.

AJ laughed. "You want to finish up here or head out for your coffee date?"

We packed up the rest of my stuff in no time. As we finished taping the last boxes, Jack and Doug showed up.

Oh God, what happened?

"Heard you could use some help," Jack said, putting my nerves at ease. Thank God they weren't here because something happened and I needed more protection.

After introductions, the guys insisted on carrying all the boxes—taking turns, so one of them was always with us. They didn't say it outright, but I had a feeling it was by design.

I didn't want to admit it, but I was grateful. My nerves were still frayed, making me jumpy.

"Maybe it's not so bad letting big macho guys do the heavy lifting once in a while," Paige joked. "It certainly helps that they're easy on the eyes."

I laughed.

As AJ walked us to the parking lot, he warned me they'd loaded everything into Jack and Doug's trucks. "They'll bring everything to my place while you and Paige have coffee."

Really? I'd never trusted a friend I enough to give them keys to my house.

He leaned down and whispered, "It's okay. I trust them."

Stupid face, showing all my emotions.

AJ insisted on paying for our order, then left us alone after directing us to a table. Understanding why, I didn't hesitate to follow his directions.

After we settled, Paige asked, "Do you think it'll be an issue for him, you being rich?"

"I don't know." I didn't think so, but it was yet another thing we needed to talk about. One more thing I needed to add to my to do list.

"Will you finish school?" she asked.

"Yes." I explained the situation. "And hopefully I don't have to retake the semester." The last thing I wanted was to lose my internship because I didn't graduate on time.

"I'm sure they'll let you," Paige offered. "Do you think he'll be okay with you working?" She tilted her head in AJ's direction.

I'd had the same thought myself, but it was stupid; the wives of the other guys at SSI all worked.

"Yeah. I think he'll support me no matter what I want to do." The truth of the statement rocked me to my core. He'd support me in a way even my father wouldn't have. A million ogres couldn't have held back my smile when I looked over and caught him staring.

His return smile made his dark eyes shine and dimples pop. Suddenly, coffee wasn't what I wanted anymore.

"Girl, you got it bad," Paige joked.

I turned back, blushing. I did, because AJ had been patient, caring, protective, and loving. And somewhere along the way, I'd fallen madly in love with him.

After dropping Paige off, AJ told me John had assigned someone to watch the house until the police released it. Apparently, Priscilla had tried sneaking past the police tape. Dallas PD had sent her away, but they didn't have the manpower to watch the house.

I wanted to be mad they'd called John instead of me, but in reality I was happy I didn't have to worry about it. *Though I should be mad he'd added services without my permission.* I doubted he did it to take advantage of me, but still.

Maybe he talked to AJ, and he volunteered to pay for it.

"What's wrong?"

I wasn't sure how to ask it, so I chose the direct route. "Are you paying for the person watching the house? I'm only asking because John didn't clear it with me, and I doubt he called my father."

He laughed. "No, though I offered when I talked to him. He brushed me off, which is John speak for he's not charging you."

Not charging me? "But, why?"

"You'll have to ask when we see him." His grin suggested he knew.

That made no sense. Before I could worry about it anymore, I got a call from my attorney.

"I have to take this," I said as I hit the answer button.

I felt AJ's eyes on me as I listened to my lawyer. She told me my father had given me full Power of Attorney, to act in his place should anything happen.

Like being incarcerated?

I don't remember signing the POA paperwork. I groaned, thinking he'd expect me to handle his accounts.

"Thank you." I stared at my phone after I hung up, shocked by the responsibility dropped on my shoulders without warning. Responsibility I didn't want.

"Everything okay?" AJ asked as he reached for my hand.

"My father named me as his primary beneficiary and gave me full Power of Attorney."

"Is that bad?"

"Yes. No. I don't know. It's just... a lot and unexpected."

"He didn't tell you?" he asked. "Don't you have to consent to being a POA?"

"You do. He must've slipped it in with other legal documents, and I signed them without realizing it." I'd been so trusting. So naïve.

How could I have been so blind? God only knew what else he'd had me sign. What if I'd signed something linking me to his crimes?

Tears pooled in my eyes and threatened to spill over.

"Blake." AJ's voice cut through the thoughts. "None of this is your fault." It was like he could read my mind.

"I trusted him."

"And he violated that trust, but that's not on you." He squeezed my hand before bringing it to his lips and kissing it. "Tell me what I can do to help."

Tell me it'll all be okay. Trust that I'm innocent, if I get accused of being a criminal.

"What aren't you telling me?" he asked.

I looked him in the eye, wanting to trust him, but I'd trusted my father. *And look where that got me.*

No. I trusted AJ. The feeling wasn't an opinion, it resonated in my soul.

"Blake, I can tell something's eating at you. Talk to me. Please."

"I'm worried about what else my father had me sign without telling me. What if I'm linked to his criminal activity?" The tears I'd been holding back spilled over.

"Do you think he would have done that?" he asked, still holding my hand.

"I don't know." And that was what freaked me out the most; I didn't feel like I knew the man I'd called Dad my whole life.

"I'll talk to John and see what he can find out. Chances are they won't tell him anything, but he can try."

"Thank you." I wiped the wayward tears off my cheek and prayed there weren't any documents linking me to my father's crimes.

And hopefully, I wouldn't get any more surprises when I met with my attorney.

"What else can I do to help?"

I sighed. "I'm not sure. I'm meeting Jocelyn at eleven tomorrow to go over the paperwork," I said. "She has a few calls to make, one of them to the family attorney, then she'll organize the paperwork for me."

"You have your own attorney?"

I could see why that might seem weird to him.

"It was a stipulation in my grandfather's will." *Now I understand why.* "Jocelyn was his attorney. It made sense for me to hire her, given her experience with his estate." And I liked her.

"That makes sense, especially since your grandfather thought your father might be in financial or legal trouble."

"Yeah." There wasn't much else I could say. Turns out Grandpa saw a lot more than I had.

Believing Priscilla would take anything of value not nailed down, I was glad the police hadn't released the house yet. I didn't have the energy to fight with her over the few sentimental items I wanted from the house.

When AJ's phone rang, he answered it on Bluetooth.

"Janerek, you're on speaker."

It was so weird hearing him announce it.

Instead of addressing AJ, John said, "Hi, Blake. How are you holding up?"

"I'm doing okay. Thanks."

"You're welcome. Janerek?"

"Yes?" AJ's asked.

"I don't want to see you in the office for the rest of the week. Unless you're accompanying Ms. Davenport."

The call disconnected as soon as AJ answered, "Yes, sir."

"Are you in trouble?"

He answered with a huge, dimple-popping grin. "No. I have a ton of accrued vacation time. This is John's way of telling me to use it."

"Oh." I'd been reluctant to ask AJ to take time off to help me. Now I didn't have to.

"You're stuck with me for the rest of the week, so you might as well take advantage of me." His eyes sparkled with innuendo and mischief.

Thinking of all the different ways I could take advantage of AJ during the week made my cheeks to glow red.

I returned his grin. "I think I can do that."

Chapter 59

AJ

The next morning, Blake insisted on making breakfast. The sight of her, in one of my t-shirts and not much else, cooking in my kitchen, made my head spin, my heart flutter, and other parts of my anatomy stand at attention.

Unable to resist the temptation to make her scream my name again, meant we were extra hungry for the bacon and eggs we had to reheat in the microwave.

Neither of us minded.

While we ate, John called to tell me the PD had released the house. Blake could go home.

"I'll see if Jocelyn can meet me there instead of the office."

Jocelyn agreed, so I drove Blake to her father's house.

Before parking, I pulled alongside Dean's car. "We're expecting Blake's attorney, Jocelyn…" I turned to Blake and raised an eyebrow.

"Robbins."

"Robbins at eleven. Call me when she gets here?"

"Will do," Dean answered.

"Thanks, man."

Blake looked shell-shocked as she walked from room to room. It looked like a hurricane had ripped through half the house. Her father's office and the library fared the worst, but the FBI left no room untouched. They'd searched anywhere they thought secrets could be hidden—which was everywhere.

I offered my quiet support, knowing there wasn't much else I could do.

"I'm afraid to go upstairs." Her bottom lip trembled.

This was her family home, one she believed was filled with love, honesty and support. The ransacked mess served as a brutal reminder of the lies and deception lurking below the surface.

I pulled her close and whispered, "You don't have to do this."

"I want to know how bad it is." She pulled away and took my hand before heading for the sweeping staircase.

Under different circumstances, I would've been in awe of the grandeur of her home. I'd only seen houses this big, this majestic, in the movies or on TV, but my concern for Blake made it impossible to enjoy.

They'd searched all eight bedrooms, but weren't nearly as disruptive as they were in the common rooms downstairs. *Except her father's bedroom.* It was still too much for Blake; she walked through her room in a daze before collapsing on her bed. A bed I assumed was made, but was now a tangled mess.

She picked up a big white teddy bear and hugged it to her chest. "I feel so violated."

I sat next to her and rubbed her back. "I'm sorry."

Her only response was a nod as she continued to look around with wide, sad eyes.

Blake's bedroom was bigger than my entire living space, and she had her own bathroom suite. *Her walk-in closet is probably bigger than my bedroom.* She'd decorated the room in pale earth tones with feminine, soft pink accents. Being in her room, which had clearly been her sanctuary here at home, felt intimate.

I helped Blake pack her clothes and personal items while we waited for Jocelyn. After introductions, I lugged Blake's stuff to my truck, and then kept Dean company while I waited for the meeting to end.

She looks exhausted. Even from here, I could see the toll the meeting had taken on her.

Jocelyn extended her hand when I met them at the bottom of the porch steps. "It was nice meeting you, AJ."

She has a firm grip. "Likewise."

I put my arm around Blake and walked her back in side. "You okay?"

"Not really. I just want this mess to be over with."

I couldn't make it be over any faster, but I could help her move her stuff. "What else do you want to take?"

"I'm taking the things my father listed as mine in his will. It's not much, and a few pieces of art that belonged to my mom. They don't have a lot of resale value, but they mean a lot to me."

Sadness hung like a cloud over her head as Blake led me through the house, trailing her fingers along furniture as she pointed out the items she wanted to take today. Occasionally she'd stop, her eyes glossing over as items brought back memories.

"I've lived here my whole life…"

Having few good memories of my childhood, and bolting from my home as soon as I could, I couldn't empathize. But I could sympathize.

Chapter 60

Blake

We padded and packed all the sentimental art, and anything of value from my room. Dean offered to let us pack his truck too, so I took everything except the furniture.

She's welcome to it.

After unloading everything into AJ's office. We offered to feed Dean. When he declined, so he could have dinner with his family, we decided to go out for pizza. Before we got to AJ's favorite pizza place, he got a call from Jack.

"You're on speaker," he said instead of answering like a normal person.

"Hey Blake," Jack said. "How're you holding up?"

Seriously? *Is 'your on speaker' code for Blake is in the car?*

"Hi Jack, I'm okay, thanks."

"How would you two feel about coming over and hanging out at Jamie's?"

When AJ looked at me, I interpreted his look to mean he was okay with it if I was. A night out sounded like a good way to take my mind off the stress of the day, so I agreed. "Can we bring anything?"

"We're ordering pizza, and have plenty of beer and wine, so I think we're good." I could hear some noise in the background. "The girls said you can bring a veggie tray so they can lie to themselves about eating healthy," he said around a laugh.

I laughed with him. "I think we can do that."

"What's your ETA?"

AJ looked at the clock. "Give us an hour; we want to change first." Then he added, "Make it one and half, since we have to stop at the store."

"Emily wants me to warn you, Flirty will be here."

"That shouldn't be a problem," AJ answered.

"Good to know."

"Later." AJ disconnected the call.

I didn't want to be that girl, but I couldn't help it. "Who's Flirty?" And why was Jack hiding her identity?

"Flirty is Ashley's call sign." He didn't sound guilty or ashamed.

"Why did Jack think he needed to warn you Ashley would be there?"

"I'm not sure. You already know Ashley and I were friends with benefits, so there's nothing to hide." He reached over and grabbed my hand. "You met her at SSI, remember?"

"Vaguely." That night had been a tornado of emotions and exhaustion. I remember her being polite, but I was so out of it,

I wouldn't have noticed if she was scowling at me the whole time.

"Hey," he squeezed my hand, "there's nothing to worry about." AJ addressed my unspoken fear. It was unnerving how easily he read my facial expressions. Better than anyone else I'd ever known.

Two hours later, we parked outside Jamie's house. We were late because AJ had carried me to the bedroom and showed me just how much he loved me.

Heat crept up my neck at the memory. *They'll know.*

AJ carried the veggie tray with one hand and held my hand with his other. He let go just long enough to knock, but before he connected, the door opened.

Jaden opened the door wide and said, "It's about time. I'm starving, but Meg and Emily said we had to wait for you to eat."

I looked down, worried I'd upset them because we were late.

"Don't be a dick," AJ said as he put his hand on the small of my back and urged me into the house.

"Sorry, Dude, but I'm starving." Jaden closed the door behind us. He sounded more cheerful when he said, "Hi, Blake."

"Hi, Jaden," I replied.

"You can call me Jay; everyone else does." He smiled. "You guys want a beer or wine?"

"That's more like it. I'll have a beer. Blake?" AJ asked.

"Wine sounds good, thanks." If I wasn't worried about embarrassing myself, I'd ask for the bottle. It'd been that kind of week.

We crossed the open space to the kitchen, where AJ handed off the tray to Jack before hugging Meg and Emily.

I wasn't expecting the surge of jealousy as I watched Ashley hug him. *Does she still want him?* What if he realized Ashley was more his type? She was thin, beautiful, and full of life.

And her father probably isn't in jail.

"Ashley, you remember my girlfriend, Blake?" he asked.

Girlfriend. It was silly, but hearing him introduce me that way for the first time made me giddy. I blushed as a huge smile spread across my face.

"Of course. Hi Blake, it's good to see you." Ashley stepped forward and opened her arms, then hesitated. "Sorry, I should ask. Are you a hugger?" Her friendly smile was infectious.

"I am." Ashley was the first person to hug me, but not the last.

The guys hugged me, too. I finally had all the J names down after getting to know them. Jamie was the oldest, and the shortest, and had compassionate hazel eyes. Jack looked just like his dad. Jaden, Jay, was the youngest, the biggest, and by far the most colorful. Tattoos covered every inch of his arms, at least the parts I could see.

I thanked Jay when he handed me a glass of sparkling rosé.

"Hope you like it; it's Emily's favorite," Meg said. It didn't surprise me to see a glass of water in her hands.

"I love a good rosé." The bubbles tickled my nose as I took a sip. "Thanks."

"Me too. Thanks for bringing the veggie tray," Emily said as she took the lid off. "Now we can pretend we're eating healthy." She grabbed a carrot and took a bite before picking up her wineglass. "Cheers."

Standing around the island, we all lifted our glasses and clinked.

"Let's eat," Jay said.

My stress slowly drained away as we ate. It felt good to let go, even if it was only for a few minutes, and relax with my new friends.

After cleaning up, we settled back down in the living room. At one point, Jay looked at Ashley and ask-yelled, "What? Do I have something on my face?"

He rubbed his hands over his messy stubble.

Ashley said, "No, I was just thinking you fit the, Jack, what did you call it last summer? Top-notch security eye candy? Anyway, you fit the mold." Everyone laughed.

Everyone except me. I didn't get the joke.

"Ashley likes being surrounded by hot alpha men," Emily explained.

Ashley laughed and said, "You say that like it's a bad thing."

I looked around; Ashley wasn't wrong. All the guys of SSI qualified as hot.

"You'll get used to it," Ashley said. "But don't stare too long. The hot alpha you snagged for yourself might get jealous."

I looked at AJ just in time to see him roll his eyes.

"He is prone to growling at anyone who notices how gorgeous you are," Jay added.

AJ turned to Jay and growled. "Shut up."

"See?" Jay held his hands up in surrender.

This time, I joined in with everyone when they laughed. Though I didn't join in when they started giving each other shit about being jealous and over-protective. I wasn't comfortable enough. *Maybe someday.*

Meg and Emily more than made up for my silence.

Before long, Meg sat by me. "You'll get used to them," she whispered, so only I heard her. I couldn't help but notice how she and Jack communicated with nothing more than their eyes and subtle facial expressions.

I want a connection like that someday.

Eventually, the group split up. The guys stayed in the living room to play video games while the girls moved to the dining room table.

We talked about everything, except Meg's pregnancy.

When Meg mentioned the women's self defense class SSI was hosting, she said I should go.

"We're all taking it," Emily said.

"I don't know." I wasn't sure I wanted to learn how to hit people.

"The class isn't about hitting people. They teach you situational awareness and the value of trusting your instincts."

I flashed back to AJ telling me to always trust my gut when things felt off.

"And how to throat punch a fucker if he tries to hurt you," Ashley added, punching the air in front of her.

"Ashley!" Meg and Emily said together.

"What?"

"You'll learn a few simple moves you can use if you have to defend yourself," Meg clarified.

That sounded a lot better than punching someone.

I asked Meg to text me the date so I could check my schedule.

"Who knows, maybe we'll even convince you to go to the range with us."

I looked towards the guys in the living room. There was no way I'd go to the range with them.

"Not with them." Emily must have seen my anxiety. "I mean, we do go with them sometimes, but we're still learning, so we've joined a women's shooting group, the Women's Shooting Club."

I shook my head back and forth. I wasn't ready to shoot a gun. Hell, I'd barely gotten over my fear of them.

"Let us know if you change your mind. Mary and Beth go with us sometimes. It's fun, and we go out for a drink after."

"Okay." I didn't think I would.

"You should consider taking a gun safety class, now that you live in a house with guns," Meg said.

It wasn't the class part that caught me off guard; it was the living with AJ part. I was staying with him until things settled, but we hadn't discussed anything long term.

"I, um, I don't know."

"It doesn't have to be at the range. Jack used a laser training gun when I first started," Meg said, misunderstanding which part of her statement had shocked me.

"I'll think about it." It was the best I could offer.

By the end of the night, I'd made three new friends. Including Ashley. It hadn't taken me long to see I had nothing to fear from her.

Before saying goodbye, we exchanged numbers. I promised I'd go to the next craft night, as long as I finished my schoolwork.

Chapter 61

AJ

I snagged a moment alone with Jack and finally told him about my childhood, the abuse, and my fears. As expected, he was empathetic and supportive.

"I love her, but I'm afraid I'll end up just like my father."

"I understand your fear, but I've never seen you treat a woman with anything less than respect," he said.

"What if I lose my temper?" Once I'd opened up, it was surprisingly easy to keep baring my soul. I'd held so much of myself back, always afraid I'd reveal too much and be judged for it. *Not anymore.* At least, not with Jack. I'd be slower to open up to anyone else.

"Listen, I've known you a long time and stood by your side during some of the worst situations a person can imagine, and I've never seen you lose your temper."

"But-"

"Never, Brother, not once." He clapped my shoulder. "I think it's time to put the past to rest and embrace your future."

I stood there, looking and feeling like an idiot. *Could it really be that simple?* And if it was, how had I missed it all this time?

"Thanks, Jack." I pulled him into a hug, grateful I could call my best friend a brother.

"Anytime," he pulled back, "Andrew."

"Don't." That name was reserved for Blake and Blake alone.

Jack chuckled. "Good to know where I stand."

"Damn straight."

Ashley pulled me aside as we said our goodbyes. "Being in love looks good on you."

It feels good too.

"Blake seems really nice, even if she is a bit overwhelmed."

"This crowd can be a bit much," I agreed with a smile. They were one hundred percent over the top, and I loved them for it.

Thinking back to what Jack had said, I asked, "Was I ever mean or disrespectful to you?"

"AJ, you were always a perfect gentleman," she answered. "Why do you ask? Did someone say otherwise?"

"No, I'm just worried about my temper." There. I'd said it. Well, I hinted at it. *But it's more than I'd normally admit.*

"Temper? I never worried about your temper." She made air quotes around the word temper. "I've seen you in work mode and you can look pretty fucking mean and scary, but that's part of your charm." She laughed. "Seriously though, I never felt anything but safe with you."

I breathed a huge sigh of relief. Maybe Jack was right; I'd learned how to control my anger along the way without even realizing it.

"Thanks." I hugged her.

"You're welcome. Now take your girl home. She's been through hell and deserves a couple of orgasms to take her mind off things."

I was on board with giving Blake as many orgasms as she wanted, but couldn't, wouldn't, talk about them with Ashley.

"Jesus." I prayed Blake hadn't heard her. "I can't discuss this with you, or anyone."

"What? I'll always advocate for my friends getting lots of big Os."

For the first time in my life, talking about sex made me uncomfortable. I didn't want to share what I had with Blake with anyone, not even someone advocating for multiple orgasms.

"I'm glad you like her," I said, desperate to change the subject.

Meg, Emily, and Ashley were the type of friends Blake needed in her life. They'd stand by her side through thick and thin, celebrate her wins, and cry for her losses.

Not that I knew many of Blake's friends. I'd only met the two, and the jury was still out on Paige, though she was growing on me now that I'd seen a different, Fuckface-free side of her. And Fuckface, well, he could fuck right the fuck off.

Ashley would be proud of the nickname I'd given him.

I looked at Blake. *Hopefully, hanging out with Ashley won't be weird for her.* They'd see a lot of each other now that we were an item.

Just say it, Janerek. You're dating. And living together. Because I had exactly zero intention of letting her move out.

Chapter 62

Blake

After spending the week elbow deep in legal paperwork and school work, I was happy when Friday rolled around and I turned twenty-five with very little fan fair.

"Happy Birthday, Sweetheart."

I woke up to those words, a dozen red roses, and a large coffee.

"Mmm, thank you." I sat up and accepted the coffee before taking the roses and inhaling deeply. "They're beautiful."

"Want breakfast in bed? Or maybe I could fill you up in other ways," he teased.

I let my eyes wonder over the tattoos on his chest. I now knew every line by heart and would never grow tired of tracing them with fingers or my tongue.

AJ flexed his pecs, making me laugh.

I lifted a hand to his six-pack abs and traced a line down the center. "Maybe a quickie before my meeting."

AJ turned our breakfast into sandwiches so we could eat them on the way to my attorney's office. Wanting his quiet support, I'd asked AJ to come with me. By noon, I had signed the paperwork transferring my late grandfather's fortune to me.

I couldn't hold back my laugh when AJ's eyes almost bugged out of his head when he learned just how much I was worth.

"You okay?" I asked.

"Yeah." He coughed as he recovered. "I didn't realize how many millions you have."

"A lot of it is in investments, but you'll never hurt for cash," Jocelyn said.

After the meeting, I accepted the collect call from my father. He wished me a happy birthday, then apologized again for getting me involved. He still hadn't accepted responsibility for his choices or crimes, instead choosing to play the victim. It was the same conversation every time. I wanted to be there for him, but he wasn't making it easy.

Later that evening, my heart sped up when AJ came out of the bathroom, dressed in a suit and tie for dinner. If I'd known how to whistle, I would have.

Unlike me, AJ could whistle perfectly, and he did as his eyes roamed over every inch of me. I didn't think I looked particularly good in my floor-length gown, but he made me feel sexy.

Because AJ looked so incredibly panty-dropping sexy, I insisted we detour to the bedroom. I asked him to leave his pink pinstripe tie on while I showed him how much I loved him.

We ended up missing dinner, so we ordered a pizza and wings.

It was the best birthday every.

All because of AJ.

When we're alone, Andrew.

My Andrew.

Before bed, he surprised me with another gift.

He asked me to move in with him. Which was insane—I'd been staying at his house, sleeping in his bed, since the rescue.

But he wanted to make it official. Since I already had keys, he gave me a new pink heart-shaped keychain.

I had to wipe away my tears before I could say yes.

Chapter 63

Blake

"I still can't believe the Sheppards invited me to Easter dinner," I said as I finished getting ready. "They barely know me." Mary invited me when I stopped by Grannie's, my new favorite place, to do schoolwork.

"I can," AJ said. "You almost done in the bathroom?"

We were still adjusting to sharing his small space, not an easy task, with only one bathroom. The only thing I missed from my father's house—my private bath. It was three times the size of AJ's, and I'd never had to share it.

Not for the first time, I wondered how attached AJ was to this house. I could easily buy us something bigger. *Or have one built for us.* I doubted he'd let me do that, which was equal parts endearing and annoying. I could buy us a nice modest house without even noticing the withdrawal from my bank account.

"I can finish in the bedroom." I grabbed my makeup bag and scooted past him. A hint of warm leather, a scent I would forever associate with AJ, filled my nose.

Not wanting to be late to dinner, I refused to give in to the desire that pooled in my belly.

When we got to John's house, Jack greeted us at the door. After hugging me, he turned to AJ and said, "It's about damn time."

"Are we late?" I asked.

"That was for AJ; he knows why," Jack explained.

Apparently, this was the first time he'd accepted an invitation to a holiday dinner. When I asked what changed, he said, "You. You helped me see past my fears, and how much they'd cost me."

Mary had insisted we didn't need to bring anything, but I felt weird going empty-handed. Instead of food, we picked up a bouquet of pink carnations with white lilies, and a bottle of wine.

The relaxed, light-hearted atmosphere was so much better than the stiff, catered events I was used to.

After Doug, Beth, and Chase, the cutest six-year-old I'd ever met, arrived, Jack asked for everyone's attention.

"Meg and I have an announcement to make."

How lucky am I to witness this?

The room erupted, making Meg blush and Jack smile.

"Let him have his moment." John raised his voice, just enough to be heard over the crowd.

"Thanks, Dad." He cleared his throat and looked at the excited faces. "As I was saying, before being so rudely interrupted."

Mary and Beth looked like they were going to burst. Jamie and Emily were holding hands and grinning from ear to ear. Jay tapped his fingers on the table, and John just leaned back, watching it all.

"Meg and I are pregnant."

The room erupted for real; this time everyone stood up to congratulate them.

After things settled down, Jay asked, "Can we eat now? I'm starving."

"You're always starving," Jamie teased him. "The grocery bill has doubled since you moved in."

"Whatever, I pay for my half." Jay laughed as he defended himself. "Come on, Dad, carve the ham already," Jay begged.

John did just that, and we all stuffed ourselves with ham and pineapple slices, Meg's bacon mac and cheese, mashed potatoes, green bean casserole, salad, and Mary's homemade rolls.

After we all settled in the living room to relax, Mary surprised me by bringing out a cake. Everyone sang happy birthday, making me blush. I laughed as I blew out the candles, not bothering to make a wish because the only one that hadn't already come true couldn't.

No amount of wishing could turn back the clock and prevent my father's mistakes.

"Welcome to the family, Blake," Mary said as she hugged me. I choked back my tears as I enjoyed the first motherly hug I'd had in over six years.

AJ wasn't the only one who embraced finding a family that day. I had a loving family as a child, but cancer and poor life choices had ripped it apart.

"Is there ice cream?" Chase asked as Mary cut the cake.

"Oh no, we forgot to buy ice cream," Meg feigned distress, winking at Beth.

"But you can't have cake without ice cream," Chase pouted.

"Are you saying you don't want cake, Little Man?" Doug asked.

"That's not what I said." Chase crossed his arms as he answered.

"Look what I found," John said, carrying in three half gallons of ice cream.

Everyone clapped except Chase—he jumped up and down, cheering.

Chapter 64

AJ

Beth, Doug, Blake and I cleaned up after cake and ice cream, while the Sheppards video-chatted with Madi, Jamie's twin. Madi was the only Sheppard Blake hadn't met, because she couldn't get leave from the Navy.

After the call ended, the guys retired to the back porch with beers, giving the girls time to gush and squeal with Meg.

Doug made sure the patio door was closed before pulling a small red velvet box out of his pocket.

"I'm asking Beth to marry me."

"Will you be doing it in an ice cream shop again?" I asked. Giving him shit about accidentally proposing to Beth, by blurting it out in an ice cream shop, was one of my favorite things to do.

Doug laughed along with the rest of us. "Your time's coming." He clapped my shoulder. "We're already placing bets."

"What the fuck?" I looked around. Every one of them avoided making eye contact, except John. He just grinned and lifted his beer in salute.

"Seriously, though, do you have a plan?" Jamie asked Doug.

"Yeah, I'm taking her out to dinner for her birthday. Chase and I have it all planned out."

"What's his silence costing you?" John asked with a laugh. As Chase's godfather, he knew how hard it was for Chase to keep a secret.

"You don't want to know." Doug laughed as he shook his head.

"Oh, but I do," John said, his voice thick with amusement.

"A new big boy bike," Doug admitted.

"Beth's going to kill you," Jack teased as we all laughed. Doug couldn't have kids of his own, so he was fully embracing his role as Chase's soon-to-be stepdad, and spoiling the fuck out of him.

"As long as she says yes first, I'm okay with it."

I looked through the patio door and watched Blake laughing, wondering if I could afford a diamond big enough to make her happy. *She's not like that.* Blake would be happy with any ring I chose for my proposal.

Sounds faded as I envisioned getting down on one knee and proposing. Images of my future flashed through my mind. Her walking down the aisle in a clingy white dress, her belly growing round with my first son, our kids playing with their Sheppard cousins.

"Who had Janerek proposing in April?" Jamie's voice disrupted the highlight reel of my future with Blake.

I turned and flipped him off with a huff. "Fuck you, Sheppard."

There was a round of, "what'd I do?" from his brothers while everyone else laughed. John's was the loudest.

Jack clapped my shoulder. "Not me, I took May. You willing to wait to help your best-friend, a father-to-be, win a bet?"

"Hey, that's cheating." Jay punched his brother's arm.

"Maybe," was all I said as I turned back to look at Blake. Because I didn't want to live another day without announcing to the world—*She's mine.*

Chapter 65

Blake

I double-checked my alarm when we finally crawled into bed. I'd be returning to classes in the morning and didn't want to be late.

I'd made good progress on my midterm make-up assignments and would turn one in early.

I was happy I was finally getting back to my normal routine. I laughed. My normal looked nothing like it had fourteen days ago. I had a boyfriend. My father was in jail. I no longer lived on campus, much to Paige's disappointment, or even in Dallas.

The commute was long, but I only had to do it for a few more weeks.

It was a mutual decision for me to stay with AJ and drive back and forth to campus. AJ wanted me here with him. And after spending a few nights curled up next to him, I never wanted to sleep without him again.

He'd laughed when I'd told him. "You'll have to suffer without me when I have overnight assignments."

"But not tonight." I'd straddled his hips and planted my hands on his chest. "Tonight, you're all mine."

My next week back flew by as I adjusted to my new routine.

Paige and I repaired our friendship. I even invited her to the SSI self-defense class. I wasn't sure about going when Meg first mentioned it, but now I was looking forward to it.

I never want to feel helpless again.

I still wasn't ready to accept her invitation to go shooting. Luckily, AJ didn't push the subject, saying, "I'm just glad you're taking the self-defense class."

He offered to take me, or find someone to teach me, but I wasn't sure I'd ever want to. I'd gotten used to living with a man who had a gun on or near him at all times, but I still didn't like them.

Friday after dinner, I grabbed my case files off the table and curled up on the couch to read. In a few weeks, I'd graduate and instead of studying case files, I'd be studying for the bar exam.

And house hunting; we definitely needed a bigger place. With any luck, we'd move before I started my internship in August.

Life was good. The only blemish was my father's eventual trial. And even that would be manageable, because AJ would be there to help me get through it.

I looked over at him. He looked so cute, concentrating as he worked on a case.

"What?" he asked without looking up.

"Have I told you yet today that I love you?"

He looked up and smiled. "Maybe, but you should probably say it again, just in case." His dimples made me contemplate skipping the case file I was reading.

"I love you, Andrew."

Six Weeks Later

Blake

AJ had been acting weird all day, and it was making me nervous.

Don't be ridiculous.

Things were great between us. We'd even made plans to move into a bigger place after I graduated.

It wasn't hard convincing him to move after sharing his small place for a few weeks. I'd turned his office into a storage room, taken over half his closet, and commandeered most of the shelves in the bathroom.

We worked at the kitchen table and ate on the couch. We were making it work, but it was cramped and it wouldn't be long before we drove each other crazy.

We wanted something with an open floor plan and a decent sized kitchen for when I learned how to cook. It had to be big enough for us to have a large home office we could share.

And room to grow.

I'd offered to pay cash, so we didn't start our next chapter with debt, but AJ argued. "The best I can do, and keep my man card, is agree to share the cost."

"I can live with that," I said. I wanted to spoil him, but AJ refused to rely on my millions. It only made me love him more.

When I joked about having all this money and no one to spend it on, he suggested donating it, or starting a foundation.

Ideas I'd considered, but hadn't put into action yet. I wanted to graduate and pass the bar before starting a business venture.

The hostess interrupted the memory when she called AJ's name. At the table, his hand shook ever so slightly as he pulled out my chair.

What is going on? Had I upset him when I offered to buy our house again? Did it make him think he wasn't good enough for me?

I wished he'd get over that feeling. Andrew Janerek was everything I wanted, and never knew I needed.

"Andrew, is everything okay?"

He turned towards me and took my hand in his. "Yeah, why?"

"You don't seem like yourself."

"Sorry, I–"

"Here you are, sir," our server said, interrupting AJ.

Damn it. I want to know what's going on in that big, gorgeous head of his.

"Thank you," AJ said, nodding towards the bottle of Champagne and two fluted glasses.

Why the Champagne? *It's too early to celebrate my graduation.*

Maybe he got a promotion.

The server filled our glasses and walked away.

"Blake." AJ shifted in his seat. "I love you."

"I love you too." It was easy to say now.

He stood up and took a knee next to me.

Oh. My. God. *Is he proposing?*

I put my hands in my lap and forced myself to remain calm.

"You're it for me. I want to spend the rest of my life with you. Will you do me the honor of being my wife?" He opened the ring box, revealing a gorgeous, sparkling square diamond set in a thin gold band.

My hands flew to my mouth as happy tears blurred my vision.

I nodded and mumbled yes through my hands.

He pried my left hand away.

"What was that?" His dimples popping as he smiled.

He'd heard me, but I was more than happy to repeat myself.

"Yes." I jumped into his arms. "Yes!"

"Oh thank God," he whispered as he crushed me to his chest.

"Were you nervous I'd say no?"

"Me? Nah. Terrified maybe," he answered. His grin showing off his dimples.

The ring fit perfectly when he slid it on my finger. I admired it for a second before wrapping my arms around his neck and kissing him.

The last eight weeks had been a whirlwind of changes. Some good, some bad. The only constant through it all, had been Andrew, no middle name, Janerek.

I laughed as I admired the ring sparkling on my finger. The man I'd called a big, dumb ogre was now my fiancé.

And I've never been happier.

Acknowledgements

Thank you, Reader, for choosing to spend some time in my world. I hope you enjoyed it.

I want to thank my Proof Reader, Nina, and my Beta readers, Kevin and Jocelyn. Your feedback was invaluable in helping me polish my story. A big thanks to Maria Secoy, and the mentor team at All Write Well—this book wouldn't be in your hands if I hadn't found them!

I also want to thank my friends, who have surrounded me with love and support while listening to me chatter on endlessly about my characters and plot lines over many glasses of wine.

Thank you all!

Also by

<u>**Sheppard & Sons Investigations:**</u>

TAKEN: Jack and Meg's story
BEATEN: Jamie and Emily's story
MISSING: Doug and Beth's story
BETRAYED : AJ and Blake's story
CAGED: Jaden and Catelyn's story

WebPage

About the Author

Eveline Rose fell in love with storytelling in a high school creative writing class. Eveline currently lives in the Chicago area with her cat, Prince, where she pours her heart and soul into her characters for your reading pleasure. She's a theatre geek who can swing a sword, and a self-defense instructor who can shoot the bullseye. Eveline spends her free time volunteering in her community, hanging out with her friends, and of course reading. One topic she can chat about for hours: Tudor history. Eveline's promise to you: every romantic suspense novel will include a strong protective male hero who will save the woman he loves, and every heroine will get her Happily Ever After. Eveline is a member of Chicago North Romance Writers Group.